Simple principles that can help you . . .

Sleep better • Handle stress more effectively • Increase your energy with diet and exercise • Attain a deeper level of calm and a higher degree of confidence • Learn from mistakes—and then let go of them • Improve relationships • Find more fulfillment in everyday events and more . . .

Energy, Peace, Purpose

Energy, Peace, Purpose

A Step-by-Step Guide to Optimal Living

G. KEN GOODRICK, PH.D.

BERKLEY BOOKS, NEW YORK

Note: This book is intended as a reference volume only, not as a medical manual. The information here is designed to help you make informed decisions about your health. It is not a substitute for any treatment that may have been prescribed by your doctor. If you suspect that you have a medical problem, we urge you to seek competent medical help.

ENERGY, PEACE, PURPOSE:
A STEP-BY-STEP GUIDE TO OPTIMAL LIVING

A Berkley Book / published by arrangement with
the author

PRINTING HISTORY
Berkley edition / August 1999

ISBN: 0-425-16996-0

BERKLEY®
Berkley Books are published by The Berkley Publishing Group,
a division of Penguin Putnam Inc., 375 Hudson Street,
New York, New York 10014.
BERKLEY and the "B" design
are trademarks belonging to Penguin Putnam Inc.

PRINTED IN THE UNITED STATES OF AMERICA

10   9   8   7   6   5   4   3   2   1

*For my boys. Here is some of the stuff you'll need
to have a good life. Also, to all those
who want to live fully.*

Contents

Preface

To the best of my knowledge, the recommendations of this book are based on methods which have been tested in behavioral research.

Please read this book carefully, and try to follow the recommendations as closely as possible. Do the homework for each chapter before proceeding to the next. To the extent that you do so, you will have success.

Note that some of the recommendations involve lifestyle changes that run counter to the prevailing values of our society. Don't let this bother you. When such conflict occurs, it will be societal values that are wrong.

I wish you well on your journey to a better life. It may be a rough road, but it is better than taking the freeway to insignificance.

Acknowledgments

Thanks be to my lifetime spouse for emotional and physical support.

Thanks to all those who have gone before. Thanks to the staff at the Estes Park, Colorado, Public Library, a great place to write books.

Energy, Peace, Purpose

A Step-by-Step
Guide to Optimal Living

1

Introduction to a Better Life

So! You're holding another ''self-improvement'' book in your hands. Why? Are you not satisfied with your life? Do you sense that your life, like the sand in an hourglass, is leaking slowly away? Do you fear you may never achieve the life you had always hoped for? Do you have a library of self-help books at home which gave only brief, if any, relief from the feeling that life is passing you by? Why do you think this book will be any different?

Why do so many people seem to lack the ability to live a life of fulfillment? Is it the age we live in? Our modern postindustrial society seems to mold us into a narrow existence. Look at Figure 1.1. Does this depict your life?

Get up, go to work, come home, watch TV, go to sleep, and repeat. Many adults spend their 20,000 days (55 adult years × 365 days) doing the same things over and over again, punctuated briefly from time to time by the experience of short-term loves, honeymoons, birth, illness, and death. These deviations from the normal grind, for a precious moment, may bring them into contact with what life is all about. For the most part, however, rather than living

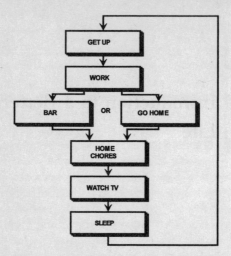

Figure 1.1. Typical Life of Meaninglessness

life, they avoid real living by relying on the distraction and stimulation provided by material possessions, electronic music and computer-game boxes, and the never-ending supply of gore, gossip, sex, and violence fulminating from the television and the Internet.

Many people become aware of the worthlessness of much of their lives, and, during short periods of lucidity, make an attempt to change course. But most fail. They run aground before reaching the distant shore. Why? Take a look at Figure 1.2.

Many people do not really know for sure what they want to achieve. They don't have answers to questions such as: How do I achieve happiness? What skills do I lack? How can I get organized? What goals are realistic, and how fast can I achieve them? They do not know how to develop a systematic plan, and they lack the energy needed to follow through. Excessive stress interferes with the time and mental resources needed to make changes. And, perhaps most

The United States: Current Conditions

To help you get a better understanding of some of the issues addressed in this book, and why it is needed, here is some information about our society.

ENERGY: Estimates from the Department of Health and Human Services show that 15 million people seek medical advice about tiredness every year. The majority of these cases are not caused by medical or psychiatric problems. So-called energy-enhancing nutritional supplements are in great demand. Only 40 percent of Americans get enough exercise to improve feelings of energy. The average diet contains 34 percent calories from fat; maximum energy is achieved at lower levels. The average American gets fewer than eight hours of sleep; this is too little by at least one hour. Most use caffeine to improve feelings of energy; but that habit actually diminishes available energy and interferes with sleep. Over-the-counter sleeping aids are very popular, and millions of prescriptions are written each year for medication. Sales of laxatives are up, and the ads tell us that we feel sluggish without a good BM.

PEACE: Up to 80 percent of Americans report having too much psychological stress, which is the feeling that they cannot cope effectively with the demands placed upon them by job and family. At least 60 percent of visits to physicians involve problems due solely to stress, or medical problems made more severe by stress. The widespread use of alcohol, and the millions of prescriptions for stress-reducing drugs, are evidence that many do not know how to cope constructively with stress. Rare is the person who seems to be at peace.

PURPOSE: Our culture is dominated by values of power, materialism, hostile competition, and vanity. Yet research shows that happiness is best achieved through a lifestyle characterized by giving, sharing in close relationships, lack of concern for possessions, constructive competition, and a focus on character rather than appearance. Many who have achieved the trappings of success have come to feel unfulfilled. They are turning to traditional religion or New Age answers to make sense out of life.

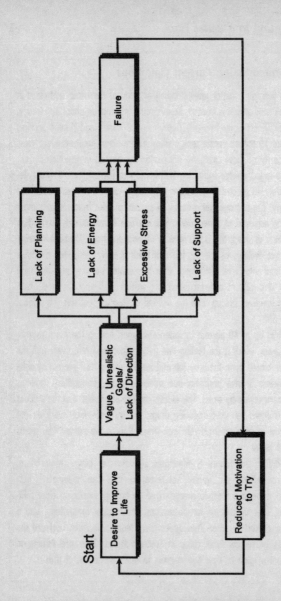

Figure 1.2. How Not to Improve Your Life

importantly, many Americans presume that "self" improvement is something that must be done by the "self," and thus they fail to get the support needed to realize their ambitions.

Tragically, the perception of failure can lead to a reduction in the motivation to continue to improve one's life. Too many failures can result in loss of hope. Depression may be the ultimate outcome of excessive failure experiences, characterized by unwillingness even to try to make things better.

Typically, those seeking enlightenment or at least some meaning and sense of achievement in life fail in their quest due to a lack of direction and skills. Few people get training in life-change skills from their parents, even fewer receive training in a solid foundation of life philosophy. The schools barely train youth in the skills needed to succeed in a career. Rare is the school that prepares students to obtain happiness and fulfillment. Religions have the right ideas, but often their teachings are not organized into an easy-to-follow plan, and the educational process tends to be exhortational preaching rather than careful counseling.

The multicultural and multireligious nature of our society can be confusing; there is no single "tradition" which can be identified and used as a guide. Most people drift somewhat aimlessly, susceptible to the influences of society which explode daily like a "dyscornucopia" of distractions and come-ons. The motivation for behavior seems to be to seek stimulation.

The nature of this stimulation reward is now being studied by neuropsychologists. The brain is designed to experience pleasant sensations when the neurotransmitter dopamine is released. The problem is that dopamine can be released by many behaviors and stimulations other than those that are good for us; recreational drugs and Nintendo are but two ignoble examples. The brain likes these things but they have no useful purpose. They do not address the problems people face: loneliness, relationship problems, coping with the medical, career, and aging crises we all experience. Repeated episodes of highly enjoyable brain stimulation do not add up to happiness. Repeated bouts of ecstasy from heroin, cocaine, loveless sex, or episodes of TV sitcoms do not lead to a sense of fulfillment.

What This Book Is Not

The best way to write a best-selling self-improvement book is to appeal to the fundamental desires of readers. People want higher self-esteem, they want more power and influence, they want sex on demand, and they want to be rich. They want to change immediately to lives of hedonistic satisfaction. And weirdness seems to add to the marketability of such books. This book doesn't fit the mold.

Someone once said, "Never try to sell people what they need. Try to sell them what they want." Sorry, but this book is going to tell you what you need, and guide you carefully through a process that can bring happiness. You will probably feel better, your self-esteem may improve, you might earn more money. But if you seek only self-gratification and power, put this book back on the shelf quickly, before you read further and discover a better way of living. Be warned that this book may stifle your quest to satisfy your greed and lusts.

Another way to impress readers with one's brilliance is to develop a complex or mysterious method of life interpretation. The more esoteric, the better. For example, one self-improvement book (*Never Be Tired Again* by Drs. David Gardner and Grace Beatty, Harper Perennial, 1990) claims to help the reader harness the energy of quantum physics for their personal benefit. The authors claim that research in high-energy physics forms their approach. They also claim the approach is related to "superstring theory." This theory postulates that the waves of energy your imagination creates communicate directly with the other forms of energy and matter in your body, and may also communicate with energy and matter outside of your body. Cool. Far out. Baloney.

Other books turn to New Age (really Old Age stuff, which used to be called witchcraft, astrology, etc.). In such books, self-improvement is achieved by exercises in which the reader is asked to "feel and enjoy a deep sense of connectedness with Mother Nature." Readers are told to recognize that "all of us need a deepening awareness of our oneness with other people and with the natural world, the wonderful web of living things." While the spiritual aspects of life are important, the normal person needs more tangible and basic methods for life restructuring. Still other books assert that happiness comes from the regular ingestion of certain herbs, or from repeated episodes of deep colonic irrigation.

It would seem that just about every psychologist (including me) writes a self-improvement book. Some are good. But many confuse the issue by fostering a method or technique which may confuse or misdirect. Some plans are just too complicated and tedious for anyone but an accountant to master. Others turn to psychotherapeutic approaches, hoping that through book reading, individuals can apply to their lives what they might get through expensive therapy sessions. However, a problem with many psychotherapeutic approaches is that they strive to alleviate negative emotions, and to help patients get what they want. This may feel good in the short term, but it will not result in happiness and fulfillment; these come from good relationships and meaningful work.

Other self-help books fail to give specific enough directions to result in meaningful life change. For example, advice to "select your friends with care" or to "be wise in your use of time" isn't very helpful. These aren't tips but obvious truths which are not easily translated into action. My favorite example of this is on a poster that provides office workers with instructions for action in case of fire. One bit of advice is, "Use judgment." As if you had some judgment in your briefcase and just had to reach in and get some! Imagine a home-repair book that told you to "use good judgment when fixing a leak in the plumbing.'' Sure, but how do you fix the leak? A good self-improvement book shows you step-by-step how to build a better life.

Some self-help books claim that reading them will help a person "take control of their life." I am not sure life can be "controlled." Perhaps improvements in *life management* are possible. Life is a continuing effort to maintain equilibrium in the face of an onslaught of challenges and barriers. One should be satisfied that one is making the best effort possible, given personal and social-environmental resources. Even those in Nazi death camps, subjected to torture, starvation, and little hope for survival, were able to maintain a sense that life was tolerable, if they focused on helpful relationships with their fellow prisoners, and put their faith in God (Frankl, 1959).

What This Book Is

Yes, this is a self-improvement book, written by a psychologist who wouldn't mind making a little money, and deriving a little fame from the book's success in the marketplace. (Be sure to watch me on all the talk shows!) However the goal of the book is to help readers find happiness. Happiness comes from mutually nurturing relationships and from meaningful (helpful, creative) work. Therefore, this book will guide you step-by-step to achieve the basic skills needed.

About Me, the Author

In order to help understand my approach to life improvement, a little bit of information about me may be in order. I think it was Emerson who said, "All great men are different." I think I have the "different" part down cold. I was raised by Phi Beta Kappa, Cornell-graduate parents. My father was a professor of political science, and then a diplomat. I still do not claim to understand either of those callings. I grew up in the U.S., Europe, the Middle East, and the Far East, in Christian, Jewish, Islamic, and Buddhist cultures. I studied engineering at Northwestern University, and became a NASA engineer, participating in the Apollo mission to the moon. If you see block diagrams and flowcharts in this book, my NASA background is why. Nobody gets to the moon and back without flowcharts, and I really think many areas of life could be better understood if depicted as diagrams.

I have always had an interest in religion, and in the "What Is Life All About, Anyway?" type questions, possibly because my grandfather and father (for a short time) were Methodist ministers. After undergraduate school, I was accepted into the University of Chicago Theology Graduate Program, but decided to be an engineer. This had something to do with the glamour of rocket science, and something to do with not wanting to be a poor student in south Chicago.

As an undergraduate I got a C in my only psychology class, but I found it interesting. So, after a few years of engineering, I got a Ph.D. in psychology. I also received three postdoctoral years of training in lifestyle change.

Since then, I have talked in depth with over 1,500 patients who were experiencing various types of life crises. Except for a small few, these people were not suffering from mental illness. They were relatively normal people who were unable to cope with what life had thrown at them. This taught me plenty. Much of the advice I gave these people consisted of skills, such as relaxation, planning, and relationship mending. I have always thought that many of these skills could be taught in the schools, perhaps replacing the required state-history courses. Suffice to say that there are millions of people walking around our society who lack basic skills for living lives that bring happiness and fulfillment. So this book is designed to be a primer.

The Purpose of This Book

Why do so many seem so lost and lacking in skills? We were meant for simpler days, when religion and morals and ethics were all of the same cloth. Communities were small enough to provide mutual support in times of trouble, as well as control through social admonishment in times of poor self-control. People acted on tradition; they knew what to do because their parents and elders taught them the traditions. Now, with both parents working, and the varied and sometimes questionable influences of the world served up conveniently right into our homes through TV and the Web, it is no wonder that we are confused about how to lead our lives.

The onslaught of stress, of challenges, sometimes makes us want to escape into drugs or materialism, or to turn to strange cults that promise relief and meaning. Because of a lack of philosophical and/or religious foundations, many are susceptible to turning away from those aspects of life which have been shown for thousands of years to bring fulfillment and happiness. The book you are holding now is based on truths which come from proven traditions, and which have been researched and validated by modern social science.

Modern technology has transformed the industrial world into a complex, noisy, crowded, and polluted place, a place in which everyone seems so busy supporting the economy through their jobs that there is no time for enjoyment. Humans were designed through evolutionary process, or by Creation (take your pick, the argument is still valid), to function best in small hunter-gatherer groups. In the rain forest, one can still find small villages in which interpersonal relationships are relatively well-defined and cordial. People get plenty of exercise, and eat well considering they have probably never met a dietitian. But I am not advocating a return to primitive living. We are too much attached to the creature comforts of urban and suburban living to regress: good medical care, air-conditioning, and Starbucks, to name but a few that are of great importance to me.

But we can improve our lives immensely by restructuring our lives in a way that brings back, at least to a small degree, the positive aspects of our simpler past. By carefully examining our lives, by creating an artificial village through small support groups, by planning our use of time and material resources, by focusing on making our work and avocations constructive and creative, and by cultivating mutually nurturing relationships, we can achieve a sense of purpose, fulfillment, and happiness in life despite the pressures of our brave new world. That is the aim of this book.

Philosophy, the love of knowledge, asks the question "What is the optimal life?" This book contends that the optimal life is one in which:

a) One feels good physically: this is achieved through a lifestyle bringing high energy and reduced risk for disease, as well as the ability to cope with stress.

b) One feels happy: this is achieved through meaningful (useful, constructive, creative) work, and mutually nurturing relationships. Focus your attention on Figure 1.3., the Flowchart of Systematic Living.

This is the design of the book. From left to right, one progresses to a higher stage of existence, first dealing with self-care through energy and peace, then to happiness through relationships and work. Note that social support is shown as helping one to achieve the changes in lifestyle; establishing social support is the first step in life-improvement. The happiness achieved as an effect of relationships and work helps motivate continued efforts to maintain life-improvement. The entire process may take up to a year to get through the first time. Of course, the flowchart describes a continuing process over one's lifetime.

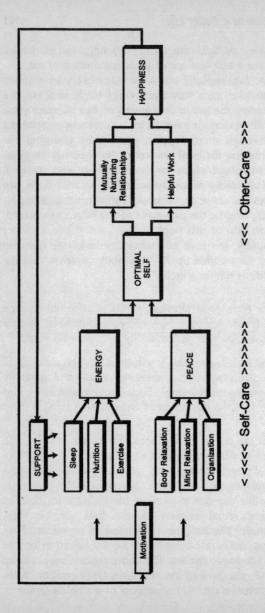

Figure 1.3. The Flowchart of Systematic Living

HAPPINESS

Mutually Nurturing Relationships

Helpful Work

Other-Care >>>

OPTIMAL SELF

ENERGY

PEACE

Self-Care >>>>>>

SUPPORT

Sleep

Nutrition

Exercise

Body Relaxation

Mind Relaxation

Organization

Motivation

The Plan

Energy, Peace, Purpose provides a badly needed, systematic plan to help readers restructure their lives for enhanced energy, a sense of peace, and greater happiness and love. There are energy books, there are stress-management books, and there are books telling one how to live a fulfilling life. Most of these works contain good advice but lack a systematic approach using lifestyle-change methods proved effective by psychological research. This book is a straightforward guidebook which integrates the physical, mental, and interpersonal components of life, based on research in lifestyle modification for optimizing health, stress, and happiness. *Energy, Peace, Purpose* is based on a systematic approach developed from experience with thousands of patients.

The approach assumes that one should first achieve a state of optimal energy with a sense of peace and control. Then, this state of readiness is used as a resource to achieve happiness through meaningful work and sharing relationships.

The three components are presented as follows:

Section 1. Energy: This is achieved through exercise, low-fat eating, better sleep, proper breathing, posture, and prudent use of alcohol, caffeine, and other substances.

Section 2. Peace: This is achieved through stress management/relaxation methods, time management, and organization.

Section 3. Purpose: This is achieved by prioritizing various aspects of life based on the principle that all behaviors should be nurturing, constructive, or creative, and that possessions should facilitate, not compete with, these behaviors.

The book has a step-by-step format, leading the reader through life restructuring using behavioral life-management methods. These methods involve a systematic way of analyzing current patterns, and designing and testing new ones. These methods include self-awareness through daily diaries, changing one's surroundings, problem-solving techniques, and use of social support. The straightforward, no-nonsense approach (remember, I was an engineer) is designed to appeal to the vast majority of Americans who have more sensible views than those expressed in many of the current self-actualization books.

Why You Should Be Glad You Bought This Book

Energy, Peace, Purpose stands out in the crowd of self-help/self-actualization books because:

1. It is based on research as well as universal truths.

2. It uses tested methods of life change.

3. It follows a logical path of first restoring feelings of energy and a sense of calm control, to be used to improve relationships and career.

4. Its lack of reliance on New Age or fringe psychotherapeutic techniques makes it easy to understand and implement.

5. It has a step-by-step format and straightforward approach.

6. The format allows for periodic evaluation of progress using self-monitoring forms.

Permission is given to purchasers of this book to photocopy these forms for personal use.

Summary of Chapters to Come

Read and ponder this section so that your brain can form an organized memory directory to place the parts of the book into an organized scheme.

Chapter 2: Social Support. The social support methods are important since interpersonal relations are critical not only to behavior change but to happiness.

Chapter 3: Energy. This includes a discussion of the concept of energy, and the psychological and physiological aspects of perceived energy, such as daily body rhythms. Lifestyle changes that enhance feelings of energy are emphasized.

Chapter 4: Sleep. Adequate sleep is the foundation for success. Methods for getting restorative sleep include moderation in use of caffeine and alcohol, taking care not to stimulate the body with food or exercise before sleep, changing the bedroom environment, selecting the ideal mattress, modifying thought patterns and emotions before going to bed, and some time management.

Chapter 5: Exercise. Developing healthful exercise, posture, and breathing habits. This includes the self-regulated-intensity exercise program which I have shown helps adults to enjoy and maintain exercise habits. The psychological and physiological benefits of regular exercise will be explained. Other motivational tips for developing a strong exercise habit include social support and modifying thoughts and attitudes about exercise. Posture and breathing also play a part in energy enhancement.

Chapter 6: Nutrition. Eating for energy, and how to avoid energy-sapping substances. Here the emphasis is on gradually switching to a lower-fat eating plan. This method has been shown to be effective for lifestyle modification in weight management. The suggested program follows methods proved in research by the author's colleagues to help adults eat substantially less fat without feeling deprived.

The use of nutritional supplements for energy enhancement is covered.

Chapter 7: Peace. Humans historically have used many methods to achieve peace of mind and relaxation. Some provide health benefits to be derived from their regular use, while some are harmful.

Chapter 8: Relaxation. Instructions for daily relaxation/ meditation methods, as well as brief relaxation exercises are provided. There is an emphasis on how to incorporate simple relaxation techniques into work and home environments. The methods include muscle relaxation and breathing techniques, as well as traditional methods such as bubble baths. Research done by the author (me) shows that some of the relaxation effects achieved after years of practice by Tibetan monks can be achieved quickly using the right method.

Chapter 9: Personal and work management for greater peace. Stress-management methods for home and office.

Chapter 10: Purpose. This overview asks the reader to explore a sense of purpose in life beyond day-to-day survival. The reader is led through a series of exercises designed to show the value of ''meaningful'' purpose, defined as purpose with goals of constructive achievement, creativity, artistry, or nurturing others.

Chapter 11: Relationships. This includes exercises to help the reader examine relationships, as well as methods to improve them. These methods include: taking the role of counselor, dealing with anger, and participating in forgiveness.

Chapter 12: Things. Exercises in this chapter have readers list all their possessions and evaluate their use with respect to meaningful purposes. The emphases are: 1) wealth is good, as long as the money is used for meaningful purposes; and 2) happiness can be achieved with or without wealth.

Chapter 13: Work. This chapter includes exercises regarding the nature of one's career, and whether a change in attitude or job is needed to establish a sense of meaningful purpose. Exercises help you examine whether the roles you play at work are constructive or destructive to you or your employer.

Methods: How to Cope with Problems

During your journey along the path of self-improvement, you will be trying to develop new habits and learn new skills. You will inevitably have some problems in sticking to your plans. This is normal and should be expected. Your *attitude* toward problems is important, for your attitude may determine whether you:

1. Persevere and ultimately succeed, or

2. Give up and feel like a failure.

Optimistic people know that problems arise, and they can look forward to the future when the problem or barrier has been overcome. Pessimists tend to see themselves as victims. Some people are rewarded for playing the role of helpless victim, since this seems to be the only way they get attention. Victims may even self-sabotage their efforts. I hope that people who buy self-improvement books do not fall into the helpless-victim category. Of course they don't.

Everyone has a different style of coping with problems. How did you develop your particular style of coping with problems? Think about the following two stories about two different families. Which one was your family like? SCENE: You are a child, about seven years old, and you accidentally spill your orange juice all over the table on Monday morning.

Family A

Father (or mother): "You clumsy idiot! Why are you always making a mess! I work hard to keep this house clean and look what you do. Go to your room. You can't have any more breakfast."

The result of this kind of reaction to a child's mistakes will teach him that mistakes are something to get emotionally upset over, and something to be ashamed of, making you unworthy of the family's love.

Family B

Father (or mother): "Oh dear! Honey, please go into the kitchen and get some paper towels and I'll help you clean this up." (After cleaning): "Now, let's analyze what happened. I think you spilled your orange juice because you moved your arm to get some toast without looking carefully. I know children have a hard time coordinating themselves. Let's work on being more careful and moving more slowly at the table, okay?"

The result of this kind of reaction to a child's mistakes is to teach the following process:

1. Do what you can to make up for your error.

2. Think about how to avoid the problem. Develop possible solutions to try out.

3. Realize that everyone makes mistakes and it shouldn't damage self-esteem or lead to emotional outbursts.

If you are reading this book because you feel you need a lot of improvement, and have low self-esteem, your ego may be closely tied to how well you perform. You may be very sensitive and get emotional when you make a mistake, or stray off the path. Try to remember that you are not the only one who has areas of your life needing improvement, and that everyone make mistakes.

If experiencing a failure results in an excessive emotional reaction and ultimately giving up, the situation becomes worse. It is possible to learn how to react to problems and mistakes *constructively* by using problem-solving methods.

Problem Solving

Problem solving is nothing more than calmly and systematically:

1. Clearly defining what the problem is.

2. Studying the problem by investigating all the factors that may have contributed to it.

3. Developing alternative approaches as solutions to avoid similar problems.

4. Deciding what alternatives may work best.

5. Trying out alternatives.

6. Evaluating how good the alternative approach is.

7. Continuing with the solution if it worked, or developing another if it didn't.

If you follow this problem-solving approach, you can find some measure of success eventually. It is always best to do problem solving with a support person or group who can check your ideas from another viewpoint, and motivate you to carry out your solutions.

You will find this approach more satisfying than reacting emotionally, although if you are a trained actor, you can revel in the emotionality of the experience for a few minutes. Compare these two reactions to a mistake:

1. "Oh no, I screwed up again. I guess this proves I can't succeed, so I might as well give up and feel like a failure." (Puts back of hand up to brow, and walks away slowly, with faint sobbing sounds.)

2. "I have made a mistake. This is perfectly natural and to be expected when anyone is changing a lifestyle. I'll call Joan and we can talk together about how I can try some other way to avoid this kind of mistake. I am still excited and optimistic that I will have ultimate success, even though I know it will take work, and I will still make mistakes along the way." (Takes a deep breath and feels energized by the challenge.)

To help you go through the steps of problem solving, the following form should be used. It is always a good idea to get your thoughts on paper; this helps you to organize your ideas.

Problem-Solving Worksheet: The Tragic Mistake

1. What the mistake or deviation was: _____
_____

2. What seemed to cause it:

a) Negative emotions b) Distractions c) Others influenced me d) I just wasn't thinking e) Other: _____
_____

3. Alternative ways of coping with similar situation:

a) Change how I feel b) Change environment c) Avoid situation d) Tell friends your goals e) Plan more carefully

Specific Plans:

_____ _____

_____

_____

_____

4. Choose plan of action: _____

_____

5. Use this plan. How did it work?

_____

_____

_____

If it worked, use it. If it didn't, analyze by going back to step 1, and finding another trial solution.

The old trial-and-error method works. Or am I mistaken?

Methods: Self-Monitoring

Even the smallest of businesses could not survive for long without keeping careful records of inventory and transactions. So it should be with your personal life. As you progress through this book, you will be asked to keep some simple diaries to record activities and thoughts. One of the most helpful ways to cope with the complexity and stress of living is to put it down on paper. Often, when things seem out of control, a careful description on paper, with all the components separated and shown in relationship to each other, may be helpful. This practice can allow your brain to perceive everything in an orderly fashion.

Research shows that the expression of stressful experiences through writing can provide psychological relief for many. The worst thing you can do is keep it all inside your head, where thoughts can become jumbled and seem more threatening than they really are. Putting it into language requires a structuring of thought into subject, object, verb, and logical phrases. More on this later in the book when mental stress is discussed.

The plan of this book asks you to spend a few minutes now and then to record your behavior and mental activities. A daily recording sheet will be used to record such things as sleep, exercise, relaxation, and time spent sharing with family. Research clearly shows that those who keep records of their behavior do much better in life-improvement programs. This may be because recording makes the tracking of progress possible, keeps you from denying lack of progress, and provides information on success.

First Homework Assignment

This involves a careful examination of your current life situation in terms of the areas you will be working on. Do not hurry to complete this assignment. You can talk with your significant others about each area to get perspective.

For each Life Area, a "Reasonable Goal" has been suggested. You can modify these if you think they are unrealistically ambitious, or not ambitious enough. But don't stray too far away from the suggestions. Record your current status, and what you have done, if anything, to improve your condition.

Table for Evaluating Your Current Life

LIFE AREA	REASONABLE GOAL
Intimate Relation	1 lifelong spouse, sharing/caring
Current Status	
What have I done for this?	

LIFE AREA	REASONABLE GOAL
Family	Nurturing relationships with children/kin
Current Status	
What have I done for this?	
Friendships	1 or 2 good ones
Current Status	
What have I done for this?	
Sleep	8–9 hours/night
Current Status	
What have I done for this?	
Exercise	4–5 hours/week
Current Status	
What have I done for this?	
Nutrition	Eat for health and enjoyment, avoid weight gain
Current Status	
What have I done for this?	

LIFE AREA	REASONABLE GOAL
Relaxed body	Lack of tension and stress disorders
Current Status	
What have I done for this?	
Relaxed mind	Feeling of well-being, peace, clear thinking
Current Status	
What have I done for this?	
Organization	Following a careful plan to achieve specific goals, using time wisely
Current Status	
What have I done for this?	
Work	Job satisfaction from performance and usefulness of work
Current Status	
What have I done for this?	
Purpose	Have good idea of what your life is about, which brings satisfaction
Current Status	
What have I done for this?	

LIFE AREA	REASONABLE GOAL
Community	Active in one organization to help improve the human condition
Current Status	
What have I done for this?	
Religion	Practice a faith based on principles of love
Current Status	
What have I done for this?	
Well-Being	Usually happy, optimistic, as result of above
Current Status	
What have I done for this?	
Energy	Able to feel energetic for 16 hours a day, with 3 or fewer cups of coffee
Current Status	
What have I done for this?	

If all the above makes you aware of many problems, and it seems overwhelming, remember that the plan is step-by-step, and that you should seek support before starting.

Second Homework Assignment

Talk to several friends who might form a small group with you to share in the experience of life improvement. Of course, they should all buy a copy of this book. The next chapter is about how to form such a group.

ATTENTION: If you or your friends think you are seriously depressed or anxious, or if you have trouble thinking clearly, or if you have no one to ask for social support, seek professional help from a psychologist or psychiatrist before starting on this book. Likewise, you should be medically evaluated by a physician if you have symptoms of low energy, sleeplessness, or any other symptoms, whether apparently psychological or medical. No claims are made that reading this book or following its suggestions is a substitute for needed psychotherapy or medical treatment, or that anything in this book can be construed as treatment for any type of illness or disorder.

References

Frankl, V. (1959). *Man's Search for Meaning*. London: Hodders & Stoughton.

2

Getting Support

GOAL: To convince you to get into a support system.

> *"No man is an island, entire of itself; every man is a piece of the continent, a part of the main; if a clod be washed by the sea, Europe is the less, as well as if a promontory were, as well as if a manor of thy friends or of thine own were."* JOHN DONNE
>
> *Two are better than one, because they have a good reward for their toil. For if they fall, one will lift up his fellow; but woe to him who is alone when he falls and has not another to lift him up.* ECCLESIASTES 4:9–10

Considerable effort and time is required to make the lifestyle changes needed to optimize energy, to maintain calm, to achieve a sense of purpose and achievement, and to enjoy sharing in nurturing relationships. Do not try to do it all alone. You need the support of others for advice, resources, motivation, and emotional support. You will be much more likely to succeed if other persons are aware of your efforts, and can hold you accountable for your prog-

ress. Humans have a tendency to slip back to their old lifestyles if they do not establish a continuing mode of support.
Religions recognize the need for lifetime support; everyone
should interact with fellow worshipers at least weekly.

Research clearly shows that people with social support
are better able to maintain lifestyle changes than those without it. But you can't get social support from just anybody.
If you were to pick someone out of a crowd, he or she
might not support the same goals you have. The "support"
you would get from such a person might be advice such
as, "Don't wimp out. The object of life is to get the most
toys by being powerful and rich."

But suppose you were able to find someone who had
goals similar to yours. Someone who had found a way
of living life fully, which led to greater happiness and
health, or who was also a beginner and willing to provide
mutual support. This is the kind of friend you need. The
biggest barrier to progress for many is the failure to admit that they cannot do it alone. Pride goeth before the
fall. Scuba divers have a rule always to have at least one
dive partner. This is a good rule for those of us above
water as well.

How Social Support Works

The most obvious way others can help you is to give
you *advice* on what to do. You can learn from others who
have "been there" and who have successfully changed
their lives. This helps you have hope; if *they* can do it, so
can you. They can also practice the techniques described in
this book with you. This can give you a feeling of self-
confidence to know that what you are doing has worked
for others. Compare this with trying to do everything on
your own; feelings of self-doubt are bound to come up:
"Am I doing the right thing? I am probably doing this the
wrong way." These are the kinds of thought patterns that

arise if you have a history of failure in your life.

When you falter, your support people are there to *comfort* you and to *encourage* you to keep on going. When you succeed, they will be there to give you praise. This will help prevent damage to your self-esteem from failures, and will boost self-esteem with every success.

Another important feature of support is that others who have made significant life changes can *share* with you the emotions and experiences they have had. This lets you know that you are not alone in the confusion and struggles you may be having in your attempt to make your life meaningful. This lets you know that you are "normal." If you felt that you were the only person with such thoughts and feelings, you might view yourself as strange; this would tend to damage your self-esteem even further.

When you are making changes in your lifestyle, you must face the truth about yourself. This can be very painful. Left on your own, you might successfully avoid dealing with issues which affect your degree of fulfillment in life. For example, if you were abused as a child, this may have a damaging effect on your self-esteem as an adult. This would make self-management more difficult. The best kind of support persons will put *pressure* on you to *reveal things about yourself* that you might want to keep hidden. Your support persons can help you deal with unresolved emotions stemming from your childhood.

Just talking about your life fulfillment goals with your support persons helps you to *organize your thoughts* about your situation. Explaining yourself to others helps you to get a perspective. If you do not communicate to others, all the emotions and thoughts you have about yourself tend to be jumbled together, adding to your confusion and anxiety. Writing a dairy of your thoughts and progress that you share with your support persons is an excellent idea.

If you have low self-esteem, it may be because you have a set of ideas and feelings about yourself that are unrealistically negative. You may have been trying to cope with feelings of low self-esteem by striving to succeed at gathering material wealth, or by being more powerful. You may have been thinking, "When I get a million dollars, then I will be a better person." When you get to know your support persons, they will *give you honest feedback* about yourself which will be more realistic than your own self-evaluations. This feedback can help you reformulate your self-attitudes and help you to be realistic in your potential for fulfillment. This can help you avoid becoming one of the many who spend their whole lives in torment because they find themselves struggling to achieve unattainable goals.

When you reveal your life goals to your support persons, you put yourself under *constructive social pressure* to meet your goals. You will want to be able to report to them that you did what you said you would do. This is very different from the social pressure you may feel from our culture, which demands conformity to values based on materialism and power. Your support persons will help you follow a plan of energy, calm and nurturing, which is gradual and allows time for personal development. They will help you through your lapses rather than reject you for your failures.

When you do have lapses, and appear to be sliding back to your old lifestyle, your support group, using the steps of problem solving, can help you *carefully analyze* what happened, and help you work out an *alternative strategy* to avoid the causes of the lapse. This kind of support helps you to continue in your efforts.

The most important help a support person can give you is to lend you their emotional support and a clear-thinking brain when you are having a crisis. A crisis is any situation in which you feel that you may be losing your sense of direction in your life. Using a friend to *talk you through a crisis* is one of the most important methods of life management you can ever learn. If you try to cope with crises all by yourself, you may fail, putting yourself into the downward spiral of failure, reduced self-esteem, and further loss of control. Reaching out to others increases your chances of success. It also provides the opportunity to make your friends happier knowing they have helped someone.

Social Support and Health

Social support is clearly a valuable resource to help us get through life with minimal mental and physical damage. Since our minds are developed through interaction with others over our lifetime, it makes sense that we feel better psychologically when life is shared with others. The effects of stress (see chapter 7) are reduced with social support. Research is now showing that good social support may support better cardiovascular health by preventing damaging stress reactions. It may reduce the insulin response to stress, reducing the chances for diabetes. It may also enhance the activity of the immune system (Uchino et al, 1996). Absence of social support appears to be associated with the onset of and relapse into depression. When people suffer negative changes in their lives, support from others may prevent the distress from becoming a psychological disorder (Paykel, 1994).

Structuring a Group

One of the best ways to structure social support is to form a support group which meets regularly. A group can be very effective in keeping you on the right track by setting up certain rules and procedures. One such rule is that if you fail to attend a group meeting, one or more other members are assigned to call you to find out why you did not attend, and to see if you are having any problems. Just knowing that they will call is an incentive to keep up regular attendance. Another rule is that all members know each other's phone numbers, and volunteer to receive calls from people in crisis. In order to resign from a group, a member is required to stand up in front of the group and explain why he no longer plans to attend. Then other members get a chance to try to convince him to stay, unless the reason for leaving is valid (e.g., moving away).

WRONG: "I don't need anyone. I am the only one who can make something of my life." This thought comes from the tradition of American rugged individualism, the pioneer spirit, an outgrowth of individual liberty taken to its illogical conclusion.

RIGHT: "I need social support to help me manage my life so that I can attain energy, calmness, a sense of purpose, and fulfillment."

There are many resources for finding a support group or starting one of your own. You may already have several friends who are willing to meet to follow the suggestions outlined in this book. You might generate some interest at your place of worship, or at your place of work. You could find a professional counselor willing to help organize a group. Whatever group you find yourself in, it is essential that the group members adhere to the principles outlined in this book.

Some may have difficulty obtaining social support. You may have very low self-esteem, or suffer from depression. This may make reaching out to form or join a group very difficult. Your social skills may be limited, making your efforts to gather support people unsuccessful. If you have such problems, you may want to consider hiring a psychologist to help you relieve your depression, and to learn the interpersonal skills needed to become part of a support group.

Awareness Exercises

At various places in this book, you will be given the opportunity to write down your thoughts about aspects of your life. This kind of journaling can be very helpful.

1. Have you ever been in a group that provided the kind of support discussed in this chapter? Describe the group and how it felt to be a member.

_____

_____

_____

2. When you were a child, did your family provide good social support? Describe the good and bad aspects of the support you got from your family.

_____

_____

_____

3. Do you think your parents had a particularly good or bad influence on your self-esteem and helping you to learn how to manage your life? Describe:

_____

_____

_____

4. Do you make friends easily? If yes, what are your characteristics that are attractive? If not, what's wrong with you?

_____

_____

Finding a Group

Finding an existing group is easier than starting your own. Psychologists and other therapists may have an interest in forming a group based on this book. Religious organizations might be a resource. Contact denominational headquarters for your area. You may be able to start a group at your place of worship. As far as I know, nothing in this book is incompatible with the teachings of the major religions. Indeed, if your religious faith conflicts with the suggestions in this book, I would like to hear about it (kgoodrick@hotmail.com). If the group consists of members of the same religious faith, then prayer and other rituals can be integrated with the plan of the book, perhaps enhancing motivation and outcome.

When you form a group, use the list below to check the quality of support offered.

Will the prospective members (including you) be:

1. Helpful and friendly?

2. Encouraging?

3. Willing to share experiences?

4. Willing to share emotions?

5. Willing to confront me with the truth about myself?

6. Willing to help me through crises?

7. Unlikely to let the group deteriorate into a whining club? (It happens.)

Starting a Group

You may have one or more friends or associates who would like to work with you on life improvement. In order to help you organize such a group, here is an organizational policy statement that you can use as a guide. Get a few friends to sign it and you are ready to roll.

Organizational Policy

Name: The name of this group will be: _____

Membership: Open to all persons who are willing to work together to:
  1) Encourage each other.
  2) Help each other follow the Plan.

  3) Develop friendships to cope with problems and bar-
     riers.

Values: Members will strive to uphold these values:
  1) People should be accepted for their willingness to be
     helpful.
  2) The goals are more energy, mental peace, physical
     health through relaxation, and balancing self-care
     with caring for others through work, family, and
     friendships.
  3) All behaviors should be nurturing.
  4) In a crisis, it is better to reach out to others for help
     than to try to control oneself.
  5) Sharing life with others and being able to help are
     the keys to happiness.
  6) The focus should be on relationships, and how they
     foster constructive and/or creative behaviors.

Meetings: Meetings will be held weekly at a member's
residence. Group meetings should have eight or fewer
members.

The format of meetings will be:
  1) Greetings and recitation of group motto, prayer,
     ritual-type stuff to build a sense of group belonging
     and cohesion.
  2) Each member shares stories of successes and mis-
     takes from the past week.
  3) Other members rejoice in success and help analyze
     the reasons for mistakes, offering suggestions for
     problem solving.
  4) Discussion about how the Plan works. Readings from
     other sources.
  5) Recitation of group's credo (based on values). Prayer/
     giving thanks that we can share with loving others.
     A promise to support each other.

Support: All members will give and get support as follows:

1) All members' home and work phone numbers will be distributed on a support list.
2) Members agree to be available by phone to help talk another member through a crisis. Visiting the member in crisis may also be needed.
3) Members will call another member who fails to attend a group meeting without calling in advance with a reason. The absent member will be encouraged to keep attending.

Resignation: Members may resign from this group only if they appear before the group to state their reasons for leaving. Other members will encourage them to stay if they feel leaving might be a step backward in progress toward life improvement. If a member fails to appear before the group to resign, other members will have at least three talks or phone calls with the leaving member encouraging reconsideration. If this fails, a card will be sent after three months to let he/she know the group is still thinking of him/her.

Summary

These are the basics of a good support group. You will want to modify the policy to fit your particular needs. But don't get bogged down in rules. The group is for support, fun, and friendship. If you have extreme difficulty in forming a group, you can settle on one good friend, or even your spouse or significant other.

Homework

Get support. Read the next chapter on sleep. You are going to need good rest in order to tackle the challenges that lie ahead.

References

Paykel, E. S. (1994). Life events, social support and depression. *Acta Psychiatrica Scandinavica,* (Suppl), 377, 50–58.

Uchino, B. N., Cacioppo, J. T., Kiecolt-Glaser, J. K. (1996). The relationship between social support and physiological processes: A review with emphasis on underlying mechanisms and implications for health. *Psychological Bulletin,* 119, 488–531.

3

Starting with Energy

GOAL: To help you discover the best path to energy.

One of the reasons many self-improvement programs fail is that people do not have the energy to carry out the plans. If physical energy is low, psychological energy will be low as well. It is difficult to get "psyched" and motivated if one feels like taking a nap. There is a strong correlation between low energy levels and depression. It has been my experience in dealing with those who are experiencing life crises that most complain of lack of energy as a chief symptom, which goes along with the feelings of helplessness that brought them to seek counsel. There is one category of patient that is an exception to this rule: I have never seen a patient who exercised regularly and complained of tiredness or depression. Anxiety, sometimes, but not depression. Of course, one might conclude that tired people are too tired to exercise. However, I believe that in most cases, an active lifestyle prevents the gradual slide into depressive states. Exercise (see chapter 5) has been shown to be as effective as psychotherapy for moderate depression (Greist et al., 1979).

In our modern society, almost no one eats for maximum energy, or exercises enough to improve fitness and endurance. Although there are some medical diseases that cause depression, I sometimes wonder how many people who are now diagnosed as "depressed" and taking one of the popular antidepressant medications might have avoided all that fuss if they had been regular exercisers. (If you are one of those on medications, see your physician before throwing away your pill bottles at the jogging path!)

I once worked with a gentleman in his seventies who had no apparent medical problems, but complained of low energy. He went to his physician, who gave him a prescription for Ritalin, a stimulant. This helped a bit. But then I found out that he never ate breakfast, skimped on lunch, and never exercised. When I was through with him, he was eating a hearty breakfast, a good lunch, walked every day, and found no need for medications to feel full of pep.

The World Health Organization has declared that a feeling of abundant energy is a good indicator of health (Dixon et al., 1993). This assumes the person is not abusing amphetamines or caffeine, and is not suffering from mania. Abundant energy means waking up feeling refreshed, having a positive attitude about the challenges and opportunities that the new day offers, dealing with the events of the day with vigor, and returning to bed tired but not worn-out.

Perhaps a personal story will provide a worthy example. When I was in my early twenties, I lacked energy. On weekdays, as a NASA engineer, I could barely drag myself out of bed to get to work. On weekends, I would sleep until the break of noon. At work, after a hearty breakfast of doughnuts, I would nod off from time to time, drinking caffeine continuously. In retrospect, I think the moon mission would have failed had all my colleagues been in such a state.

I was saved by a health-nut friend ("If you're not a health nut, you're a sickness nut," he would say). He showed me that I could get up and exercise, become fit, and feel energetic. I became a jogger, back when people driving by would stare and honk at such a novel phenomenon, a person actually choosing to exercise. I reduced coffee consumption, and learned the miracle of nutrition. Thirty years later, even with children to raise, I have more energy. I get up about seven A.M. (but not unless an alarm device has been set to get me to work on time) and feel fairly energetic, at least when my total body is awake, which takes time for anybody.

What Is Energy?

From a *physiological* standpoint, energy comes from the conversion of calories in the food we eat into sugars that the muscles and organs can use. Food is converted into glucose (sugar), amino acids (proteins), and fat. Glucose and oxygen produce ATP, the energy molecule for muscles. In this way, muscles are able to turn chemical reactions into physical movement. They also turn physical movement into chemicals, such as lactic acid, which builds up to cause tiredness in overused muscles.

The process of muscular force involves the metabolism of oxygen, which is why we breathe. The ability of the body to metabolize oxygen is the measure of cardiorespiratory fitness, which is calculated as the volume of oxygen used per minute. If you have an exercise test on a treadmill, you may be breathing into a mask with two hoses attached. The difference in oxygen content between the intake and output hoses is the oxygen you metabolize. If you have been exercising regularly, your lungs and blood vessels are adapted through larger size and greater absorption ability to take in more oxygen, and to expel more waste gases. Lack of fresh air at home or in office buildings may be a cause of low energy from oxygen depletion. Fortunately, one doesn't have to be an exercise physiologist to have abundant energy. In the absence of disease, it is merely a matter of good sleep, good exercise, and healthful eating.

Energy Cycles

The energy we feel follows a biologically determined circadian (Latin: during the day) rhythm over each day. This level of energy closely corresponds to body temperature. If you have a good lifestyle, you may notice feeling colder about four A.M., but find that you get warmer just before waking up naturally. Energy increases gradually from awakening to a peak at about lunchtime, then sags for a few hours, increases some at dinnertime, then slowly returns to a low level at bedtime. Judicious use of latté can help to get you over the afternoon slump (but no caffeine after four P.M.!). You might try going without coffee in the morning to see whether your gradual increase in energy is due to that first cup, or due to naturally increasing energy.

Each individual has a slightly different pattern of energy. Some people are "morning people," who follow the credo "Early to bed, early to rise, makes a man healthy, wealthy, and wise," and, one could add, "despised" by the other group, the "evening people." The latter group follow the credo "Wake up when your eyes open, and party/work on into the wee hours." I believe that "evening people" can, through careful lifestyle changes, be converted into "morning people." However, as a "morning person," I have never been able to tolerate an "evening people" lifestyle.

In the plan of this book, you will be recording your energy levels regularly to see how they change and improve. To some extent, you can adjust your schedule to take advantage of the high-energy times to do such things as hold meetings, and save the routine matters that do not require much mental energy for your low-energy periods. If you are a shift worker, or red-eye flight attendant, good luck. Your energy cycles will be out of synchrony with what your body must do.

For women, hormonal shifts and menstruation may alter feelings of energy and tension, resulting in decreased energy. There is some controversy about this, except among women, who know what they are talking about. Low energy, low mood, and irritability are associated with the late luteal and early premenstrual phase (Redmond, 1997), but only about 10 percent of women in the reproductive years experience significant changes in mood and energy level (Steiner, 1992). Whatever PMS may be, many report that the types of lifestyle change recommended in this book are helpful in alleviating the intensity of the symptoms.

Energy may fluctuate on much slower cycles over longer periods. In regions that have a winter, some people are depressed and tired during cold months, possibly due to the lack of sunlight, possibly due to less exercise, and possibly due to less fresh air. Some may have a chemical imbalance. This is called Seasonal Affective Disorder. One treatment involves daily exposure to bright light. Perhaps regularly shoveling snow outside might be helpful. In the warmer parts, such as south Texas, I have noticed a similar pattern of low energy and depression associated with the summer months, when everyone stays inside with air-conditioning, getting less exercise and less fresh air. The air-conditioning also provides more mold and fewer negative ions, which could contribute to the problem.

Energy: Psychological Factors

From a *psychological* standpoint, energy is a feeling of well-being and strength that is partly due to the metabolism in your muscles, but is also influenced by motivation, a sense of purpose, and/or a sense of hope. Thus, in addition to lifestyle energy enhancers such as nutrition and exercise, it is important to have the right frame of mind. This can come from your upbringing, religious, or philosophical training. Continuing support from others who subscribe to the same mind-set is essential to keep you on the right path.

Of Rats and Men

When rats are placed in an inescapable bucket of water, they will swim to keep afloat for many hours, but eventually run out of steam and drown. If, however, you take a rat out of the bucket well before the normal drowning time, and then place the rat in the bucket several days later, the rat will swim for much longer than the normal drowning time. (I don't do these experiments, I just report about them.) The theory is that rats which have been removed from the bucket swim much longer, and seem to have more energy, because they have a hope of being removed again. So you have to ask yourself, "Who is going to rescue me from my drowning bucket?" If you can't think of any salvation resources, then your energy may fade, and you will go under. But there is hope. You have a support group! (Remember the previous chapter?)

A study of college students (who often serve as substitutes for rats in experiments when the budget doesn't allow for rats) provides another example of how energy is affected by psychological factors. Students were asked to memorize some difficult material to win a prize. Some were told that they didn't have a rat's-rear-end chance of succeeding. Others were told that the chances were high that they could succeed and win the prize. The subjects in the latter group reported higher self-perceived energy than the low-chance-of-winning condition (Wright & Gregorich, 1989). This is why fans yell, "You can do it! Go for it!" to encourage, and to increase perceived energy level in the athletes they favor. This is why you should provide encouragement to those in need of a boost in a time of crisis.

However, even with maximum support from others and maximum hope, you don't want to push forward without first building up your energy through lifestyle changes. This is why this plan begins with energy improvement, the first step in self-care. There are some people who feel uneasy taking care of themselves, perhaps because their self-esteem is so low that they feel worthy of love only if they take care of others, at the expense of their own comfort. An extremely important theme throughout this book is: *Take care of yourself first, so that you can then have the energy to take care of others,* in balance with self-care. Maintain the balance of self-other care as much as possible. Too much *self-care* is narcissism, too much *other care* is co-dependency. More on this when you get to the section on Purpose.

Perceived energy can be increased through a positive mood state such as that induced by the encouragement of friends. Likewise, it can be reduced through negative mood induction, such as the sudden realization that you are doing everything wrong, or when someone unkindly points out that you are going to fail, as usual. The relationship between moods and energy level has been studied thoroughly by Professor Robert Thayer at California State, Long Beach (his book is required reading. See Thayer, 1996). Thayer has defined four major mood states:

a) *calm-energy:* the most desirable state, associated with positive moods. It represents optimal mental and physiological states. In the Oriental philosophies associated with the martial arts, this is seen as the ideal state, because it combines mental alertness with potential energy.

b) *calm-tiredness:* this is also a good-mood state, which might be ideal for late evening as one prepares for sleep after achieving a good day's work.

c) *tense-energy:* the energy of this mood is that associated with stress, frustration, and perhaps some anxiety. However, the energy is there to deal with these negative aspects.

d) *tense-tiredness:* this is a bad mood situation. Fatigue is mixed with nervousness, tension, or anxiety. This is the mood of depression.

The plan of this book is to help you develop a step-by-step method to increase the chances that you are in the *calm-energy* state, and that you will tend to stay in that state during the day.

Lifestyle Factors Associated with High Energy

Although some people seem genetically more energetic than others, the way you live from day to day is what determines, to a large extent, how much energy you will enjoy. Studies of people who feel energetic show that energy is related to:

1. *Low-fat eating*. Most people feel tired, and sleep more, on a high-fat diet. That is why a high-fat diet may lead to overweight. Not only does fat have 2.5 times more calories than other nutrients, but eating too much of it makes you less likely to exercise.

2. *Exercise*. People who exercise regularly and are physically fit clearly have more feelings of energy and well-being than couch potatoes.

3. *Sleep*. It is obvious that lack of sleep can make us feel tired. Many Americans get only seven hours of sleep a night. When they get eight hours, they report feeling much better.

4. Feelings of *peace and relaxation*. This may help the immune system.

5. *Poisons*. Nicotine, alcohol, and caffeine can reduce your feelings of energy. Even one glass of wine or beer can reduce the body's ability to use oxygen for 24 hours. Smoking reduces the ability of the lungs to get oxygen into the body. Caffeine blocks the signals to the brain telling you to rest, and interferes with sleep; most people report feeling more energetic after giving up coffee.

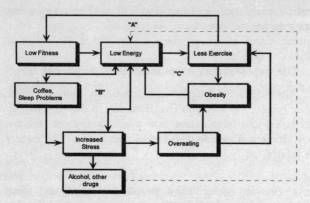

Figure 3.1. Lifestyle and Energy Cycles

The relationship between energy, habits, and weight is shown in Figure 3.1.

Study this figure. Note how low physical fitness results in low perceived energy, which in turn makes exercise less likely, which in turn reduces physical fitness (Cycle A). Most Americans seem to be caught in this vicious cycle. Note also that people with low energy may have a harder time coping with stress, and have more perceived stress because of low energy levels (stress is the perception that one's ability to handle problems may be inadequate). Overeating or abuse of other substances may be the result.

Many turn to caffeine to compensate for feelings of low energy. Now that people are willing to pay three dollars for a cup of coffee, it is clear that caffeine is becoming a serious drug habit. Caffeine interferes with sleep, increases feelings of stress, and reduces feelings of energy after the initial buzz wears off (assuming you don't have your arm hooked up to a coffee intravenous drip system). This is shown as Vicious Cycle B.

The reduced likelihood of exercise can lead to obesity, which in and of itself may be a physiological burden causing increased feelings of tiredness. I have dealt with many patients seeking treatment for obesity. A common complaint is lack of energy. This is depicted in the figure as Vicious Cycle C.

The way to escape from these vicious cycles is to get sleep, increase exercise, and eat fewer calorie-dense foods. These are the topics for the next three chapters.

About Fatigue and Medicine

Our health system is disease-oriented rather than health-oriented, partly because insurance covers only diseases, and researchers are more likely to get grant money if they focus on diseases. Thus, people talk in terms of fatigue more than in terms of energy. Fatigue is increasing in prevalence in the United States, possibly because of decreasing sleep (Bliwise, 1996), increasing stress, and decreasing exercise (Anonymous, 1996). The prevalence of chronic fatigue (being tired all the time, but not *chronic fatigue syndrome*) has been estimated at about 20 percent of the U.S. adult population (Buchwald et al., 1995). In primary-care-medical-clinic settings, as many as 25 percent come with fatigue as a major problem (Kroenke et al., 1988). Individuals with excessive tiredness are more likely to be frequent users of the health-care system, and have mood, anxiety, or psychosomatic disorders (Walker et al., 1993).

Although the complaint of chronic fatigue is widespread in primary care, physicians, who prefer a medical problem focus, may be lax in performing a comprehensive evaluation which includes psychological and behavioral (exercise, diet, sleep) assessments (Ward, DeLisle, Shores et al., 1996). Increasingly, the pressures of managed care result in a lack of time for physicians to delve more deeply into each patient's lifestyle problems. Sometimes they dismiss the patients as ''cranks'' or ''whiners.'' They may prescribe an antidepressant.

However, unless someone in the health-care system re-

fers the patient to a course in lifestyle change, the problem
may linger. Fatigue as a symptom is persistent; some have
found only about one fourth of patients improved at a one-
year follow-up (Kroenke et al., 1988). This places a cost
burden on the economics of the health-care system, which
is ultimately paid by (you guessed it) us, the healthy working class.

When patients complain of chronic fatigue, the majority
seem to get a psychiatric diagnosis (Wessely et al., 1996).
In a study of 565 patients with at least six months of unex-
plained fatigue or chronic unwellness, researchers found
that almost half had a psychological disorder that started
before the fatigue. About one fifth of the patients had a
possible medical problem causing fatigue. One fourth of the
patients were diagnosed with chronic fatigue syndrome, and
another fifth had none of these problems (Reyes et al.,
1997). Again, I wonder how many would suffer from fatigue, and get a diagnosis of depression, if they had established a regular exercise habit earlier in life.

Energy BS

Because there is so much fatigue in our society, there is
a high demand for solutions to this uncomfortable problem.
Whenever there is a high demand for solutions, there is an
opportunity to make money by selling substances and devices. Of course, caffeine has been around for many years,
it works, and is relatively harmless for most people if used
wisely. Amphetamines will boost your feelings of energy,
but the withdrawal crash is so discomfiting that use becomes addictive as well as illegal. Ginseng is now touted
as an energy enhancer, but there is scant evidence that it
works. Pregnenolone, part of the natural hormone system,
was found to increase energy in studies done after World
War II, but there has been no recent scientific validation
for it. Peppermint as an aroma can boost alertness temporarily, but alertness and energy are not quite the same thing.

True energy can only be derived from a healthy body, properly rested and fed.

However, since there are many people looking for easy answers to life's problems, savvy businessmen are willing to sell you a wide variety of energy-enhancing products. Some of these I found on the Web include:

- the Secrets of Feng Shui, which is supposed to make you feel better through the arrangement of furniture in your room, and by discovering specific points in your home or office associated with energy and success. There are also two Feng Shui symbols, worn about the neck, which increase yin and yang energy, according to the purveyors.

- Gem Essences, which are supposed to increase energy through the "emerging modality of healing in vibrational medicine." The molecules of your body are supposed to resonate with the vibrations in the quartz crystal you wear around your neck.

- Life Force Energy Disks, which are supposed to be very useful for those who spend a lot of time in front of a computer, for the purpose of reducing fatigue and "other harmful effects of electromagnetic radiation."

- Quan Yin symbols: a statue of Quan Yin hung or placed in a room is alleged to have the "power to cleanse the environment of any unpleasant energies."

If I really wanted to make *BIG MONEY* by writing energy enhancement books, I would use language like this (also found on the Web at www.energyenhancement.co.UK/med.htm:

My Plan will lead you to the most advanced methods of conscious healing and the most advanced course of using psychic powers to get in touch with the Higher Self, ground negative energies, integrate the separated selves and master relationships through the Three Initiations leading towards Enlightenment.

Energy Enhancement is the latest and most advanced message channeled from Ascended Masters and based on years of research with living Masters using hidden techniques over 5000 years old, for the benefit of humanity for the next Millennium.

However, if I ever went on a talk show and started blathering like that, I would risk the danger of doubling over with uncontrollable fits of laughter, and thereby losing what little credibility I have.

Summary

Feelings of energy are best obtained through proper lifestyle, including plenty of exercise, and avoidance of poisons. There are no substances or devices that have been proved to be of benefit. However, I do like my double latté at about two P.M.

Homework: Medical Evaluation

Regardless of your level of energy, it is wise to get a thorough medical checkup before starting on a life improvement plan to enhance energy, achieve calm, and find your life purpose. There are so many things that can be out of kilter in the human body, many of which can alter the way you feel and think. A list of some of them that might cause reduced energy includes:

- diabetes
- coronary heart disease
- cancer
- hypothyroidism
- anemia
- multiple sclerosis
- lupus
- chronic obstructive pulmonary disease
- depression
- undereating
- HIV

- kidney disease
- liver disease
- sarcoidosis

- prescription medications that can cause tiredness.

Ask your physician to clear you for a moderate exercise program. This may involve testing depending on your current health status and age. If it turns out that you have a serious disease, then you will need to work closely with your health-care providers to determine your limitations regarding the lifestyle changes recommended in this book.

Homework

Continue meeting with your support personnel.

Begin keeping a diary, which should look something like this:

Name: _____ Weekly Report: _____

	Sun	Mon	Tue	Wed	Thu	Fri	Sat
Sleep hours							
Exercise minutes							
Relaxation minutes							
Mood							
Energy							
Nutrition: Breakfast							
Lunch							
Dinner							
Snacks							

COMMENTS:

_____

_____

SCALE: Add the following symbols as appropriate to each box:

   ☹   very bad, or very low

   ⌢   bad, or low

   ⌣   good, or high

   ☺   very good, or very high

Example: Exercised Monday for 20 minutes and it felt very good:

Exercise minutes	20☺					

Example: Energy level seemed low on Wednesday:

Energy				⌢		

Your reports for relaxation, exercise, and nutrition will change as you learn more about the specifics of these aspects of energy building in forthcoming chapters.

Important Point: Note This!

One rule of the plan is this: BE NICE TO YOURSELF. Your life-improvement efforts are designed not only to add energy to your life, but also to be enjoyable (mostly) while you develop your new habits. The forthcoming chapters will show you how to luxuriate in great sleep, to enjoy exercise, and to eat like a gourmet. Think of making lifestyle changes as an *adventure*, a *new and interesting experience*. Too often people think of life improvement efforts as a *burden* requiring *great effort*. Forget that thought with this plan! With this plan, it should be clear that *the burden of doing nothing about your life* is far greater than the effort it takes to develop yourself into a *healthier, high-energy* person.

Read that last sentence again aloud.

References

Anonymous (1996). State-specific prevalence of participation in physical activity Behavioral Risk Factor Surveillance System. *Morbidity and Mortality Weekly Report*, 45, 673–75.

Bliwise, D. L. (1996). Historical change in the report of daytime fatigue. *Sleep*, 19, 462–64.

Buchwald, D., Umali, P., Umali, J., Kith, P., Pearlman, T., Komaroff, A. L. (1995). Chronic fatigue and chronic fatigue syndrome: prevalence in a Pacific Northwest health care system. *Annals of Internal Medicine*, 123, 81–88.

Dixon, J. K, Dixon, J. P, Hickey, M. (1993). Energy as a central factor in the self-assessment of health. *Advances in Nursing Science*, 15, 4, 1–12.

Greist, J. H, Eischens, R. R, Klien, M. H., Faris, J. W. (1979). Antidepressant running. *Psychiatric Annals*, 9, 134–140.

Kroenke, K., Wood, D. R., Mangelsdorff, A. D., Meier, N. J., Powell, J. B. (1988). Chronic fatigue in primary care. Prevalence, patient characteristics, and outcome. *JAMA*, 260, 929–34.

Redmond, G. (1997). Mood disorders in the female patient. *International Journal of Fertility and Women's Medicine*, 42, 67–72.

Reyes, M., Gary, H. E., Dobbins, J. G. et al. (1997). Surveillance for chronic fatigue syndrome—four U.S. cities, September 1989 through August 1993. *Morbidity and Mortality Weekly Report*, 46 (No. SS-2), 1–13.

Steiner, M. (1992). Female-specific mood disorders. *Clinical Obstetrics & Gynecology*, 35, 599–611.

Thayer, R. E. (1996). *The Origin of Everyday Moods: Managing Energy, Tension, and Stress*. Oxford University Press.

Walker, E. A., Katon, W. J., Jemelka, R. P. (1993). Psychiatric disorders and medical care utilization among people in the general population who report fatigue. *Journal of General Internal Medicine*, 8, 436–40.

Ward, M. H., DeLisle, H., Shores, J. H., Slocum, P. C., Foresman, B. H. (1996). Chronic fatigue complaints in primary care: incidence and diagnostic patterns. *Journal of the American Osteopathic Association*, 96, 34–46.

Wessely, S., Chalder, T., Hirsch, S., Wallace, P., Wright, D. (1996.) Psychological symptoms, somatic symptoms, and psychiatric disorder in chronic fatigue and chronic fatigue syndrome: a prospective study in the primary care setting. *American Journal of Psychiatry*, 153, 1050–59.

Wright, R. A., Gregorich, S. (1989). Difficulty and instrumentality of imminent behavior as determinants of cardiovascular response and self-reported energy. *Psychophysiology*, 26, 586–92.

4

Sleep, the Foundation of Energy

GOAL: In this chapter you will be asked to examine your philosophy of life and how it affects your sleep attitudes and habits. Exercises will help you enhance your awareness of how childhood influences and current lifestyle may be getting in the way of good sleep. By transforming the sleep experience into an enjoyable, sensual event, you will be more likely to develop a sleep style that will enhance feelings of energy.

Sleepless in the U.S.

Lack of sleep is epidemic and unfortunately routine in our lives. Humans need about nine hours of sleep every night, especially if they are getting a healthful amount of exercise. Many Americans now average seven hours. Stress and pressures from work, the hectic noise of urban existence, family needs—all these are conspiring to make peace and contentment scarce commodities. And now that we especially need sleep as a physical and mental restorative, we find ourselves getting less and less precious rest. We long for relief, but never can seem to get the control over our lives to make time for, and prepare for, the deep and rejuvenating sleep our bodies are designed to obtain. But we can do better. Let me take you figuratively by the hand, and lead you to more fulfilling sleep.

In my experiences as a psychologist, I have seen hundreds of patients. It never ceases to amaze me how many of these individuals, who come with feelings of anxiety and / or depression, lack adequate sleep. Some lack good sleep because of their troubles. But some seem to get into trouble by leading lifestyles which demand more of their bodies than nature allows. Lack of sleep can be a major contributor to the inability to cope with relationship, family, and job problems. These challenges might not seem so demanding if the individual had the energy that comes from a lifestyle properly founded on good sleep. Therapists know that in crisis management, the first step after ensuring safety is "decompressing" and rest. Bad sleep and depression go together; lack of sleep leads to tiredness, which might make depression worse; depressed people often arise too early, worrying about their sad state (Moffaert, 1994).

Despite the obvious need for good sleep, the problem of inadequate sleep is widespread. Up to one half of Americans experience sleep disorders at some point in their lives, and it would seem that most of the other half aren't doing very well with sleep either. There are many factors that may be causing this sorry state of affairs. Over the last 30 years economic trends have made it more difficult for the average person to make a decent living within normal working hours, or with only one parent working. We work harder and longer to maintain our standard of living. Many are forced to move to the distant suburbs; the long and stressful commute robs them of valuable time which could be used for more sleep. To make matters worse, there appears to be a growing spirit of unhealthful competition (dog-eat-dog), compelling many to excessive work hours. A new credo is emerging: "The early bird gets the worm, lunch is for wimps, and the way to get ahead is to work late." The habit of overwork and staying up late is already notoriously damaging the psychological health of many Japanese. A study of middle managers found that 70 percent were working more than 10 hours a day, affecting their sleep patterns. There is now a campaign in Japan advocating that people work fewer hours (Maruyama & Morimoto, 1996).

Only about 25 percent of households with children consist of two parents with a stay-at-home mother. The breakdown of the traditional family places an extreme burden on many single mothers, who find it difficult to make restorative time for themselves, much less increase their sleep hours.

Modern technology has given us "conveniences" which disrupt sleep patterns. The advent of electric lighting makes it possible to stay awake to all hours; it was not long ago that the sunset brought about a reduction in activity as lanterns provided dim light. And of course one can accuse television of being a major contributor to excessively late bedtimes. TV lures us into late-night viewing through the enticement of worthless sensory stimulation, spiced with the pornography of violence and sex, and embellished with fantasies of wealth and adventure.

Given all these pressures against good sleep, how can you achieve a good night's rest? You cannot change society. But you may be able to change yourself. This change can occur if you restructure your priorities, so that restorative sleep becomes the foundation for your mental and physical health. You can develop a new approach to living, a new philosophy of life, which will help you make needed changes in your sleep style.

In chapter 1, a description of the plan divided activities into two categories: self-care and other care. Sleep is the most basic self-care "activity." In order to motivate yourself to develop a better sleep style, you need to recognize that you have a right, duty, and privilege to get good sleep, since it is required for self-care, and to provide you with the energy to provide other care. The self-caring aspect of life allows you how to make sleep an extremely *enjoyable restoring experience.* Learning to make sleep a "gourmet" event will motivate you to maintain your new habits of enjoyable sleep. You can make everything about sleep part of a beautiful experience, from pajamas to aromas to sex. In this age all of us must strive to be gentler on ourselves. The best place to start a significant change in lifestyle is to embrace the night as a wonderfully restoring period of relaxing activities and deep sleep. Then you can arise each day to face the challenges of life with renewed energy and health!

Developing a Philosophy of Sleep

Sleep is a good place to start a new emphasis on self-care, because it is a private or semi-private aspect of your life, and you have freedom to make changes in your sleep style. Also, good sleep provides the foundation for an energy-filled life. Feelings of energy come from good sleep,

---

Thought for the Day

To provide a focus and direction for this major lifestyle change, a different orientation to life is needed. Everyone operates according to a set of principles for living, whether consciously or not. Some learn these principles from experience, some from parents, some from religion. A philosopher would be concerned with how a set of lifestyle principles helps a person live a "good" life, in terms of optimizing happiness for himself and others. However, it seems that many people are living according to the philosophy of fear: work harder and longer to stay ahead of the payments for a lifestyle full of activities which we hope will give us a sense of enjoyment or importance. It is a struggle that will never meet our needs for peace, unless we change our life orientation, and let this philosophy guide us in every aspect of our lives.

regular exercise, and a low-fat eating style. But a good sleep lifestyle is needed before an exercise program can begin, and tiredness often reduces eating self-control. Not to mention the relationships that fail due to the irritability that lack of good sleep can produce.

In order to develop a positive attitude toward sleep, and a philosophy of life that makes good sleep a high priority, you should examine what perspectives and feelings many people seem to have about sleep. The ideal sleep attitude should have been formed in childhood. Do you remember sleep as a child? For some readers, reflecting back to childhood will bring fond memories of caring parents tucking you in to bed, reading you a story, singing a lullaby, telling you everything is going to be all right, turning on the night-light shaped in the image of a favorite cartoon character, leaving your door open slightly, being assured that Mommy and Daddy were just down the hall, and not to worry about the bogey-man stories which your older brother told you. If you had an idyllic childhood, as I did, it is time to make sleep as beautiful an experience now as it was then.

Without even thinking about it, many have developed a negative attitude toward sleep. There are the unfortunate few who dread the night because, as children, unspeakable acts were committed against them as they lay in bed.

Researchers now refer to ''Adverse Childhood Experiences (ACE),'' which may include incest, physical abuse, or alcoholism. As many as one third of Americans may have experienced ACE. Those with ACE are now known to have a much higher likelihood of a variety of stress and behavioral disorders in adult life, including insomnia. Without therapy, good sleep may be difficult. If you had such a traumatic childhood, you may need to recondition yourself to learn that sleep can be a time of peace. (Talk to your doctor or a psychologist; but don't just take sleeping pills.)

Thinking About Your Childhood Sleep

Here is an exercise designed to help you get in touch with childhood factors that may now be affecting your sleep habits and your attitude toward sleep.

1. Describe your childhood sleep experiences: your bedroom, stuffed animals you may have slept with, and siblings with whom you shared a bed or room. Was your bedroom a happy place? If not, why not? Is your bedroom currently a nice place to sleep? If not, read on.

2. What was the emotional tone in your family as you went to bed; what was the emotional tone in the morning?

3. How were you awakened?

4. Was there physical or sexual trauma associated with sleep?

5. Were you unusually frightened of the dark? What did you do about this fear? What did your family think? Are you comfortable in the dark now?

6. Do you think the memories of your childhood sleep experiences affect the quality of sleep you get now?

7. Can you feel secure sleeping without covers over your body?

Some avoid good sleep because, consciously or subconsciously, sleep is viewed as a form of death. We have all heard the bedtime prayer, "Now I lay me down to sleep . . . If I should die before I wake . . ." It is adaptive for animals to feel in control of their surroundings; sleep makes us give up control. In sleep we are susceptible to attack without warning. Humans naturally fear or avoid darkness, because our vision is adapted to daytime. Without a feeling that we are in a secure environment, a sense of heightened vigilance works against relaxation and sleep.

Some individuals see sleep as interfering with opportunities to achieve more work or to enjoy more play. A work-aholic, who works mainly to feel important in order to overcome low self-esteem, or to become wealthy at the expense of spiritual and interpersonal values, may push well past midnight. Eventually, the productivity of a workaholic will fall below that of someone who has more moderate work hours.

There is a branch of Jewish tradition which calls for the minimizing of sleep, because the desire for living is seen as a struggle against the desire to sleep. Oversleeping is seen as robbing one of life's opportunities; it dulls the mind. Individuals are urged to push on through the night if they are excited about a project. There is a Jewish custom called "Mishmar," staying up all night on Thursdays to complete a project or discussion. However, the tradition does call for one to average eight hours of sleep a night.

Differences in attitudes about sleep may even be genetically determined. There is a genetic variation in which the brain requires more than the usual amount of stimulation to "feel comfortable." People with this variation tend to be thrill seekers (e.g., bungee jumpers, sky divers, and so forth), or they may seem to be constantly busy at something which keeps their brain very active (video-game addiction); they may have a sense that sleep interferes with a chance for excitement. They tend to be night owls, and their sleep habits may not fit well into the world of workers who must rise early, Monday through Friday. The majority of people, without the thrill-seeking genetic variation, strive for order and calm in their lives, minimizing stimulation; they are comfortable quietly reading a book. Thus, there are "morning" people who function well earlier in the day and look forward to sleep in the evening, and there are "evening" people who want to party at night. If you are an "evening" person, you may have found conflict between your need for good sleep and the world's demands upon you in the morning.

Bad Sleep Is Like Bad Sex

For the human body to respond properly and enjoyably to sex, a receptive mood must be set. The environment should be secure and peaceful. A sequence of behaviors should unfold slowly and caringly so that the organs may respond with facilitating fluids and maximal sensitivity. So it is with sleep. If one views sleep as an important and vital part of optimal living, then it should be treated with care and loving attention to detail, in the same way as one might prepare for sex. Sleep should be experienced in the same way a gourmet experiences a great meal: mood, surroundings, senses, and food are all carefully woven together in a sequence leading to a sense of fulfillment and contentment.

Compare these two sleep lifestyles:

1. After a hard day's work and a few drinks with friends at the neighborhood bar, Cindy comes home to her apartment at about 8:30 P.M. She watches TV and snacks until ten-thirty, then irons clothes, cleans up the kitchen, then she remembers she must pay some bills to be mailed the next day. At 11:30 P.M. she is dead tired, and flops into bed. She arises six hours later (to the sudden detonation of her alarm clock) so that she will have time to get ready for work and catch the seven A.M. bus.

2. After a hard day's work and a good workout at the gym, Susan comes home at eight-thirty. She has a nutritious, low-fat vegetarian dinner, then goes through her mail and makes a list of things to do the next day in her planner. She makes sure her daily plan is consistent with her spiritual beliefs. While listening to restful classical music, she meditates and relaxes in candlelight for 20 minutes. The candles emit a re-laxing aroma. She then slowly goes to her bed, and experiences the peace of floating on a water bed. She

is lulled to sleep by the electronically generated sounds of waves on the shore, with distant thunder. She arises 7.5 hours later to the sound of soft and gentle classical music. Breathing exercises restore her full energy level as she goes over her plan for the day.

Which example is most similar to your sleep experiences?

Stop Torturing Yourself

Intelligence agents use sleep deprivation as a standard technique to break down the will of captives. They wake them every 30 minutes in an unpleasant way so that adequate sleep cannot be obtained. Eventually, the captive's mind becomes frazzled, and resistance to suggestions to sign confessions is broken. Yet many deprive themselves of sleep, and wonder why they lack the ability to lead productive and happy lives.

The Right to Sleep

Every human has the right to at least eight hours of restorative sleep every night. Any interference should be viewed as a violation of a basic human right. This includes interference from spouse, children, and pets.

One way to look at the self-care orientation to life (and sleep) is to examine how well people take care of themselves compared with the care they give others. There are two extremes:

1. *Overcare of Others.* Some people, because of a traumatic childhood, have very low self-esteem, and are constantly trying to care for others at the expense of their own self-care. They do this to try to ''look good'' to others, in order to be loved. Someone at

this extreme might say, "Oh, that's all right. You go to bed, I'll stay up to finish the laundry." This same person is first up in the morning to make sure everyone gets what they need for breakfast. The problem with this extreme, which is called "codependency" when it applies to those involved in alcoholic families, is that the person burns out on giving. The people she is trying to help see her as an overcontrolling person searching for attention through martyrdom. Mutual resentment often results, and the caregiver fails to get the love she seeks.

2. *Overcare of Self.* Some people, perhaps those spoiled as children, have the view that they deserve royal treatment; they want to wallow in self-indulgence. They demand to sleep late, and make demands on others while they themselves remain comfortable in bed. Needless to say, resentment may build up in this type of situation as well. It is important to note that some with low self-esteem, when feeling frustrated, will become temporarily self-indulgent, but then feel guilty for caring for themselves. Others who are overstressed may seek sleep as a form of withdrawal; be kind to them, they need more caring. Excessive sleep can be a sign of depression.

The ideal life orientation is to care *optimally for others by first caring optimally for yourself.* This means that one should get good sleep, exercise, recreation, and nutrition not only for personal energy and enjoyment, but also to have the energy to be a helpful resource to others, and to be able to share life with others. Compare your current lifestyle with the examples given in this table:

Table 1: Typical Lifestyle Compared with Nurturing Lifestyle

AREA OF LIFE	TYPICAL LIFESTYLE	NURTURING LIFESTYLE
Work	Worry, fear, insecurity, hostile competition, lose sleep over work	Work is seen as opportunity for constructive cooperation. Feelings of accomplishment make for sound sleep.
Family	Little interaction; watch TV together at best. Lack of family team spirit. Hostility disrupts sleep.	Family acts as a team to help each member achieve good relationships, meaningful activities/work, and good health with good sleep.
Health	No time for exercise. Eats high-fat fast food. Neglects need for relaxation/restoration of body; sleep given short shrift.	Good health seen as basis for happy life; regular exercise, good nutrition, regular rest and sleep.
Emotional	Uses substances to alter mood; does not practice relaxation; worries about selfish interests. Poor health habits and interpersonal conflict prevent good sleep.	Actively tries to solve mood problems; uses stress management; knows happiness comes from good relationships and tries to balance self-care with caring for others. Knows that good sleep can enhance mood.

Take a highlighter and mark the phrases that describe you in this and the other tables.

Here is a table outlining the *nurturing sleep style*.

Table 2: Typical American Sleep Style versus Nurturant Sleep Style

SLEEP FACTOR	TYPICAL AMERICAN SLEEP STYLE	NURTURANT SLEEP STYLE
Presleep Activities	Stimulating, worrisome activities	Presleep ritual designed to optimize sleep
Presleep Food/ Beverage Use	Use of substances/food that are disruptive of sleep	Selects food and drink to ensure restful sleep pattern
Presleep Sex	Sex late in evening, postponing sleep	Sex planned to optimize sleep, and to enhance enjoyment, following hormonal rhythms
Presleep Emotional Coping	Worries and sadness take hold as other stimulations are reduced at nightfall	Uses methods to control anxiety and improve life organization so that the mind is clear for perfect sleep
Philosophy of Sleep	Sleep viewed as another event in hectic, tiring lifestyle; sleep viewed as a problem area	Sleep embraced as wonderful restorative process with enjoyable and helpful pre and postsleep rituals

Sleep Factor	Typical American Sleep Style	Nurturant Sleep Style
Attitude Toward Sleep	Exhaustion controls the body; mind may fight sleep if sleep is seen as interference in finishing tasks	Recognition that problems will be more easily solved if good sleep comes first.

Time Management for Good Sleep

Time management should begin with a nine-hour period for sleep rituals (30 minutes before sleep, 30 minutes upon arising) and sleep (eight hours for most people). Work backward from the time you must awake; for example, if you must arise at six A.M. to get to work on time without sleep rituals, then you should plan on beginning the sleep process at nine P.M. This may seem an unreasonably early hour to retire; many of the most popular TV programs start at nine P.M. But how many of these programs add to the quality and beauty of your life and relationships? How life enhancing are these programs compared with the feelings of energy and optimism that can be derived from optimizing sleep? Perhaps the valuable TV programs could be taped for viewing on the weekend. Some may say that social obligations often require staying up well past nine P.M. Again, ask yourself which of these social events really enhances your life. Perhaps you can persuade your friends to plan parties for afternoons on the weekends. Some singles (and some marrieds) have a habit of looking for romance or sex by hanging out at bars or clubs late into the night. Again, relationships begun in this way tend to be short-lived and medically dangerous, and not as gratifying sexually as the intimacy that can be found in relationships developed and nurtured over time in the light of day, and with the commitment to lifetime bonding (marriage).

No Time for Sleep?

Patients who lack adequate sleep typically complain that they haven't enough time. Often there really is no extra time. In these cases, consideration should be given to altering lifestyle factors such as job hours, location of residence, etc., to help make good sleep a priority. In most cases, there really is enough time for good sleep if you make sleep a priority.

The following table shows an example of time well managed around a foundation of good sleep. If you feel that this schedule is *unrealistic* given the demands placed on your time, try thinking of the *demands* as unrealistic instead (times may be shifted earlier or later for individual needs, without changing the duration of the sleep process).

Table 3: Weekday Time Management for Optimal Sleep

ACTIVITY	START	END
Awakening ritual	5:30 A.M.	6 A.M.
Stretching, relaxation, bath, breakfast	6 A.M.	7:30 A.M.
Commute	7:30 A.M.	8 A.M.
Work (includes 30 minutes for lunch, and three 10-minute energizing/walking breaks)	8 A.M.	5 P.M.
Commute	5 P.M.	5:30 P.M.
Exercise	5:30 P.M.	6:30 P.M.
Supper	6:30 P.M.	7 P.M.
Family	7 P.M.	8 P.M.
Self/spouse	8 P.M.	9 P.M.

ACTIVITY	START	END
Presleep ritual	9 P.M.	9:30 P.M.
Sleep	9:30 P.M.	5:30 A.M (8 hours)
Television	limit to 0–2 hours/week	
Shopping/socializing	plan for weekends	

Keep a similar diary to see where all your hours go. Can some of them be converted to sleep and sleep preparation?

Your children's sleep problems become your sleep problems. Consider this case study: Sarah and Michael are corporate workers with two children, Chris (age eight), and Amy (age four). Collecting the children from school and day care, overseeing homework, dinner, baths, leftover chores, planning for the next day, and "working" to get Chris and Amy to bed consume most evenings.

Change can begin with the parents prioritizing for themselves and their children. They decide relaxing and healthy "unwinding" is an important goal for the evening. They start a family custom of embracing the night. After baths and pajamas, they gather to stretch. Slow stretching for sleep and positive talk about sleepiness and bed helps children prepare for nighttime separation. Once the custom is in place, the tug-of-war over sleep lessens. The children will incorporate the positive signals of bedtime. Now Sarah and Michael's time begins.

Sleep Quality Questionnaire

Circle the score for each aspect of sleep. The purpose of this questionnaire is not to give you a "sleeping score," but to call to your attention areas where improvement might be needed.

ASPECT OF SLEEP QUALITY	SCORE (CIRCLE BEST ANSWER)				
Ability to fall asleep easily	Very Good	Good	Fair	Poor	Very Poor
Feeling of relaxation while preparing to sleep	Very Good	Good	Fair	Poor	Very Poor
Sense of peace before going to sleep	Very Good	Good	Fair	Poor	Very Poor
Feeling of energy upon arising	Very Good	Good	Fair	Poor	Very Poor
Sense of calm upon arising	Very Good	Good	Fair	Poor	Very Poor
Sense of peace and optimism upon arising	Very Good	Good	Fair	Poor	Very Poor
Sense that sleep is a wonderful experience	Very Good	Good	Fair	Poor	Very Poor
Emotional content of dreams	Very Good	Good	Fair	Poor	Very Poor
Ability to sleep all through the night	Very Good	Good	Fair	Poor	Very Poor
Ability to go back to sleep quickly if you wake up during the night	Very Good	Good	Fair	Poor	Very Poor
Bed	Very Good	Good	Fair	Poor	Very Poor
Bedroom	Very Good	Good	Fair	Poor	Very Poor
Sound, noises, temperature	Very Good	Good	Fair	Poor	Very Poor
Smell	Very Good	Good	Fair	Poor	Very Poor
Sense of peace if awake in middle of night	Very Good	Good	Fair	Poor	Very Poor

Sleep should not be experienced as a physiological imperative that overtakes the body when it is driven to exhaustion by the demands of the day. Sleep, or rather the *sleep experience,* should be a wonderfully enjoyable part of your life. It should be like a gourmet dinner, savored slowly, from appetizer to dessert and aperitif.

John Keats (1817) from "Sleep and Poetry"

> What is more gentle than a wind in summer?
> What is more soothing than the pretty hummer
> That stays one moment in an open flower,
> And buzzes cheerily from bower to bower?
> What is more tranquil than a musk-rose blowing
> In a green island, far from all men's knowing?
> More healthful than the leafiness of dales?
> More secret than a nest of nightingales?
> More serene than Cordelia's countenance?
> More full of visions than a high romance?
> What, but thee Sleep? Soft closer of our eyes!
> Low murmurer of tender lullabies!
> Light hoverer around our happy pillows!
> Wreather of poppy buds, and weeping willows!
> Silent entangler of a beauty's tresses!
> Most happy listener! when the morning blesses
> Thee for enlivening all the cheerful eyes
> That glance so brightly at the new sun-rise.

The Bedroom Environment

We spend one third of life sleeping, so the bedroom should be a special place, even if lovemaking didn't occur there.

MATTRESS: Let's start with the mattress. The basic principles of good "mattressology" are:

1) Firm and flat enough to support your spine so that the spine is level when you lie on your side. This includes the support of a pillow. Have someone look at your spine while you are lying down. I have found that box springs and the traditional thick mattress system can allow for mid-bed sag. My solution, based on years of sleeping in Southeast Asia, is a thin (four inches thick) mattress, placed on unyielding wood (I bought mine at Ikea, the Swedish furniture store). Over this is placed a one-inch mattress cover made of a wonderfully soft substance. This provides proper support, but feels soft. This system does not allow for the bouncy-bouncy effect for children who use beds as trampolines, but that is their problem.

2) The material that touches your body should be capable of dispersing body heat so that hot spots do not build up. Hot spots is one cause of what sleep professionals call "tossy-turny" sleep disorder.

The type of mattress I recommend is relatively inexpensive. You should try out different beds to find one that feels good to you, as long as it provides spinal support. Some interesting products on the market that I don't necessarily recommend, but which seem promising (if one doesn't lose sleep worrying about financing), are:

1) Tempur-Pedic: This is made of a material developed by NASA which conforms to your body shape, preventing pressure points. They say that this "Anti-gravity effect" reduces tossing and turning by 83 percent. It comes with matching pillows.

2) The SAMINA bed system from Toronto is made of a set of slats which adjust to body position and forces. Over this is a thin, latex mattress, with a natural, "Bioactive" shorn wool cover. It is noted that no metal parts are used so that the natural magnetic field

is not disturbed. I have found no research that magnetic concerns are important for sleep, but it might affect my magnetic personality.

3) DermaSafe mattresses help you to "defy gravity" with variable foam density matched to body parts.

4) The Sobakawa Pillow is "filled with thousands of tiny, natural buckwheat husks that quickly conform to your head, neck, and shoulders." The use of husks allows for air circulation.

5) The Prenatal Baby Cradle maternity mattress by Maternal Concepts: This is an inflatable mattress with breast and abdomen chambers so that a woman can lie on her stomach without pressuring these areas.

6) The Select Sleep Comfort System, a mattress with air chambers that can be inflated individually so that your sleeping partner can have soft, mushy support while you pump up to a firm mattress experience.

7) The MagnetiCo Sleep Pad, developed by a dentist, is based on the hypothesis that the human body works best when it is exposed to a magnetic field similar to what existed thousands of years ago. So this system contains magnets which, it is claimed, improve strength and endurance, relieve symptoms of arthritis, alleviate headaches and sleep disorders, and improve the immune system. This may be true, but I'm not spending $1,000 for a queen-sized version until I see research published in *The Journal of the American Medical Association.*

SOUND: For me, there are only three sound environments conducive to sleep:

1. The cacophony of millions of frogs and crickets of a summer's night, laced with gentle breezes, the lonesome cry of a coyote, and distant thunder;

2. The steady drone of an air conditioner, or air cleaner;

3. Absolute silence.

Since absolute silence is hard to achieve, and since urban existence requires closed windows to keep out pollution and crime, the answer for many is number two. However, there are now devices that electronically simulate the sounds of surf, rain, waterfalls, crickets and frogs, etc., which I find very pleasing and soothing.

ATMOSPHERE: Many have advised sleeping in a room with an open window, to provide fresh air, assuming there is fresh air outside. This is generally a good idea, but perhaps today, in the city, one could devise a through-the-wall vent, with a fan and microparticulate-absorbing filter so that outside air could be drawn in, in a controlled and clean way.

COLOR: I have found that dark green walls are conducive to relaxation. They help control excessive light when low-level illumination is desired. A dark ceiling might also be considered. On such a ceiling, one can place star and planet stickers which glow after the lights are extinguished. Yes, I know those are for kids, but have you ever lain in bed and looked up at a vast array of glowing stars?

TEMPERATURE: This may be a matter of individual taste. In my youth, I enjoyed sleeping in the tropics (low temperature 80 degrees F, 95 percent humidity) with an electric fan blowing over my body. I also enjoy sleeping under a down quilt at 45 degrees F. One consideration is that cold germs proliferate in warm air, so keeping one's bedroom toasty is probably not such a hot idea.

SMELLS: People are increasingly becoming aware of their environmental odors. Aroma therapy works in the sense that if you think a smell is pleasant, your mood will be lifted. The odor of peppermint can be stimulating, so this might be useful in the morning. Lavender is the smell for relaxation. This odor is available in candles, bath oils, massage oils, and mists.

LIGHTING: Soft lighting is conducive to relaxation and sleep. Lavender candles could be tried, taking care to have the proper equipment to prevent fires, which are not conducive to sleep.

PAJAMAS and SHEETS: Explore the variety of materials now available. In winter, I have enjoyed flannel sheets. I have also enjoyed satin sheets and pajamas, but more for their sensuality than for sleep.

MATTRESS VIBRATION: Vibration units are available for regular and water beds. Unless you have a medical condition that might be exacerbated by shaking, such as the dislodging of a blood clot (yuck), vibration can be very relaxing, and many people find that sleep comes easily after a few minutes on a gentle agitation cycle.

> What about your bedroom environment while traveling? Hilton Hotels now has "Sleep-Tight" rooms, which are being designed and studied in cooperation with the National Sleep Foundation. These rooms have environmental and white-sound machines, special mattress systems, and even special lighting systems that have been used to realign circadian rhythms. Of course, decaffeinated beverages are supplied, along with earplugs, sleep masks, Serta pillows and mattresses, relaxing classical music CDs, and Teledyne Water Pik Original Shower Massage® showerheads.

The Presleep Ritual

If you were to tell someone that you were going to put yourself into a state of unconsciousness for eight hours, they might become alarmed. But restorative sleep is calming, not alarming. To get the best rest, you should have a routine presleep ritual to follow, rather than do what most of us do, which is have a sudden realization that "It is already eleven P.M. and I have to get up early to prepare for that important presentation and if I don't get enough sleep I'll appear tired and won't do a good job and Sue will get the promotion instead of me, oh dear, etc." So here is a suggested plan for winding down before sleep:

1. Stop all exercise and use of caffeinated beverages at least four hours prior to sleep time. Sexual exercises are permitted, as they do not seem to interfere with sleep, and in fact can help produce good sleep, if you start early enough to get your nine hours (of sleep, that is).

2. Stop eating all foods, especially high-fat or spicy foods, at least two hours before sleep time. Nonsugary beverages are okay. Many people find that eating high-sugar desserts late in the evening is a no-no for deep sleep.

3. Have a nice hot bath or shower, using fragrant soaps/oils, lit by candlelight, to the sound of soft, relaxing music. Avoid stimulating content (sex, violence, most news) on TV, if you must watch TV at all.

4. Keep a pad next to your bed. Write down all the potential worries and problems you may have, to get them on to paper and out of your mind. Tell yourself: "There is no use worrying about these things now. They will be right here on the pad when I get up, and my restored mind can then better deal with them." However, it is not a good idea to let the sun set without resolving anger, so do what you can (see chapter 11), or make plans for the near future, well before going to bed. If your bedroom scene is a potential source of anger, seek counseling.

5. Practice a relaxation technique, such as muscle relaxation (see chapter 8).

6. Pray as recommended by your religious faith.

7. Activate sound and other environmental control systems, as required.

8. Drift off into soothing slumber.

During Sleep

In case you should awaken during the night, maintain low lighting. In fact, you can take a tip from pilots and ship captains: they know that red lighting allows one to see things that might otherwise go bump in the night, but red light does not activate the visual sensorium in a way that causes arousal and increased wakefulness. So you can keep a red light burning all night. It is all right to urinate (in the proper location), and quietly return to bed. Try to arrange your clock so that you cannot see it during awakenings. Often people will awaken at three A.M., and become upset when they notice the time. Let the actual time be a mystery to you. It should be enough to know that your alarm is set.

Postsleep Ritual

ALARM: The ideal way to wake up would be from natural causes. Most people, if they eat and exercise healthfully, and go to sleep eight to nine hours prior to the time of awakening, can learn to wake up at the appropriate time. However, most of us are burdened with the apprehension of waking up too late to get the kids to school on time, or to catch the bus/train. For us, an alarm system is needed. There are clock radios that will start with low-level music, then increase the volume, and then blast you with a buzzer if more than 15 minutes have passed. Something gradual is a good idea. The ideal awakening would be in response to gentle caresses from your spouse, adorned with whispered assurances of love and support.

LOVEMAKING: Speaking of gentle caresses, research has shown that sex hormones are at a high level early in the morning. Some like to take advantage of this natural phenomenon; it really can set a positive tone for the rest of the day. It beats jumping out of bed to rush to work. Careful time management and judicious use of breath cleansers can allow sex to be switched to mornings. This is an advantage for those who have limited time, and who feel less enthusiastic later in the evening when the kids have finally gone to sleep, and are too drained to enjoy much of anything.

BREATHING: Buddhist monks practice the ''breath of life'' upon arising. This is done as follows: 1) Stand by your bed; 2) Bend forward as you exhale, folding your arms around your chest; 3) As you rise up to a standing position, breathe in deeply, until you are fully filled with fresh air, and you are stretching your arms up and slightly backward. Hold this condition for about five seconds, then completely relax and exhale. Do this a few times, thinking about how oxygen is getting into the little nooks and crannies of your lungs which have become stale from the suboptimal position and respiration of sleep. You can do this breathing exercise outside in your garden, unless the weather is inclement, or your urban environment is impure/unsafe.

PLANNING: Take a brief look at the list of projects you keep, and your schedule book. Make your mind clear about what you will and won't do during the day. Uncertainty is death to proper motivation.

Treatment of Insomnia

The suggestions in this chapter are generally well founded. However, the disorder of insomnia can have psychological and medical causes which are not adequately addressed by the approach herein described. About one third of all Americans report sleep problems, most likely due to lifestyle (not enough exercise, too much caffeine or alcohol) and stress. While use of medication may help an insomnia victim get needed rest, regular use is usually not indicated. Behavioral treatment consists of teaching insomniacs to have enjoyable bedtime rituals, to sleep at regular times, and to learn how to avoid obsessing over worries (including the worry of inability to sleep). Seek professional help from your physician and a psychologist if you seem unable to get good sleep. Get information from the sleep resources listed below.

Sleep Resources

These resources can start you on the path of becoming an amateur sleep expert:

Better Sleep Council, P.O. Box 13, Washington, DC 20044

The National Sleep Foundation, 122 South Robertson Blvd., Suite 201, Los Angeles, CA 90048.

American Sleep Disorders Association, 1610 14th St. NW, Suite 300, Rochester, MN 55901.

Stanley Coren. *Sleep Thieves: An Eye-opening Exploration into the Science & Mysteries of Sleep.* New York: Free Press, 1996.

Homework

1. Redesign your bedroom according to the suggestions. Continue to keep your weekly diary, and continue to discuss your progress with your support group.

2. Practice good sleep habits; make sleep a higher priority.

References

Maruyama, S., Morimoto, K. (1996). Effects of long work hours on life-style, stress and quality of the life among intermediate Japanese managers. *Scandinavian Journal of Work, Environment & Health*, 22, 353–59.

Van Moffaert, M. M. (1994). Sleep disorders and depression: the "chicken and egg" situation. *Journal of Psychosomatic Research*, 38 (Suppl 1), 9–13.

5

Exercising for Energy

GOAL: Reading this chapter will help you make exercise a higher priority, and it will show you how to make exercise an enjoyable habit.

Inactive America

Now that you are rested from a good night's sleep, it's time to think about exercise. Feeling energetic is difficult without a regular exercise program. Mammals, including us humans, really don't operate well without exercise. The attitude we should have about exercise is that it is as important as sleeping and eating. True, some people live seemingly happy lives without ever doing exercise. But most of the people I have talked with, and most of the research, demonstrate that exercise and energy go together. If you are already a regular exerciser (three to five hours of brisk exercise a week), then you can jog to the next chapter. If not, then tune in to the fact that exercise is the main energizer. Using the approach described in this chapter, you can change your attitude toward activity so that never again will you think of exercise as a burden, but as an opportunity for invigoration and fun.

About 50 to 60 percent of Americans lead sedentary (seated at work and at TV) lifestyles. Inactivity is a risk factor for (makes it more likely that you will get) heart disease (Fletcher et al., 1992) and terminal cancers (Blair et al., 1989). An active lifestyle can bring benefits such as fat mobilization (don't we wish it would go somewhere else?), improved insulin action (good for blood sugar control), reduction of blood pressure, reduced blood cholesterol, and weight/fat control (STEFANICK, 1993).

How did it come to be that we as a culture have so few people that get enough exercise for health? Why are most of us exercising less and less, and getting fatter and fatter? I have predicted that all Americans will be very fat in about 200 years, based on current trends (Foreyt & Goodrick, 1995). The increasing prevalence of obesity is most likely due to reduced activity, as well as overconsumption of food. Before the industrial revolution, almost everyone had to do some manual labor on the job or at home to survive. Walking was the most common means of transportation, and even riding a horse used some calories. Even as late as 100 years ago, many Americans were farmers. Farming was not so easy back then. No one plowed a field in John Deere air-conditioned comfort with a four-speaker sound system. Farmers' wives had to chop wood, maintain a garden, do laundry, and clean house using their own muscles for power. Farming is still not the easiest profession. However, back then, farmers did the equivalent of ten miles of jogging every day to run their farms; their wives put in the equivalent of about seven miles of jogging every day. How does your lifestyle compare?

There are still parts of the world where humans live in primitive conditions. According to a *National Geographic* TV program I saw many years ago, there are still small groups of people who have lifestyles involving adequate exercise. Deep in the rain forests of Peru, a hunter may spend all day running after a monkey, trying to fell it from the treetops with a blowgun loaded with poison darts. After about five miles of jogging, and after climbing about ten 100-foot-tall trees, the hunter is able to make the final kill, and get about five pounds of lean meat. The monkey meat is lean because a monkey performs aerobics several times a day just to survive, and doesn't eat fast food.

The question we must ask ourselves in modern times is: How much effort did we expend the last time we bought a bag of potato chips? (*Note:* A one-pound bag of potato chips has 2,600 calories. Five pounds of lean monkey meat has about 2,800 calories.)

Early farmers and monkey hunters show us that if we want to achieve physical fitness, we need to change our thinking about exercise. We are designed as a species to spend a good deal of time and energy in getting enough food to eat, chasing after a potential mate, and protecting our mate, children, and territory from predatory animals and those who would take what we have. But we are so clever that all normal needs can now be obtained without much physical effort at all. (Except perhaps in some blighted, inner-city areas.)

In chapter 3, I explained how lack of exercise is a common cause of low energy. Lack of exercise decreases physical fitness, or the ability to metabolize oxygen. This makes the everyday activities of life seem more tiring, since low fitness is like low horsepower in a car. A low-horsepower car will struggle over small hills. Less exercise means lower fitness, which means more tiredness, and less inclination to exercise; this completes the low-energy/inactivity cycle. The more you don't exercise, the more you don't want to exercise.

People who have been feeling tired or run-down for years probably haven't been exercising much. (If you have been exercising a lot and still feel tired, perhaps you need

to slow down. The principles of this book still apply.) The
goal of becoming a regular exerciser may seem very distant
and, for some, painful. But gradual increases in exercise
can be made without excessive pain. As the body adapts to

Exercise Quiz
(for nonexercisers only)

TRUE OR FALSE

1. The last time I exercised was in high-school gym class when my doctor
   started charging me extra for excuse notes.

2. I wait for another day to visit my friends on the second floor if the
   elevator is out of service.

3. If I start thinking about exercise, I lie down until such thoughts go
   away.

4. I am so tired every morning that I need verification from another human
   before I am convinced that I am awake.

5. My heart rate at rest is over 65 beats per minute, even when I am
   not being romanced. (A very physically fit person will generally have
   a resting heart rate below 60; average is 75 to 80. What's yours?)

6. I might exercise if I had more energy, like enough to get out of my
   chair.

7. Once I drank enough coffee to get up enough energy to exercise, but
   within two minutes I had to go to the bathroom.

8. Exercise makes me tired.

9. Exercise hurts.

SCORING: If you had one or more "Trues," consider how fortunate you are
to be getting the valuable information and motivation contained in this
book.

---

more and more exercise, feelings of energy will increase. It may take up to six months, but eventually you will get to the point where you look forward to your exercise, and feel bad when you miss a session. When you reach this stage of fitness, "motivation" is usually not a problem.

There are many habit-enhancing methods to help a person develop regular exercise patterns. Some of these involve changing the way you think about exercise. Some involve use of "self-management" methods, which include time management and arrangement of your environment. Another important method is to make sure that exercise is perceived as enjoyable. You can learn to exercise at an intensity that is set by how you feel. This ensures that exercise always feels as good as it can. My research studies have shown that people are more likely to stick with an exercise plan if they use this self-regulated intensity principle (Goodrick, Malek & Foreyt, 1994).

A researcher asked people about their attitudes toward exercise. Regular exercisers said they enjoyed exercise, and that it gave them more energy. Those who did not exercise said they did not enjoy exercise, and that exercise made them tired (Riddle, 1980). Who do you think knew the truth about regular exercise?

Case Study 1

A young man in his mid-twenties was an engineer with a rather boring job. His routine included coffee and sweet rolls for breakfast, and enough coffee during the day to stay awake. He was asthmatic as a child, and suffered attacks when he tried to exercise. Often, he would find himself nodding off at his desk. This was a very uncomfortable feeling. How awful it must be to have a strong desire to lie down on a cozy bed, but be forced to stay put at a desk trying to focus your brain on complex mathematics. This was at age 25. Now, 28 years later at age 53, with proper nutrition and regular aerobic exercise, this person rarely feels tired during the day, and is able to write lengthy, knowledgeable books on enhancing energy. He has more

energy in middle age than then he had during what should have been his
roaring twenties.

The key to becoming an enthusiastic exerciser is energy.
If you don't feel energetic, you won't develop and maintain
an exercise habit, unless you enjoy self-punishment. People
who feel energetic want to exercise. They look forward to
it, just as do children and dogs. (If you owned a show dog,
or racehorse, you would not keep it confined to a small
cage, but would let it run free daily. Are you keeping yourself in a small cage?) High-energy people feel frustrated if
they can't exercise. They enjoy exercise so much that they
need no willpower to exercise regularly. A few years ago
a university tried to do a study of what happens to very fit
men when they stop exercising for two months. They could
not get any volunteers. You can be like them—compelled
to regular exercise.

Behavior Change Methods

The ways to develop an unshakable motivation to exercise regularly include:

1. Learning to enjoy exercise

2. Changing your thinking about exercise

3. Mind control

4. Increasing awareness of your exercise behavior

5. Controlling your exercise environment

6. Using visualization to experience the unseen effects
   of exercise

If taken one day at a time, in a step-by-step fashion, use of
these methods can result in the development and maintenance of a regular exercise habit.

1. Learning to Enjoy Exercise

Did you hate physical-education classes? Did you always get PE class early in the morning so that you felt sweaty and unkempt during the rest of the day? Was exercise used as a punishment for not doing enough exercise or for being late? Were you reluctant to participate because of a complete lack of athletic ability? These experiences may have led you to be less than enthusiastic about exercise. But it can become an enjoyable activity. (Be sure to get a checkup from your physician before increasing activity. There are some diseases that may need attention first, so that you don't drop dead on your way to enhanced energy.)

Self-Analysis: Exercise

Answer these items to help yourself gain perspective about your relationship with the concept of exercise.

1. Describe your experiences with vigorous exercise from childhood on.

_____

_____

2. If you are not currently exercising, what are the barriers within yourself?

_____

_____

3. Are there any barriers outside of yourself that prevent your exercising?

_____

_____

4. Visualize how your life would be different when you become fit with regular exercise. What do you have to look forward to?

_____

_____

I hope you are able to walk. If not, you will need to consult with your physician and a physical therapist to determine if there is a possibility of getting exercise in some other way, such as using an exercise bicycle designed for the arms. If not, you may need to focus on meditation (see chapter 8). But I assume you can walk. I assume you can walk around the block. That is all you need to get started. All you have to do is follow these two rules:

A. Rule One of developing an exercise habit: Exercise at an intensity (or speed) and duration that feel *invigorating* but never *strenuous*. In other words, go as fast and long as you can without discomfort, and without being overly tired later.

B. Rule Two of developing an exercise habit: Never give up. (Unless your physician tells you to stop.)

I have found that if unfit individuals follow these rules, using the walking program described at the end of this chapter, they can learn to enjoy exercise and make it a lifelong habit. It could also be called a "longlife" habit, since regular exercise seems to be associated with longevity.

In one of my research projects, I taught sedentary adults how to enjoy walking. They kept records on their exercise and how they felt during and after exercise. After one year, I found that 65 percent were still doing healthful exercise. The records also showed that almost everyone reported feeling "good" or "excellent," both during and after each exercise "experience." The exercise plan I used in this research was designed after the ideas of John Greist, a psychiatrist who pioneered the use of exercise in the treatment of depression (Greist et al., 1979). He found that regular, gentle jogging was as helpful as psychotherapy in alleviating moderate depression.

> After many years of research, the evidence is growing that exercise is good for mental health (Landers, 1997). Exercise can produce an anxiety reduction similar in magnitude to other treatments (e.g., drugs), but with the added benefit of the healthful benefits of activity. The antidepressant effect of exercise may begin as early as the first session, and may be suitable even for the severely depressed. Exercise can be as effective against depression as psychotherapy and behavioral treatment. Adding drugs to an exercise program does not substantially increase the antidepressant effect.

I like to call exercise sessions "experiences" because it is important to focus on all the pleasurable experiences involved in exercise. During a walk, for example, you can experience the rhythmic actions of your muscles and lungs, the sight, sound, and smell sensations of your walking path, the thoughts that come to you as you spend some time alone in a natural setting. Yes, walking can be a form of recreation. Or, you can enjoy your favorite TV program as you walk briskly on your living-room treadmill (you will sell your couch as unsuitable for your new lifestyle).

2. Changing Your Thinking About Exercise

You can change your thinking about exercise by learning how to do it so that it is enjoyable. But it is also helpful to fill your mind with information about the benefits of exercise to keep you motivated. I have found that most of the unfit people who learn to enjoy exercise have a chance of making it a lasting habit. But others stop, even though they enjoyed exercise. The reason most of them quit seems to be due to what could be called ''life stress.'' The life stressors include divorce, job changes, moving to another house, and other events that had nothing to do with whether they should exercise or not. Apparently, under stress, exercise was edged out by other concerns, even though these individuals knew that exercise was good for reducing feelings of stress.

To make activity a higher priority in life, filling your brain with all kinds of facts about the wonderful effects of exercise may be helpful. Often it seems that when you have to make a decision, there are two ''debate teams'' challenging each other in your head. The team that wins is the one with the most persuasive argument based on the most facts. If you are filled with facts in favor of exercise, then, when life stressors occur, your ''proexercise debate team'' can win. One might say, ''It's all right to argue with yourself as long as you don't lose to the side that's against you.''

So fill up your brain with the benefits exercise. Here they are:

Benefits of Exercise
HEALTH BENEFITS:

- Heart muscle is made stronger and more efficient

- Helps reduce blood pressure

- Reduces resting heart rate

- More oxygen gets to cells

- Fats in blood are reduced

- Fat deposits on body are reduced

- Reduces risk of having heart attack

- Elasticity of arteries is increased

- Reduces risk of osteoporosis (brittle bones)

- Prevents reductions in metabolism caused by eating less

- Slows down the aging process

- Improves lung efficiency

- Tones up muscles

- Improves sleep

PSYCHOLOGICAL BENEFITS:

- May alleviate anxiety

- Reduces uncomfortable reactions to stress

- Helps you feel good and fight depression

- Makes you feel more energetic (because you have more energy!)

- Improves self-esteem and "body image"

- Improves appearance, makes you thinner

- Gives you an enjoyable experience

- Keeps your mind alert as you age

- Helps keep your physical reactions quick as you age

- Some say it makes you sexier and improves sex (there is only one way to be sure about this)

- You can feel superior to those who remain inactive and unfit.

Another motivational tool is to look at the other side of the coin, or the

Disadvantages of Not Exercising

- Makes you more likely to get dreaded diseases (diabetes, for example)

- Makes you tired

- Makes you age more quickly

- Makes you fatter

- Makes you jealous of your friends who have become fit

Question: When you are older, do you want to be thought of as someone who needs to take a nap, or someone who has the *vitality* and *energy* to participate fully in enjoyable recreational activities?

3. Mind Control

When humans decide whether or not to do something, they weigh the pros and cons of the behavior in their minds. They think of the advantages and disadvantages of each course of action, such as those for exercise listed above. Suppose, for example, that you have thought about the advantages of exercising. Suppose you are just about to put on your walking shoes and take an enjoyable walk. But then something strange happens in your mind. From somewhere, deep in your subconscious, comes a jumble of distorted thoughts. Soon these thoughts become clearer, and you realize that you are dealing with your less desirable side. Up from the depths of your mind come *excuse thoughts*. An excuse thought is a reason that your high intelligence has created to allow you *not* to exercise.

A typical excuse thought goes like this: "I should exercise today, but there is a show on television I want to see, and I can always exercise tomorrow instead." Presto! You have a reason for not exercising. If you have enough excuse thoughts in your head, you can come up with reasons not to do many things you should do. Intelligent people are sometimes much more able to generate excuse thoughts, and in this way their intelligence works against them.

> Let's face it. Most people do not behave in an ideal fashion. There is a big difference between what we know we should do and what we actually do. Most of the major religions recognize this problem. "There is good I should do, but I do it not. There is evil which I should not do, but I do it. I see a force in me which battles against the logic of my mind"
>
> ROMANS 7:14–25

Identify all the excuse thoughts (ETs) you may have regarding exercise. I have listed some possibilities below. Then come up with a counterargument (CAs) for each one. After developing a counterargument for an excuse thought, you will have more difficulty when you try again to subvert your own good intentions.

ET: "Exercise makes me too tired."
CA: Exercise improves feelings of energy.

ET: "Exercise takes too much time."
CA: It takes only 5 percent of your waking hours.

ET: "Exercise is painful."
CA: A gradual program won't hurt. The discomfort of being unfit is much greater.

Now list some of your own excuse thoughts:

Excuse Thoughts	Counterarguments
_____	_____
_____	_____
_____	_____
_____	_____

You may want to copy these excuse thoughts and their counterarguments and post them on the wall in your house for repeated readings.

PONDER THIS: Self-control means running out of excuses not to do the right thing.

4. Increasing Awareness of Your Exercise Experience

In order to develop a habit, you will need to be totally aware of your exercise behavior. One way to do this is to keep careful records of your exercise sessions, and of the times when you did not exercise as planned. Most people can't accurately remember whether they did or did not exercise on any particular day a week ago. If you write down your exercise experiences, you will be aware of how frequently you are exercising, how long you exercised, and how you felt during and after exercise. You can see your progress over a long period of time.

You can also make a note of the times you didn't exercise as planned, and why you didn't. Was your excuse valid or invalid? What could you do to prevent this barrier to exercise from occurring again? The weekly self-monitoring diary is designed to record your exercise experiences. Put comments and notes about problems in the back of it. Talk with your support group members about your experiences and problems.

If you faithfully record your exercise on these forms, you will maintain a high level of awareness about your habit formation. You will be less able to fool yourself about whether you are making progress or regressing. I sum up this section with another secret of motivation:

Success in behavior change is highly correlated with faithful self-monitoring. People who keep records are more likely to succeed. So do it.

In addition to the self-monitoring forms, get a whole-year calendar (poster style) upon which you can record your daily exercise for 365 days. This should be posted prominently at home and/or office. Since developing solid habits takes some people six months or more, keeping track on a calendar for one year is a very good idea.

5. Controlling Your Exercise Environment

External factors or events, which psychologists call "stimuli," trigger much of our behavior. For example, a red light is a trigger for stopping. If you want to trigger good behavior, such as exercising, you can set up your environment so that exercise becomes more likely. Here are some examples:

- Set aside a particular time for exercise so that it becomes a part of your schedule. This way a certain time can be a trigger for exercise, instead of you trying to "fit" exercise into random periods of spare time. Make exercise a priority, as important as sleeping and eating. Early in the morning is a good time to exercise without conflicting with your daily schedule. If you are not a "morning person," you might become one when regular exercise gives you a higher level of energy.

- Make sure your exercise clothes and equipment are ready and visible to you so that you can immediately get ready for exercise before a dreaded excuse thought takes control despite your better intentions.

- Arrange to exercise with one or more people. Then

they can trigger you to exercise. Use your support
group for partners and encouragement.

· Execute a contract with family members, friends, and/
or coworkers which says that you will get some reward
if you stick to your exercise plan. This can be highly
motivational since most people want to look good to
others.

· Subscribe to a walking or exercise magazine that is
filled with informational and motivational material.
Then, every month a uniformed representative of the
United States Postal Service will deliver to your residence a reminder that you are an enthusiastic exerciser.

· Join a fitness club. But beware! Many people sign up
for years of membership in such clubs when they are
highly motivated and influenced by the salespeople and
equipment. But many new members fail to keep using
the club, because it becomes too much trouble to go
there when motivation is lower. Think carefully about
the advantages of exercising on your own before sign-
ing a contract. Do you know for certain that you will
use it regularly for a long time?

· Buy a treadmill (I have a NordicTrack Walkfit) and
put it in front of your TV. Dr. John Kakicic at the
University of Pittsburgh found that formerly sedentary
adults could maintain more consistent exercise habits
if they were given treadmills for home use. Americans
spend hundreds and thousands of dollars on home entertainment systems. Why not spend a few hundred on
a good treadmill? Exercise in the privacy of your own
home while watching TV. Remember—enjoyable
brisk walking is all that is required.

You can see that environmental control means that you
do something *now* which changes future stimuli in a way
that makes exercise more likely *later*.

6. Visualization

In order to realize a goal, you must have a clear picture of the goal in your head. Not just a picture of the benefits of achieving the goal, but a picture of the good feelings you will have about your accomplishment. I have already discussed some of the psychological and health benefits of exercise. In this section I present some mental exercises to help your brain focus on the emotional aspects of exercise.

The next time you find yourself inactive, think about what is happening. As you sit watching TV, imagine your motionless body getting stale. Lack of movement prevents proper blood flow and stagnation of tissue. Nutrients are converted to fat instead of feeding muscle. The body slowly loses its ability to use oxygen to make energy. Lack of strong blood flow to the head fosters feelings of fatigue.

In contrast, think about the healthful effects of exercise. The next time you take a brisk walk, imagine oxygen flowing from your lungs throughout your body. Feel the blood pumping strongly to bring nutrition to the muscles and to remove waste materials. Sense that your muscles are becoming stronger and firmer. Enjoy the feelings of energy that flow through your body.

Exercise, if done gradually and using self-regulated intensity, can be enjoyable. It can become a habit, using self-management methods and by enlisting the support of others. Eventually, it will become its own reward. It will provide you with the sense of energy you need to persevere in your life-change efforts.

Exercise Motivation: Staying on Track: It may take a few months to develop an exercise habit that will stick for life. For years, you may have developed a pattern of living which did not include exercise. It isn't easy to add six hours a week to what may already have been a busy schedule.

If you let exercise go for a few days, or a week or more, then you need to analyze what happened (unless you were sick). Using the problem-solving method, be your own exercise troubleshooter.

Exercise-Lapse Troubleshooting

Ask the following questions about your lapse:

1. When and where were you when it became apparent that sessions were to be missed? Was something unusual going on in your life, like divorce, a job change? Were you on a trip? If the situation was very unusual, then you don't have to worry about it since it is unlikely to occur again.

2. Were others trying to influence you to exercise or not exercise? Your support people should be urging you to exercise, and hopefully they are exercising with you. If others are trying to urge you *not* to exercise, try to encourage them to exercise.

3. What did you do instead of exercising? Did you watch TV, take a nap? Do something that was absolutely necessary and unavoidable? Reexamine your priorities about exercise if you find yourself doing something other than exercising when you have scheduled exercise.

REMEMBER: If you choose to stop exercising, you are also choosing to give up your chances for optimal energy.

4. How tired were you at the time of your missed session? If you felt tired, and this was due to inadequate sleep or illness, then you shouldn't have exercised. If there is no apparent cause for tiredness, give exercise a try for a few minutes to see if your energy level doesn't perk up.

5. What started the chain of events that led to a missed

session? Did you begin to have excuse thoughts about missing exercise long before your appointed time? Did you say to yourself, "I can always exercise tomorrow instead"?

6. What were the barriers to exercise? Try to make exercise as convenient as possible.

7. What is your overall explanation for missing sessions? Put it into your own words, and explain it to your support people. Often, when trying to explain the reasons to someone else, the problem becomes clearer, and your faulty reasoning, or excuse thoughts, become less valid when presented to someone else. In life management, it is sometimes easier to fool yourself than it is to fool others.

If you find yourself missing exercise for a long period (a "relapse" to old patterns of inactivity), ask yourself the following questions:

1. What events in your life seemed to cause relapse (e.g., family, job, health, other stress factors, emotions)?

2. Do you plan to restart your exercise regimen? When? How?

3. What emotions do you have about relapse?

4. What is your overall explanation of this relapse?

5. How much was this relapse caused by your problems, and how much by circumstances and situations out of your control?

Discussing these issues with others will help you get your mind back on track.

REMEMBER: It is never too early to start exercising. It is never too late to start back again.

Posture: Many people who are chronically tired, and some who are depressed, can be helped to have more energy simply by postural changes. Many tired and sad people tend to hunch over, and let their shoulders hang forward. This compresses the chest, making full breathing difficult. Sit up straight, keep those shoulders back! To help bring the shoulders back, exercises such as push-ups may be helpful.

Homework: Your Exercise Plan

Now that you have had an opportunity to think about exercise as an enjoyable activity, it is time to develop a plan to build up gradually to four to five hours of vigorous activity each week. Remember, whether an activity is "vigorous" or not depends on how *you feel* about it. Within a few weeks, "vigorous" and "enjoyable" can be experienced in exercise at the same time.

Develop a schedule for gradually increasing the time you spend each week in exercise, and to learn more ways to be motivated to be a regular exerciser. Here are some good guidelines for increasing exercise:

1. Start at a comfortable level. Even five minutes per walk may be enough if that's how much you feel you can tolerate. Start with three walks per week. Exercise at a pace that seems invigorating but not strenuous. You should be able to breathe without much effort. You should be able to talk with a friend as you exercise.

2. Add five minutes to each walk each week. That means next week your walks will be ten minutes long, the next week they will be fifteen minutes long, etc. This way, in about twelve weeks you may be walking about forty-five minutes each time. Or maybe an hour each time.

3. If you think the exercise is making you feel tired, slow down your progress. Take two or three weeks before you add five minutes per walk.

4. If you miss a week of exercise, restart at the level before that week.

5. If you feel tired but have had enough sleep, and are not sick, then try exercising for five minutes. Then see how you feel. If you feel better, continue exercising as long as you feel all right. If you still feel tired, stop and rest. Wait for another day. Not every day can be ideal for exercise.

6. By the way, don't exercise less than three hours before going to bed. The activation of your body due to exercise may interfere with getting to sleep.

7. A good exercise program may take up to 6 hours per week. This is only about 5½ percent of your waking hours. Your increased energy during the day will make you more productive even though you have 5½ percent less time. Of course, if you exercise during your normal television times, you won't "lose" any time exercising. Exercise should be considered important enough to take up some time. *Note:* The average American spends 28 hours a week watching TV.

8. Plan ahead. On your calendar, mark the times for the next 30 days when you will exercise. Don't let other activities interfere.

9. Keep your weekly diary going.

The Right to Exercise

You have a right to exercise. You have a duty to yourself and your loved ones to take care of yourself so that you can have the energy to take care of them. Too often in our culture, some people, especially women, feel they must take care of others at the expense of neglecting themselves. If you put your health first, then you will be able to be a healthy helper for others. If you put your health last, then soon you will not be able to help others so much, and you may become resentful about not getting your share of exercise and recreation, and irritable due to lack of energy.

Resources for Exercise

YMCAs, YWCAs, JCCs
President's Council on Physical Fitness and Sports
200 Independence Ave., Room 738H
Washington, D.C. 20201

References

Blair, S. N., Kohl, H. W., Paffenbarger, R. S., Clark, D. G., Cooper, K. H., & Gibbons, L. W. (1989). Physical fitness and all-cause mortality: a prospective study of healthy men and women. *JAMA,* 262, 2395–401.

Fletcher, G. F., Blair, S. N., Blumenthal, J., et al. (1992). Statement on exercise: benefits and recommendations for physical activity program for all Americans. *Circulation,* 86, 340–44.

Foreyt, J. P., Goodrick, G. K., (1995). The ultimate triumph of obesity. *Lancet,* 346, 134–35.

Goodrick, G. K., Malek, J. N., Foreyt, J. P. (1994). Exercise adherence in the obese: Self-regulated intensity. *Medicine, Exercise, Nutrition and Health,* 3, 335–38.

Greist, J. H., Eischens, R. R., Klein, M. H., Faris, J. W., (1979). Antidepressant running. *Psychiatric Annals,* 9, 134–40.

Landers, D. M., (1979). The influence of exercise on mental

health. *Research Digest,* 2(12), 2–8. Washington, DC: President's Council on Physical Fitness and Sports.

Riddle, P. K. (1980). Attitudes, beliefs, behavioral intentions, and behaviors of women and men toward regular jogging. *Research Quarterly,* 51, 663–74.

Stefanick, M. L. (1993). Exercise and weight control. In Holloszy, J. O. (ed.), *Exercise and Sport Sciences Reviews.* Vol 21. Baltimore, MD: Williams & Wilkins.

6

Eating, Drinking, and Pill-Popping for Energy

GOAL: To reduce calorie density in foods, and to avoid most pills and supplements.

All right, folks! Now that you are getting better sleep and have started on an exercise program, it's time to think about what kind of fuel to put into your system for highest horsepower. I need to tell you that I have no credentials in nutrition, but this hasn't stopped anyone in the history of nutrition/diet books from promulgating an amazing variety of eating recommendations. Most of these have been interesting, but most have been useless, and sometimes dangerous. Check with a registered dietitian before you follow my recommendations. I can only tell you that the plan in this chapter is based on the recommendations of federal-government agencies and panels of distinguished nutrition scientists.

What to Eat?

The bottom line is: For maximum energy, every day you should eat fruits and vegetables, lots of grains, a little meat, fish, or vegetable protein, and some low-fat dairy products. Avoid nutritional supplements for added energy; there aren't any that benefit the average person. That's it in a nutshell. Now for the details.

The Dietary Guidelines for Americans developed by the U.S. Department of Agriculture and the American Institute of Nutrition Steering Committee on Healthy Weight are as follows:

- Eat a variety of foods.

- Balance the food you eat with your physical activity to maintain or improve your weight.

- Choose a diet with plenty of grain products, vegetables, and fruits.

- Choose a diet low in fat, saturated fat, and cholesterol.

- Choose a diet moderate in sugars.

- Choose a diet moderate in salt and sodium.

- If you drink alcoholic beverages, do so in moderation.

If only everyone had training in nutrition, and if knowledge were virtue! If only high-fat fast foods were not so easily available (one of the corporate goals of McDonald's is that no urban or suburban American should live more than four minutes away from a McDonald's).

Let's begin by discussing the kinds of foods to avoid if the goal is to have high energy. There are several categories to consider. Food types associated with low energy include: high sugar, high-calorie density (basically high fat), and low fiber. Two points to note here: 1) These types of food seem to be very popular with Americans, and 2) These types of food are rare in a diet of foods obtained directly from nature.

After-meal tiredness doesn't seem to be affected by the kinds of food in the meal (Orr et al., 1997), but larger meals will induce more tiredness than smaller ones. Lions lie down and sleep after eating gazelles; don't you wish you could lie down at work at two P.M. after going to the all-you-could-eat buffet? So smaller meals might be one way to keep up energy; four or five small meals a day rather than two or three large ones might work.

Fiber

A high-fiber diet is not often thought of as an energy booster. However, if you think about all those laxative advertisements which show how sluggardly people feel when they are full of constipation, then it becomes apparent that good and regular bowel movements are important for feeling spry, as well as for digestive-tract health. One rule of thumb to use is this: You are eating enough fiber, and drinking enough liquid, if you have one substantial bowel movement each day. Ask you doctor for details on whether this applies to your particular medical situation. The diet recommendations in this chapter normally would make laxatives unnecessary. Also, you must promise that when you are older, you won't talk about this topic very often (see chapter 11 on Interpersonal Relationships).

Fluids

Be sure to drink lots of fluid. A survey (Yankelovich et al., 1998) found that the average American drinks nearly eight daily servings of hydrating beverages, such as water, juice, and decaffeinated soft drinks. However, of these eight, five are servings of caffeine- or alcohol-containing beverages. Caffeine and alcohol act as diuretics, causing the body to lose fluid it needs to retain. The body is 70 percent water, and water plays a central role in nearly every major bodily function, including all those that make us feel energetic, such as carrying nutrients and oxygen to the cells and removing waste. Not drinking enough can zap your kidneys.

Most people feel fatigued with dehydration. However, the urge to drink—thirst—lags behind the need to drink more water. So make drinking water a habit; for example, drink after each urination (about every two to three hours). I have noted that I drink plenty in dry climates, but never get thirsty in humid zones. This may have something to do with the sensation of dryness in the mouth caused by low humidity. Further research is needed.

Food, Depression, and Energy

Larry Christensen, a professor of psychology at the University of South Alabama, has reviewed the relationships between foods and depression in his book *Diet-Behavior Relationships: A Focus on Depression* (Christensen, 1996). His major conclusions are:

1. The eating of simple carbohydrates (sugars) can induce feelings of fatigue in some people. (This makes sense because eating sugar tends to produce a sudden increase in blood sugar, followed by an increase in blood insulin. The insulin is designed to help get the sugar into the cells to be used as food, and has the effect of reducing blood sugar level. However, there is usually a surplus of insulin left over, causing the blood sugar to fall below where it would have been without the sugar intake. This could cause feelings of tiredness. Robert Thayer (1987) showed that a sugar snack caused a short-term rise in feelings of energy, but then caused reduced energy and increased feelings of tension and irritability. So, when the candy bar companies tell you to eat their products for energy, don't believe it. When you crave sweets, eat a banana.)

2. Since depression and fatigue are so closely related, and since dietary sugars are associated with fatigue, Dr. Christensen tried to alleviate depression in patients by eliminating sugars. The result was an increase in energy and a decrease in depression. The depression came back when the old sugary diet was restored. Depressed people might eat sugary stuff for the temporary energy high it gives them; in the long run, they feel worse because of it. In another study, emotional distress was significantly reduced after only two weeks on a sugar- and caffeine-free diet. Caffeine will jazz up your metabolism and thought processes, which

is not needed in emotional distress situations. Relaxation is needed. (The optimal state for functioning is high energy and relaxed, which, in case you have forgotten, is the thesis of the first two parts of this book.)

3. Tryptophan, found in foods such as dairy products and turkey, may increase drowsiness, and may slow down mental functioning, since it is changed into serotonin in the body. The major antidepressant medications act by increasing the available serotonin in the brain. However, research has failed to show that eating tryptophan will cause impairment in the performance of various tasks requiring mental alertness.

4. Despite what the "carbohydrate addicts" say, there is little evidence that complex carbohydrates (grains, potatoes, etc.) have an effect on fatigue. (I would also like to point out that those who say Americans are eating too many complex carbohydrates [getting out of the "zone"] do not have much research support for their recommendation to eat more protein.)

High-Fat Foods and Energy

Everybody talks about eating too much fat. Too much fat in the diet may cause cancer, obesity, and heart disease. But a high-fat diet is also associated with lower energy. I have noticed in several research projects that the amount of fat that people report eating is inversely related to their reports of energy and well-being. After a high-fat meal, the risk of heart attack and stroke may increase, because the fatty foods increase the activity of blood coagulating factors (Larsen et al., 1998). This may also reduce the ability of the blood to transport nutrients and oxygen, a definite energy downer.

Rats in captivity given rat chow will normally have periods of activity during each day, even if they don't really need to exercise to survive. But if their diet is changed to one similar to what Americans eat (pizza, chips, and other high-fat treats), they will slow down and sleep more (Danguir, 1987). This indicates that high-fat eating might not be ideal for high energy. Not to mention that chronic eating of a high-fat diet may lead to obesity, which is not a high-energy state. It is interesting and a bit sad to note that Americans who own pets generally have less healthful diets than their dogs and cats. They feed their animals a good diet which is based on extensive research done by the pet-food industry. How much careful research went into the diet you ate last week?

In humans, there is evidence that high-fat diets are de-energizing. One study in Boston compared two diets that had equal calories (Bandini et al., 1994). One was high-fat (83 percent of calories from fat), and the other high carbohydrate (83 percent carbohydrate). Human subjects ate one diet for 9 to 21 days, then, after a break, ate the other diet for up to 21 days. In five of the seven subjects, total energy expenditure was higher on the carbohydrate diet than on the fat diet. This was explained by greater physical activity on the high-carbo diet. Thyroid hormone profiles also changed in the direction of less metabolic energy expenditure, although metabolic rate did not decrease. Guess what? Subjects reported feeling lethargic on the high-fat diet.

Alcohol and Energy

Alcohol reduces the ability of the body to metabolize oxygen, and is basically a poison which will reduce feelings of energy. Other recreational drugs, downers or uppers, will reduce feelings of energy in the long haul. If you can't stop drinking or drugging, get help before reading further. Call Alcoholics Anonymous, and see your physician. Enough said.

Going to Pot with Caffeine

Caffeine is the only drug I regularly use. It has no place in the healthful optimizing of energy. Caffeine fools the body into thinking it has more energy, but only wears it down, to create a need for more caffeine. Just four to five cups of coffee a day may raise blood pressure (Lane, 1998). Abuse of caffeine is a real psychiatric diagnosis which can be found in the doctors' big books of diseases (American Psychiatric Association, 1994). The symptoms include: restlessness, nervousness, insomnia, flushed face, excessive urination, stomach troubles, muscle twitching, rambling flow of thought and speech, rapid pulse and heart rhythm disturbances, and agitation. I have met hundreds of patients who feel at their wit's end, frazzled, can't sleep, can't think, feel panicky, and all because they were drinking up to 12 cups of coffee a day.

A gradual program of withdrawal from caffeine should coincide with your efforts to sleep, exercise, and eat more healthfully. In order to avoid headaches, reduce your coffee drinking by one cup per day per week. If you are drinking five cups a day this week, next week drink four cups a day, etc. I have found myself feeling more relaxed, with more energy, during the times when I have avoided caffeine. If you really like coffee, stick to two cups a day: one to wake up, one to get over the postlunch lethargy. But remember, no caffeine after four P.M. to avoid sleep problems. Read labels on soft drinks, medicines, etc. Caffeine is lurking in many products! Wrigley's has just come out with a caffeinated gum. This may be a gum you should eschew.

Nutritional Supplements

Many individuals turn to nutritional supplements that promise increased energy. More than 100 companies are marketing "ergogenic aids" and "energy enhancers," with over 300 products containing over 230 ingredients, such as wheat germ, bee pollen, Ma Huang (ephedrine), guarana, amino acids, ginseng, and other herbs and mineral combinations that have no scientific validation that they improve energy in any way (Herbert & Barrett, 1994). In 1996, total sales of such products exceeded $204 million.

When customers accessed a new computer-based nutrition-supplement teaching program at 400 stores of a major health-food chain, "fatigue" was the most-asked-about symptom (McCarthy, 1997). It ranked above free radicals/antioxidants, cholesterol, concerns related to aging, and colds/influenza concerns.

The use of nutritional supplements is increasing as the public turns to alternative methods to improve health. In 1984, a survey of 128 patients in an urban family health center found that 31 percent used supplements, motivated chiefly by a desire for increased energy; a survey of the physicians revealed that they did not usually discuss nutritional supplements with patients (Pally, Sobal & Muncie, 1984). In a rural family practice, a survey of 199 patients showed nutritional supplements used by 54 percent, with good nutrition and less fatigue given as the reasons (Sobal, Muncie, & Guyther 1986). Eliason et al. (1996) surveyed 200 consecutive patients at a family practice clinic, and found that 52 percent had taken supplements during the previous year. Over half of these supplement users took them for energy enhancement. The media was the principal source of patient information regarding supplements. Only one third of these patients had told their physician about supplement use. Patients with a higher educational level took more supplements than those who had only graduated from high school. Eliason et al. (1997) also telephone-surveyed 136 customers visiting health-food stores, and found the average respondent used six different supplements, most often to prevent a health problem. Ginseng, commonly used for energy, was one of the herbs most frequently used. Although 85 percent of the respondents had a regular physician, typically they did not consult their physician about dietary supplements.

All of this use, and I still know of no supplement I could recommend to the average person which would increase their feelings of energy in a healthful way. Supplements that might be useful for athletes include creatine and sodium bicarbonate (Williams, 1995), but don't rush out to try them. Of course, if your physician determines, through testing, that you need some form of supplementation of vitamins, minerals, or whatever, then take them. Otherwise, stick to the prudent diet ideas shown in this chapter.

Nutritional Supplement Mythology Found on the Web

Here are some examples of the plethora of nutritional supplements which promise more energy. I am not saying they are fraudulent. I am only saying, if I were you, I would wait until the effectiveness and safety of these supplements was proved and published in respectable scientific journals. Until then, let the buyer beware!

Cordyceps, a grasslike mushroom. "Over 1,500 years ago, herdsmen noticed that their livestock were more vigorous after eating cordyceps that grew in their high Tibetan pastures." Now, a formula developed during the Ming Dynasty harnesses the power of these mushrooms. You can become a champion in 30 days; the product is used by Olympic athletes! I would like to know why the cows were more vigorous before I take this stuff.

Ginseng is advocated by some very prominent people in broadcasting, but where is the evidence?

Guarana will temporarily boost your feelings of energy due to its caffeine content. This is not a healthful way to boost energy.

Bee pollen lacks evidence of an ergogenic effect. Even though it may be all the buzz, don't get stung by sellers of this.

Glandular extracts are supposed to work by rejuvenating the body's organs. Ask your physician about this treatment, which requires injections. Don't be surprised if she laughs.

Androstenedione is a steroid hormone found in all animals. It is a precursor of testosterone, and is claimed to help the body be "robust and hardy." I couldn't find any evidence that this is worthwhile.

Smell Your Way to Greater Energy?

Aromatherapy has been around since the dawn of noses, but it is becoming more popular as alternative healing approaches gain acceptance. According to researchers at the Institute for Circadian Physiology in Cambridge, Massachusetts, the aroma of peppermint may help improve alertness and performance during times of sleepiness (Stampi et al., 1996). Adult men were studied for two nights, one with, and one without the smell of peppermint. The aroma was diffused into the room from the ventilation ducts of the air-conditioning system. The subjects were asked to perform a battery of tests including a driving simulator of the type used in driver's education. During the early part of each session, no difference was found for peppermint. However, in the sixth and seventh hour, late at night, peppermint had an alerting effect, as demonstrated by quicker reaction times. The effect was also seen for "lane deviation variability." If you are driving down the highway late at night, you do not want "lane deviation variability."

I have on my desk a bottle of aromatherapy beads containing oils of peppermint, lemongrass, and eucalyptus (California Fragrance Company, Los Angeles, 800-424-0034). I think snorting the fumes perks me up, and it also helps to relieve clogged nasal passages. Other than the improved breathing effect, aromas, like caffeine, do not actually give your body more energy. But they smell nice. Other aromas thought to be enlivening are jasmine and rosemary.

Motivating Yourself to Eat for Energy

To eat for energy, most people in the U.S. need to eat fewer calorie-dense foods. This means fewer calories per cubic inch. The easiest way to reduce calorie density is to avoid high-fat foods. But high-fat foods taste really good. So some tips on eating lifestyle change may be helpful.

This section will help you rethink your thoughts and attitudes about food, and the crazy food environment we live in. When I give talks, I first show a slide of the wilderness, and remind the audience that this is the kind of environment we are adapted for in terms of diet: low fat and high fiber, and usually not large meal sizes. The next slide shows a block in Houston that has a Taco Bell, a McDonald's, a New York Pizza, a Wendy's, a Burger King, and a Kentucky Fried Chicken. Fat City, no doubt.

Remember the Peruvian who spent all day chasing after some monkey meat in the rain forest? He has the proper balance of good exercise and low-fat eating. He needs no willpower to control his eating. Low-energy eating doesn't occur in his village. But poor modern man. Calorie-dense foods are everywhere. And inexpensive. A century ago, Americans used to spend up to 40 percent of their family budget on food. Now food only costs us about 15 percent of our income (yes, there are some poor people in our country who spend more than that on food, but we are talking averages). According to the National Association of Restaurateurs, Americans are now spending $354 billion dollars a year on food and drink at restaurants, up from about $55 billion in 1970. A lot of this food is calorie dense.

The food available to us is high in calorie density (and usually fat also). Thousands of years ago, humans ate a diet that was about 10 percent fat; now Americans eat about 38 percent of calories from fat. This is due in large part to the practices of the food industry. Take, for example, chickens. They used to run around the farmyard eating corn. Now chicken farms consist of massive buildings which each hold 10,000 chickens. These birds live in little cages. One conveyor belt runs by their cage with food. Another belt runs under the cage to remove chicken waste. You can imagine that such chickens are not in a state of peak physical condition.

When you buy one of these chickens at the store, examine it closely. You will see clumps of yellow fat attached to the muscle. Depending on the quality of your store, there may also be giant hunks of yellow fat hidden under the meat. These chickens were obviously on their way to serious obesity and heart disease. However, they are sacrificed at a young age so that we humans may eat their fat and become obese and get heart disease.

Beef is a good source of protein and some vitamins, but the kind you buy in the grocery is calorie dense due to fat. When you eat beef, are you eating the fit muscle of a proud animal that was recently roaming the range? Or are you eating the fatty muscle of an emasculated creature that has been kept penned-in prior to slaughter to add the desired "marbling" of fat?

Chips seem to be gaining in popularity. In some stores, chips now take up a whole aisle. But is this any way to eat? There is a brand of potato chips which says on the bag that their chips are simply "fried slices of potato, one of nature's nutritious foods." There are more words designed to make the purchaser of these chips feel good about the nutritional value of chips. You can calculate the nutrition of potato chips from the information printed on the package. In terms of calories, a baked potato has about 20 calories per ounce. Potato chips are made out of potatoes and fat, and have about 160 calories per ounce. You can conclude that potato chips are *seven* parts *fat* and one part potato.

I wrote to the manufacturer of these chips with some recommendations. I pointed out that the wording on the package suggested that potato chips were nutritious and that eating them was a good idea. I felt this was fraudulent, since chips have too much fat, especially when compared with unfried potatoes. I was so bold as to suggest that to be perfectly honest, their product should be called "Fat Chips," in order to reflect the main ingredient. The response I got suggested that I should mind my own business.

However, in the last few years, this same company has developed baked potato chips which are low in calorie density and fairly tasty. They also have fat-free potato chips made with Olean©, the controversial fat substitute. It is controversial because some people claim that it causes gastrointestinal problems. But research shows that fat-free chips aren't any more a problem than regular fat-slave chips. I eat the fat-free kind now and then.

The Economics of Eating Chips

In nature, a squirrel must defend a territory to protect his food supply. Within that territory, there will be just so many nuts per season to eat. When a nut is eaten, there is one less nut available for survival. Compare this with an urban human who eats chips. When humans buy and eat potato chips, the companies that produce chips notice that the demand is up. So, to make more money, they make more chips. They also make more varieties of chips, since a wider variety of products usually ends up selling more, perhaps because variety tends to increase appetite. Then other companies notice the opportunity to make money in the chip business, so they enter the competition, and prices may get lower. The supermarkets get a good profit from selling chips, so they devote lots of space to chips, thus increasing the temptation to buy. Advertising on television increases, thus inducing us to buy and eat more. Conclusion: In nature, food supply is limited, and eating diminishes the supply. In Western industrial human society, food supply tends to increase with demand, and changes occur to promote more eating. This effect is greater with the tempting high-calorie-dense foods. In this way, diets associated with reduced energy levels and obesity are fostered.

A growing number of people are demanding lower-calorie-density foods. The food industry is trying to make changes. In addition to reduced-fat potato chips, you can get baked rather than fried corn tortillas. You can get ''light'' beef from special breeds of cattle which have been fed a good diet without hormones. You can buy frankfurters made from turkey, and even fat-free beef, and vegetarian hot dogs, if you really must have a frankfurter. You can go to a salad bar or get a baked potato at many fast-food hamburger franchises.

You can now get no-fat yogurt and cottage cheese. There is fat- and sugar-free frozen yogurt which actually is very good. There are fat-free sweet rolls and pound cake. Fat substitutes made from proteins are the new rage. So there is hope. With the *new* modern food technology, we are beginning to solve the problems of the *old* modern food technology.

Our food environment may actually be losing some of its fat. But Americans, especially our children, are still exercising less and less, and getting fatter and fatter, year by year. There are still large areas in the supermarket which contain only high-sugar and high-fat items, such as the soft-drink/chips aisle, or the ice-cream/frozen-pies-and-cakes section. Yes, it is still too easy to eat high-fat foods. We need to get our children to eat for energy, and then get out and exercise.

Beware of "High Energy" Foods

What should you eat to maintain a high energy level? Foods with lots of energy? Fat has 2.5 times more energy in terms of calories per ounce than does protein or carbohydrate. Should you eat fat for energy? No. I once found a product sold at a "health food" store that was labeled "Energy Drink." It claimed to give you "2.5 times as much energy as protein." This is because it consisted entirely of fat. This energy drink was merely vegetable oil and some vitamin E. It is true that this drink would give you more "energy" than protein, but in terms of calories, not pep.

Motivational Secrets of Low-Calorie-Density Eaters: How to Reduce Your Desire to Eat High-Calorie-Density Foods

Do you crave high-calorie-density foods (high fat and/or high sugar)? Of course you do. They are tasty. They are tasty because humans are designed to go after the high-calorie-density opportunities to eat. We do this because our appetites are adjusted to earlier times when calories were scarce. Back then, we had to search out food, and work to get it. Now we have to put our effort into avoiding too much food.

In order to control eating, here are some methods to help stay in control:

Stop Dieting

One of the most important things to do to gain control over your eating is to stop restrictive dieting. Dieting can lead to serious self-control problems in eating, including binge-ing and purging. To curb cravings for calorie-dense foods, you will need to eat three meals a day, with two between-meal snacks. For snacks eat pretzels or fruit. The idea is that sensible eating spread out over the day will stabilize your blood sugar so that hunger never gets to be much of a problem.

Sensible eating means eating according to the recommendations of the surgeon general, the American Heart Association, and the American Cancer Society. Fortunately, these organizations agree on what's good for us. Isn't it nice to know that the recommended diet for high energy is also good for reducing the risk of heart disease and cancer? As recommended by these groups, we need to eat more complex carbohydrates and less protein and fat. In your nutrition books you will discover that complex carbohydrates are metabolized more slowly than simple ones, so that blood sugar level and appetite tend to be more stable.

Easy Does It

If you have been an eater of calorie-dense foods most of your life, you will not want to shock your system by suddenly switching to healthful eating. It is also difficult to make big changes in lifelong habits. One alternative is gradually to increase the number of "low-fat-sugar" eating days that you have each week. A low-fat-sugar eating day is one in which everything you eat is relatively low in fat and sugar.

Advantages of Low-Calorie-Density (LCD) Eating

One way to keep yourself motivated to stick to low-calorie-density eating is to remember that *you can eat more food*. If you enjoy eating, then LCD eating is for you. Because LCD food has fewer calories per volume, you may find yourself eating a larger *quantity* of food than you did when you were less careful.

For example, you can eat 8 ounces of broiled tuna, or 3.6 ounces of prime beef, or 2.5 ounces of Cheddar cheese, or half a small chicken pot pie, or 1.7 frankfurters, or 2 tablespoons of peanut butter. They all have about the same number of calories, but they are listed in increasing order of percent fat. If you were in a restaurant, and the waiter asked if you would prefer an eight-ounce fish steak or two tablespoons of peanut butter, which would you order?

Another advantage of eating LCD foods is that because of the greater quantity of foods you will be eating, you should be getting a better variety of nutrients in terms of vitamins and minerals. When you start on your quest to become an LCD eater, you can also maintain enthusiasm as you discover the new recipes and even new foods which you may have overlooked before.

Minding Your Mind

Filling your mind with many good thoughts about LCD eating and so many bad images of high-calorie-density (HCD) foods may help you to avoid HCD foods easily. Rather than being tempted by them, they will make you think about the energy and health consequences. However, for times of temptation, it may be helpful to recognize the *excuse thoughts* which can creep into our minds when sumptuous foods somehow present themselves to us.

As you may recall from the previous chapter, excuse thoughts are designed to help justify your bad behavior so that you can go ahead and give in to temptation. Why are excuse thoughts so able to do this? It may be because most people would rather feel guilty than anxious. When you are tempted, you become anxious because you fear you may succumb to temptation. But anxiety is a very uncomfortable emotion. Thoughts of the desired food do battle with thoughts of your nutrition goals. An excuse thought then pops up in your mind. Such a thought can be construed to be a ''compromise'' solution to the conflict. You will eat the HCD food, but you will make up for it at a later date by eating more LCD foods. But tomorrow is another day, which comes with its own set of excuse thoughts. So you move into the future always just a few footsteps behind self-control, without ever catching up.

Excuse Thoughts for HCD Eating

- ''I have done so well lately that I can splurge just this once.''
- ''I will eat this now, but tomorrow I will:
  1) walk 25 miles over mountainous terrain
  2) not eat anything
  3) eat only grapefruit, including rinds.''
- ''Cheesecake contains protein, a very important nutrient.''
- ''These potato chips are made from potatoes, one of nature's wonderful foods.''
- ''If I don't eat this fried chicken, Grandma will be offended, and she weighs 260 pounds.''
- ''Adolescent Deformed Ninja Lizard Sugar Flakes can be part of a nutritious breakfast, so I'll eat this box for a late-night snack.''
- ''I paid $19.95 for this buffet, so I guess I have to eat as much as I can stuff in my face.''
- ''All those experts on heart disease, cancer, and obesity just might be wrong about these fried chicken nuggets.''

What are your excuse thoughts for eating HCD foods? Write them here, along with counterarguments.

_____

_____

Visualization

One way to change the way you think and feel about HCD foods is to visualize what is happening inside your body when you eat them. Think about the fat ending up as deposits in your blood vessels, or stored in fat deposits. Think about the sugars causing imbalances and reducing energy. Examine meats and poultry you have brought home from the supermarket. Feel the fatty tissues. Take a 12-ounce can of soft drink, and then spoon out 10 teaspoons of sugar onto a plate next to the can. Realize that they both have the same amount of sugar. Take a piece of sausage about seven inches long. Put it next to a whole stick of butter. Realize they both have the same amount of animal fat.

Changing Your Food and Eating Environments

We do not live in the rain forest. HCD eating opportunities are thrust upon us everywhere. Can you drive to work without passing the exhaust vent of a fast-food restaurant? Can you go to the grocery store without seeing the mile-long *aisle of chips*? Most people can't. This is unfortunate because mere exposure to the sights and smells of HCD foods can cause your body to increase insulin output, which lowers blood sugar level, which causes hunger to increase. But this hunger is usually not the hunger related to food deprivation. This hunger is usually the instinctive hunger to store up calories as fat which was helpful thousands of years ago when food was scarce.

There are ways to change your food and eating environment to minimize the chances that you will be tempted to eat HCD foods. Here are some methods you can try:

1. Keep HCD foods out of the house. If your spouse demands to have HCD foods, let him/her go to buy and eat them elsewhere. If your children demand HCD foods, let them know who is boss. (Consult with your pediatrician about when to reduce the fat in your children's eating. Some parents have overdone this and stunted their kids' growth.)

2. Throw away all deep-fat fryers you have.

3. Avoid restaurants that feature HCD foods (most do). Many now have healthful selections identified on the menu.

4. Eat with others who know about your goals.

5. Subscribe to an LCD magazine, such as *Cooking Light*.

Urge Breakers

No matter what you do, there will be times during your switch to LCD eating when you will have urges to eat HCD foods. Urge control can be helpful in these situations. Try these techniques. Many have reported that they are not only able to resist urges, but that continued practice of these techniques seems to reduce the frequency and intensity of the urges.

1. The best urge control technique may be to call a friend.

2. Bring to mind the visualizations about HCD foods mentioned above.

3. Practice sitting down at your dining table with your most tempting HCD foods. Smell it, look at it, study it carefully, but don't eat it. Not even a little taste.

Think about the fat and sugar hidden in it. Sit this way for at least 20 minutes. Write down your thoughts and feelings. Then either throw this food away or give it to a friend. Immediately eat an LCD alternative food. Do this with someone watching so that you don't eat the HCD stuff. This exercise trains you to be exposed to food temptations and to learn that you can be exposed to them, not eat them, and still live to see another day.

4. Allow yourself to become deeply relaxed. Most urges to eat HCD foods will go away after a few minutes, especially if you put some distance between yourself and the food. Relaxation can increase self-control in other areas. Relaxation is covered in chapter 8.

5. In addition to relaxation, immediately do some alternative behavior that is incompatible with eating. Go for a walk, take a shower, call a friend, mow the lawn, or read a book.

A basic approach to good nutrition is to eat like people do in third-world nations, where people eat naturally a diet that has developed over hundreds of years of tradition. Amazingly, most of these diets seem to "work" in terms of providing good nutrition, even though no dietitians were consulted. For example, the Tarahumara Indians of northern Mexico eat a lot of corn and beans, which provides a complete protein mix. They eat very little meat, so they don't have cholesterol problems. Similarly healthful diets can be found in New Guinea, the backcountry of Thailand, and the farmlands of China. What many of these traditional diets have in common is that the basis for meals is a large portion of complex carbohydrates: rice, pasta, potatoes, bread, corn mush, etc. These people do much more physical work than we do, and this is what they eat. Carbohydrates for energy. To the portion of complex carbohydrates, small amounts of nuts, cheeses, or meat can be added. Fruits and vegetables are unlimited. This diet has been advocated by Colin Tudge in his book *Future Food* (1980). A return to a more primitive diet has also been recommended by others more recently (e.g., Eaton et al., 1988).

The Food Pyramid recommended by the U.S. Department of Agriculture (1995) is about the same as the primitive approach, with modern food availability taken into account. Here is what you should eat daily according to the pyramid:

	Servings per Day
Vegetables:	3–5
Fruits:	2–4
Grains: breads, cereals, rice, pasta:	6–11
Milk, yogurt, cheese (low fat):	2–3
Meat, poultry, fish, beans, peas, nuts, eggs:	2–3

(serving = 3–4 ounces)

Calculating calorie density of foods: Calorie density is defined as calories per volume. Generally, calorie density is related to calories per weight. To compare two foods of similar size and weight, the one with more calories is more calorie dense. You have to be careful about certain foods, and be sure to read the nutrition labels. Take your calculator to the store and check out foods before you buy them. Some "fat-free" products are more calorie dense than the original versions. "Reduced calorie" mayonnaise is still 90 percent fat.

If you stick to eating foods as they can be found in nature, calorie density will be low. There are some exceptions, such as nuts and avocados. If you substitute nuts for meat, go for an equivalent amount of calories, compared with four ounces of lean meat. Do not eat a jar of peanuts in one sitting.

Homework: Starting an LCD Eating Plan

1. Your goal is gradually to reduce calorie density and fat to a level corresponding to about 25 to 30 percent of calories from fat. If you don't want to spend time becoming an amateur nutritionist, then eat only foods as they come from nature. This includes fruits and vegetables, wild game, ocean fish, grains. To get started, use the following self-monitoring form to record your daily eating. Photocopy the form and keep one in your pocket or purse at all times. In each box, record an "H" or an "L" showing whether the serving was high-calorie-density/high-fat, or low-calorie-density/low-fat.

Date: _____

Vegetables: ☐ ☐ ☐ ☐ ☐

Fruit: ☐ ☐ ☐ ☐

Grains: ☐ ☐ ☐ ☐ ☐ ☐ ☐ ☐ ☐

Dairy products: ☐ ☐ ☐

Meat, bird, fish, beans, peas, eggs: ☐ ☐ ☐

Fluid, 8-ounce serving
(no sugar or caffeine): ☐ ☐ ☐ ☐ ☐ ☐ ☐ ☐

After a few weeks of filing out this form, you will be able to follow a good eating plan. But you can carry this form as a reminder to yourself. NOTE: Serving sizes can be adjusted to fit how much you care to eat each day.

2. Continue with your weekly diary, and your weekly meetings with your support group. Sleep well, and exercise.

Resources

American Dietetic Association Consumer Hotline: 1-800-366-1655

Foreyt, J. P., Goodrick, G. K., (1994). *Living Without Dieting.* New York, Warner. (Highly recommended)

References

American Psychiatric Association (1994). *Diagnostic Criteria from DSM-IV* Washington, DC: American Psychiatric Association.

Bandini, L. G., Schoeller, D. A., Dietz, W. H. (1994). Metabolic differences in response to a high-fat vs. a high-carbohydrate diet. *Obesity Research,* 2, 348–54.

Christensen, L. (1996). *Diet-Behavior Relationships: Focus on Depression.* Washington, DC: American Psychological Association. (To order, call 1-800-374-2721.)

Danguir, J. (1987) Cafeteria diet promotes sleep in rats. *Appetite,* 8, 40–53.

Eaton, S. B., Shostak, K., Konner, M. (1988). *The Stone Age Health Program: Diet and Exercise As Nature Intended.* New York: Harper & Row.

Eliason, B. C., Kruger, J., Mark, D., Rasmann, D. N. Dietary supplement users: demographics, product use, and medical system interaction. *J Am Board Fam Pract* 1997, 10, 265–71.

Eliason, B. C., Myszkowski, J., Marabella, A., Rasmann, D. N. (1994). Use of dietary supplements by patients in a family practice clinic. *J Am Board Fam Pract* 1996, 9, 249–53.

Herbert, V., Barrett, S. J. *The Vitamin Pushers: How the "Health Food" Industry Is Selling America a Bill of Goods.* Prometheus Books.

Lane, J. D., Phillipsbute, B. G., Pieper, C. F. (1998). Caffeine raises blood pressure at work *Psychosomatic Medicine,* 60, 327–30.

Larsen, L. F., Bladbjerg, E. M., Jespersen, J., Marckmann, P.

(1998). Effects of dietary fat quality on postprandial activation of blood coagulation factor VII. *Arteriosclerosis, Thrombosis & Vascular Biology,* 17, 2904–09.

McCarthy, L. (1997). Report on use of the computer-based bio-nutritional encyclopedia. South Norwalk, CT: New Paradigm Ventures, unpub report.

Orr, W. C., Shahid, G., Harnish, M. J., Elsenbruch, S. (1997). Meal composition and its effect on postprandial sleepiness. *Physiology & Behavior,* 62, 709–12.

Pally, A., Sobal, J., Muncie, H. L., Jr. Nutritional supplement utilization in an urban family practice center. *J Family Practice* 1984, 18, 249–53.

Report of the American Institute of Nutrition (AIN) Steering Committee on Healthy Weight (1994). *Journal of Nutrition,* 124, 2240–43.

Sobal, J., Muncie, H. L. Jr., Guyther, J. R. Nutritional supplements use by patients in a rural family practice. *J Amer Coll Nutrition* 1986, 5, 313–16.

Stampi, C., Aguirre, A., Macchi, M., Moore-Ede, M. (1996). Peppermint aroma as a countermeasure to sleepiness during driving simulation. *Sleep Research,* 25, 112.

Thayer, R. E. (1987). Energy, tiredness and tension: effects of a sugar snack versus moderate exercise. *Journal of Personality and Social Psychology,* 52, 119–25. See also Thayer's book, *The Origin of Everyday Moods.* New York: Oxford, 1996.

Tudge, C. (1980). *Future Food: Politics, Philosophy and Recipes for the 21st Century.* New York: Harmony Books.

U.S. Department of Agriculture (1995). *Dietary Guidelines for Americans,* 4th ed. Washington, DC: USGPO, Home and Gardening Bulletin No. 232.

Weidner, G., Connor, S. L., Hollis, J. F., & Connor, W. E. (1992). Improvements in hostility and depression in relation to dietary change and cholesterol lowering: The Family Heart Study. *Annals of Internal Medicine,* 117, 820–23.

Williams, M. H. (1995). Nutritional ergogenics in athletics. *Journal of Sports Medicine,* 13, Spec. Nos., S63–S74.

Yankelovich Partners for the Nutrition Information Center at New York Hospital–Cornell Medical Center, International Bottled Water Association (1998). *Survey of Water Drinking Habits of Americans.* (See http://www.bottledwater.org.)

7

Do You Have Peace?

GOAL: To help you achieve a sense of calm control.

Do you feel that your life is progressing in a wonderful way, and that you are achieving and experiencing just about everything you could have ever hoped for? If you think so, then you are either very close to God, or very far from reality. Life is a continuing series of challenges, and there is no real peace, because as soon as one challenge seems to be finished, another one begins. Or many challenges could occur simultaneously. In our modern age of family disintegration, urban crowding, and loss of fundamental values, many seem to live a life of torment rather than peace.

But let's define peace more precisely. The dictionary definition (Merriam-Webster) defines peace, in a personal sense, as "freedom from disquieting or oppressive thoughts or emotions." Peace might also be used to describe a life in which:

1. There is an absence of troublesome challenges (never happens).

2. The is a sense of control over all challenges, or

3. There is a feeling of acceptance about those challenges that cannot be controlled.

Peace depends on one's interpretation of life as much as on the characteristics and conditions of life itself. For example, I know people who have enough money to retire and live in great wealth, but they have no peace because they are always trying to make more money, and worry excessively over business decisions. I know of others who are quadriplegic, and have no money, and yet, because of religious faith and acceptance of their condition, seem to be at peace. Perhaps they have peace because they know they can no longer struggle. I have seen villagers in Southeast Asia who had nothing but family and a few acres of rice paddy who displayed no sense of anxiety or worry, only contentment. Perhaps they have peace because they don't know any better.

But most of us can struggle, and we are driven to struggle to make things better. This is especially true of those who buy self-improvement books. In order to achieve some sense of peace, we need to develop life skills which will help us better manage life's challenges, and help us to minimize harmful psychological and physiological reactions to the stress they create.

As a self-assessment of your current state of peace, let's bring back the table from chapter 1 which lists the important areas of life. For each area, list your current challenges, and rate how stressful/unpeaceful that area is for you. This will help you reflect on your current peace status. Be sure to discuss this with your support group, or take it with you if you seek therapy.

Table for Evaluating Your Current Life Challenges

LIFE AREA	CURRENT CHALLENGES
Intimate Relation	
Current stress perceived	*Extreme Heavy Moderate Minimal None*
Family	
Current stress perceived	*Extreme Heavy Moderate Minimal None*
Friendships	
Current stress perceived	*Extreme Heavy Moderate Minimal None*
Sleep	
Current stress perceived	*Extreme Heavy Moderate Minimal None*
Nutrition/weight	
Current stress perceived	*Extreme Heavy Moderate Minimal None*
Organization	
Current stress perceived	*Extreme Heavy Moderate Minimal None*
Work	
Current stress perceived	*Extreme Heavy Moderate Minimal None*
Lack of Meaning in Life	
Current stress perceived	*Extreme Heavy Moderate Minimal None*
Religion	
Current stress perceived	*Extreme Heavy Moderate Minimal None*

LIFE AREA	CURRENT CHALLENGES
Mental Functioning	
Current stress perceived	*Extreme Heavy Moderate Minimal None*
Fatigue	
Current stress perceived	*Extreme Heavy Moderate Minimal None*

If you circled a fair number of "extreme," "heavy," or "moderate," then you may have too much stress (I define stress as the perception that current life challenges are too much to handle). Too much stress is associated with mental and physical deterioration. This is because, as animals, we are designed to respond to the kind of stress that requires running away from predators, or fighting those who would try to take away our food or mates.

Potential Effects of Chronic Stress

This table shows why the "stress response" is a helpful, automatic system for protecting our bodies when stress involves fighting or fleeing. However, if we experience social or work stress, and it is inappropriate to bash the boss on the head or to run away from the office, then stress reactions may lead to some physical problems. Because we must react to stress without getting physical, we are left to "stew in our own juices."

Stress Response: The Good and the Bad

IMMEDIATE EFFECTS (Good in primitive times)	POTENTIAL CHRONIC EFFECTS (Bad in modern times)
To Feed Muscles	
Blood pressure increases	High blood pressure
Heart rate increases	Heart rhythm disturbances
Breathing rate increases	Anxiety
Adrenaline released	Anxiety
Lung passages widen	Asthma
Blood to stomach decreased	Indigestion, increased risk for ulcers
Increased sugar from liver	Increased risk for diabetes
Fats increase in blood	Heart and blood vessel disease
To Prepare for Action	
Increased mental activity	Anxiety, confusion, poor judgment
Eyes dilate	Eyestrain
Muscles tense	Back and jaw trouble, tension headache, fatigue
Metabolic rate increases	Sweating, fatigue
To Reduce Bleeding and Disease	
Surface blood flow decreased	Cold hands and feet, migraine
Blood clotting factor increased	Stroke
Immune response activated	Immune system weakened
Bowel and bladder muscles loosen	Ileitis, colitis, urological problems

If you feel you are stewing in your own stress juices too often, you may already have some signs of stress-related disorder. Here is a list of symptoms that might be caused by, or made worse by, stress. If you have any of these, see your physician to make sure there is no underlying medical problem. *Stress Symptom Checklist:* Indicate which of these you have by putting a number in the blank. Rate each symptom "1" if its a small problem, "2" if a moderate problem, and "3" if severe.

Table for Evaluating Your Potential Stress Symptoms

Symptom	Rating	Symptom	Rating
lower-back tension	1 2 3	yelling/anger	
jaw tension, grind teeth		hyperventilating	
upper-back/neck tension		asthma	
sleep too much		strained breathing	
waking at night		frequent colds or flu	
feel tired when arising		headache	
bad dreams		chest pain	
can't get to sleep		stuttering	
overeating		feel faint	
undereating		hot spells, sweating	

Symptom	Rating	Symptom	Rating
gas		cold spells	
constipation		heart racing	
diarrhea		itching	
heartburn, reflux		muscles twitches	
cramps		cold hands, feet	
nausea		fatigue	
ulcers/ileitis/colitis		depression	
frequent urination		mistakes/accidents	
hemorrhoids		forgetfulness	
can't concentrate		apathy	
irritable		sexual disinterest	
worry too much		reduced productivity	
anxiety		abuse of alcohol and other drowner drugs	
		TOTAL SCORE	

You can add up your score, and see how this score may change over time. Don't compare your score with others. Since stress is a matter of individual perception, comparisons would not be meaningful. People are different in the way they react to life challenges, as the following section describes.

Personality and Peace

Family of Origin: The peace we experience in life may be determined in large part to the way we were raised. Some families are prone to interpret life challenges as crises. In such a family, the children learn that dealing with crises means that one should display lots of negative emotions, including alarm, frustration, irritability, and despair. Yelling, flailing of arms, making accusatory remarks, assigning blame, and calling out blasphemously to a deity are all part of the crisis family agenda. Recall how your family reacted to life challenges. How do you react now as an adult? What example do you set for your children? Therapy for persons who grew up in this kind of family would involve relearning how to face challenges, using the skills outlined in this book.

Type A: The Type-A person is generally characterized as a hard-driving competitor. Symptoms include: posture of muscle tension, hostility, finger tapping, interrupting others, overuse of gestures, ticlike drawing back of the corners of the mouth exposing teeth, hostile/jarring laugh, fist clenching, frequent use of four-letter words, excessive forehead and lip perspiration, trying to do many things at once, trouble waiting in line, irritable with others, thinks in terms of quantities instead of qualities.

Obviously, this is a high-stress-type person. How do people get that way? One theory postulates that early in life, a child develops a sense of insecurity and low self-esteem (Everly, 1989). In order to compensate, an excessive need for achievement is created. A desire for the power to obtain the resources needed for achievement is next. The need for power involves a strong need for control, and fear of loss of control. This is accompanied by a sense of time urgency, and a need to achieve as many things as possible in the shortest possible time. A hostile attitude is cultivated against others who are seen as competitors or barriers to achievement. All this is associated with an extremely high physiological reactivity to perceived challenges. In this way, Type-A individuals are more prone to certain stress-related disorders. Hostility has been shown to play a potential role in the development of heart disease in these types (Dembroski & Costa, 1988).

Therapy for Type-A individuals does not involve trying to get the person to relax. Type-A people find the concept of relaxation abhorrent. They want to work hard and achieve! Dr. Ethel Roskies, a Type-A researcher in Toronto, once tried to recruit Type-A men for a study by promising to "help them relax" (Roskies et al., 1986). No one answered the ad. Later, she put in an ad describing Type-A individuals and said she had a program that would "help them improve their efficiency." Three hundred fifty people called immediately. The treatment, which helps them become less hostile and to slow down a bit, actually does increase efficiency. This is because a real Type-A person eventually burns out. Few Type As reach the top of corporations because they can't handle the stress, and because few want a hostile person in leadership roles.

Type-B people are the opposite of Type A. They tend to be calm, noncompetitive, and not easily angered. They focus on the qualitative aspects of projects and are willing to be part of a team. Generally, they are more secure than Type As. However, under great pressure, a Type B may show Type-A characteristics. There are really no pure types; some people are somewhere in the middle of A and B.

Reward Insufficiency Syndrome: Some people seem unusually compelled to seek out stimulation. This could be stimulation from rock climbing, bungee jumping, parachuting, or aggressive competitive sports. These are the thrill seekers. Other seek stimulation from drugs. They always are doing or taking something to keep their brains entertained. One theory is that these people, who may represent up to a third of the population, have a genetic difference in their brains (Blum et al., 1995). The areas of the brain that receive dopamine, the ultimate rewarding substance, are defective. This means that more dopamine must be produced to get the same reward effect that others of us get with less intense lives. Dopamine is involved in the rewarding effects of eating, exercise, sex, and some drugs. Genetic testing is now available to determine if this genetic syndrome is present.

Optimism/Pessimism: Optimistic people look forward to positive outcomes when they meet most of life's challenges. This helps them face the task and continue working toward a solution, in hopes that there really will be a brighter day. A classic example is the story of the two salesmen who were assigned to sell shoes. Their territories were in the rain forests of Brazil. The pessimist returned to headquarters very distressed. "These people don't buy shoes. They always go barefoot!" The optimist returned jubilant. "What an opportunity! No one in my territory has shoes yet!" Or the story of the young boy who returned to his room to find a large pile of horse excrement put there as a joke by his brothers. "Oh, wow! This must mean that Daddy finally bought me a pony!"

Nothing is either good nor bad, but thinking makes it so. That's what the Greek philosopher Epictetus wrote. There is always a more positive way to look at any situation. This is the basis for what is now called "cognitive psychotherapy." This approach examines the patient's thoughts and attitudes, and the goal is to make thoughts more accepting and positive. Take a moment to think about something in your life that you don't like. Is there an alternative way of viewing the situation? Talk to a friend about it. Often, another person can more easily see the positive aspects of a situation. Even people facing imminent death have been known to maintain a sense of peace, and a positive, loving attitude. Accentuate the positive, eliminate the negative, and don't mess with Mr. In-between. Count your blessings first. Optimistic people tend to be psychologically and physically healthier than pessimists (Scheier & Carver, 1992).

Selfishness and Selflessness: Those who are overly concerned with satisfying their own needs at the expense of others will never have peace. There will always be a sense of competition, and a feeling that others are always trying to take something. Peace can come only when relationships are mutually nurturing, and there is trust in a norm of fair sharing of resources. Ask your friends to give you honest feedback about this aspect of your life. If you have no friends you can trust, take it as a sign you need more work in this area. More on selfishness later, starting in chapter 10.

Selflessness, or the concern for helping others without expectation of reward (altruism) is certainly a good trait, and is one of the secrets of happiness. However, helping others excessively, at the expense of personal emotional and physical health can be stressful for all concerned. Such attempts to help others excessively may stem from a motivation to make up for low self-esteem or an attempt to control others' lives. Nobody likes a meddling martyr. Those who are helped will end up rejecting the helper who sought love and attention.

Peace: The Result of Good Life Management

Regardless of your personal assets and liabilities, peace can be optimized through careful life management. I define life management as following a step-by-step plan of action outlined in this flowchart:

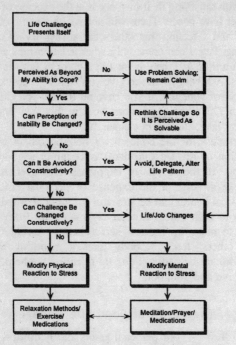

Figure 7.1. Flowchart for Life Management

Life management to achieve some sense of peace consists of the following elements (refer to the Flowchart for Life Management):

1. Calm investigation of the problem/challenge.

2. Developing a plan to solve the problem presented by the life challenge, or to tolerate/accept it.

3. Using a plan to mitigate the mental and physical effects elicited by the aspects of the challenge which are perceived as stressful.

These are the elements involved in good psychotherapy. In fact, the flowchart could serve as a therapy model in most cases seen by psychologists.

Life Challenge Perceived As Beyond My Ability to Cope: It is this perception that initiates the stress response. But careful reflection upon the challenge may reveal a new way of understanding its nature. Seeking counsel from others and getting their views on the nature of the challenge is critical; too often people get caught up in fits of anxiety and panic over things which, when reinterpreted, are not really so imposing.

Example 1: "I can't write a 200-page book by the deadline! It's impossible! I will fail and never be a famous author!" This is an example of catastrophizing. Counsel from a friend might be: "Look, calm down. You can only write one chapter at a time. Write down a schedule, plan to work evenings and weekends for a few months, and everything will turn out great."

Example 2: When driving to an appointment across town involving a very important business deal, a colleague and I got stuck in freeway traffic due to an accident ahead. We knew we would be very late. (This was before cellular phones.) But since we are both psychologists, we reinterpreted the situation in the best way. First, we noted that there was nothing we could do about the situation, so there was no use in screaming, honking, or cursing, fun as those activities might be. Second, one of us noted that the seemingly endless line of brake lights extending before us looked, when you took off your glasses, like a beautiful string of bright rubies. Then I decided to use the time constructively by practicing a relaxation technique. No, we were not on drugs. But we used humor to turn a bad situation into a laughable one. *Note:* This is the type of situation in which the Type-A person might go bonkers. Road rage is getting to be a more popular way of settling the challenges of the highways.

Another aspect of seemingly overwhelming life challenges is lack of appropriate training and skills. If there is time, perhaps a course of learning would enable one to meet the challenge constructively. One should welcome the life challenge as a motivation to get more education. For example, I took a twelve-week course in financial planning, which considerably eased my stress over money matters, even though it did not substantially increase my wealth.

Can a Life Challenge Be Avoided? If a challenge is viewed as within your ability to master, then calm problem solving, planning, and persistence will win the day. If, however, you and others agree that the challenge is too much, then the possibility of avoiding the challenge needs to be considered. This is a possibility only if it can be done without shirking responsibility, or duty to family or country.

Example 1: Your boss has given you an incredibly large project to finish before tomorrow. Can you delegate this to an underling? Can you use this as a motivation to quit and find another position?

Example 2: Your commute takes 45 minutes each way every day. Can you get permission to travel either before or after the rush hour? Is there an alternate route which is shorter, or which takes just as long but is more scenic and doesn't involve so much congestion?

Can the Challenge Be Changed? Often we have the power and skill to alter a life challenge so that it becomes a set of problems we can solve. In interpersonal relationships, effectively communicating your needs and working to achieve a negotiated change in others' demands may result in a more favorable situation for you and for the others. This is the rationale for what has been called assertiveness.

If the life challenge cannot be changed, or reinterpreted,

or avoided, and you perceive it to be more than you can cope with, then you will need to work on modifying your physical and mental reactivity to stress. These methods are described in the next chapter. Study and practice them well.

Poetry Corner

What technological marvel better serves our need to hurry and rush more than the automobile? Would life be less stressful if we all rode bicycles, or walked? Here is my poem about it:

Ride On!
(or, Wordsworth in a Porsche Turbo Carrera)

Ride on with freeway's frantic haste,
Man in your ferrous carapace.
With urgent goal, and breakneck pace,
Compelled to run, to win some race.

Volatile vapors sparked to blast
The pounding pistons turn the shaft.
Tires claw and strain, to spin and turn.
Bright flashing chrome and rubber burn!

Hurling onward, into bright day
Ignoring flowers along the way
Rushing, flying, past trees that sway
Trees that can never go away.

But I, like trees, prefer to rest.
I am at home, I've done my quest.
Swing on the porch, coffee in hand,
Birds on the wing, blooms on the land.

So ride on man with lightning speed
Of pastoral calm, take no heed.
Octane driven, overdrive on
Keep pushing on, keep pushing on.

The World Is Too Much with Us
William Wordsworth (1806)

The world is too much with us; late and soon,
Getting and spending, we lay waste our powers:
Little we see in Nature that is ours;
We have given our hearts away, a sordid boon!
The Sea that bares her bosom to the moon;
The winds that will be howling at all hours;
And are up-gathered now like sleeping flowers;
For this, for everything, we are out of tune;
It move us not—Great God! I'd rather be
A Pagan suckled in a creed outworn;
So might I, standing on this pleasant lea,
Have glimpses that would make me less forlorn;
Have sight of Proteus rising from the sea;
Or hear old Triton blow his wreathed horn.

Homework, Part One

Make a lot of copies of the following Life Challenge
Self-Assessment and Plan Development Form (or, for the
benefit of former government-acronym-aficionado workers
like me, the "LCSAPDF"). Fill out the form for as many
life challenges as you can think of. Use this form for the
rest of your life to help yourself get a mental handle on,
and to develop a plan for, meeting life's challenges constructively.

Life Challenge Self-Assessment and Plan Development Form

Describe the Life Challenge:	What aspects of the Life Challenge are stressful, and why?
_____ _____ _____ _____ _____ _____ _____	_____ _____ _____ _____ _____
Can you confront this challenge successfully? If yes, go to right.> If no, go below ↓	Use careful problem-solving methods.
List ways to reinterpret the challenge in less stressful ways: _____ _____ _____ _____ _____	<HINT: Get opinions of others.
List ways the challenge might be avoided constructively: _____ _____ _____ _____ _____	List here possible ways to delegate the challenge, or alter your life pattern. _____ _____ _____ _____

List here how the challenge might be changed:

_____

_____

_____

_____

_____

_____

<HINT: Can you negotiate for a more favorable situation, or get someone to help you?

_____

_____

_____

_____

List mental-stress-reduction methods here, such as meditation/prayer:

_____

_____

_____

_____

<HINT: If you feel really out of control, and nothing you do seems to help, seek professional help.

List physical relaxation methods you will use:

_____

_____

_____

_____

_____

_____

_____

_____

<HINT: If you really can't relax, you can see a physician to get medications for relaxation and sleep. But don't rely on these for more than a few weeks. Dependence on medications is not a solution, but another serious problem. If you have been diagnosed as chemically dependent, medication is only an option of last resort.

Homework, Part Two

Write down a brief history of your life, noting the particularly big life challenges you have experienced, and how you handled them. Based on this, do you feel that you have a high or low ability to handle challenges? Talk about this with your support people.

Homework, Part Three

Write down a few paragraphs describing why you feel you have a high (or low) feeling of peace in your life, and why. Discuss this with your support people.

Homework, Part Four

How can a person attain maximum peace in life? Talk amongst yourselves about this topic. Dealing with life challenges successfully, and knowing how to relax and be organized, helps enhance feelings of peace. But true peace comes from following the right life course, or purpose. (Don't cheat by reading the last third of this book first.)

As usual, keep up your weekly diary, meet with your support group, exercise, and eat prudently for energy.

References

Blum, K., Wood, R. C., Braverman, E. R., Chen, T. J., Sheridan, P. J. (1995). The D2 dopamine receptor gene as a predictor of compulsive disease: Bayes' theorem. *Functional Neurology*, 10, 37–44.

Dembroski, T., Costa, P. (1988). Assessment of coronary-prone behavior. *Annals of Behavioral Medicine,* 10, 60–63.

Everly, G. S. Jr. (1989). *A Clinical Guide to the Treatment of the Human Stress Response.* New York: Plenum.

Roskies, E., Seraganian, P., Oseasohn, R., et al. (1986) The Montreal Type A Intervention Project: major findings. *Health Psychology.* 5, 1, 45–69.

Scheier, M. F., Carver, C. S. (1992). Effects of optimism on psychological and physical well-being: theoretical overview and empirical update. *Cognitive Therapy and Research,* 16, 201–28.

8

Physical and Mental Peace

GOAL: To learn how to control your muscles and mind for relaxation.

Focusing on Relaxation

This chapter describes a variety of ways to help you relax your body and mind. Unless you are in grave physical danger, it is usually best to be as relaxed as possible. The martial arts and Eastern philosophies regard the ideal state as one in which you have high energy but are calm inside. In order to remain calm, you should strive to be aware of your bodily and physical tension at all times. Just sitting down and thinking about how your body feels can have a very relaxing effect. Hypnosis works by strengthening an inward focus.

Think about your body right now. How do your feet feel? Tense? Hot? Numb? How about your shoulders? Often tension builds up over the day, but it goes unnoticed, since we are focused outward, and distracted by all the pressures of work and responsibilities. Take a deep breath, and as you exhale, let all the tension in your body flow away. Watch the second hand of your watch. As it sweeps around for 60 seconds, tell yourself to relax more and more as it comes back to its starting position. Even simple relaxation methods can have a profound effect. The trick is to remember to do them, and to focus inward from time to time to prevent a nasty buildup of stress that can lead to illness or conflict.

Some people can immediately sense a feeling of deep relaxation when asked to focus on their bodies. Others have been tense all their lives, and do not know how to experience relaxation. Some of these people may have grown up in tense families, or in families where maintaining some tension was part of being prepared to ward off attacks by siblings or angry/drunk/incestuous parents. Others came to believe that tension was the appropriate muscular condition if one was going to get ahead in life through aggressive competition.

I want you to try the following relaxation methods. Some will work better than others, depending on your individual characteristics and predilections. After trying them out, and choosing your favorites, you can integrate them into your daily and weekly schedule. Remember, relaxation is an important part of self-care. You can justify taking the time, and enjoying the experiences, because relaxation keeps you healthy in order to help others. Failing to relax may cause burnout, with poorer health and troubled relationships.

The types of relaxation techniques include those focusing on physical relaxation and mental relaxation. Physical relaxation is conducive to mental relaxation, and vice versa. I recommend adding several enjoyable relaxation activities to one's lifestyle, replacing perhaps a few hours each week of senseless and useless television viewing.

Substances, Smells, Sounds, and Sights
for Relaxation

Due to the increasing stress of modern life, there is a great demand for easy ways to relax. One of the easiest ways is to pop a pill or take substances. Alcohol is the traditional favorite, but it has some rather grievous psychological and physiological costs attached to its use. As mentioned earlier, even a small amount of alcohol can reduce the body's ability to produce energy from oxygen. It is also a depressant, and who needs a downer to cope with stress? Overuse of alcohol can lead to many embarrassing outcomes, not the least of which might be unsafe sex, losing your job, your spouse, your family, and your life. I used to provide mental-health services to industrial workers. Many of them seemed to have the idea that it was normal to work an eight-hour shift, and then to come home and drink a six-pack of beer (more on weekends). But the truth is, anyone who drinks more than two drinks a day is getting into a danger zone. There are many books and organizations treating the evils of alcohol and street drugs. Call Alcoholics Anonymous for more information.

What About Prescriptions?

You can see your physician and get a prescription for tranquilizers. But I would suggest you talk to the doctor in great detail about the benefits and costs of getting on a mood-altering pill. Depending on medication may be necessary in crises, but the realization that one needs medicine to cope is not good for self-esteem, and sets a pattern for wimping out on life's challenges. There are many such drugs available today. Their widespread use is most likely an indication that people lack life-coping skills, more than it is that humans have built for themselves a culture in which their own bodies and minds cannot deal with the pressures.

The most popular tranquilizers were introduced in the

1960s. Librium was the first of the class of drugs called benzodiazepines, which were developed in an attempt to make a tranquilizer without the sedative properties and potential for abuse, addiction, tolerance, and dependence of the earlier barbiturates and other sedative/hypnotic drugs. The popularity of the benzodiazepines rose steadily to a peak period in the mid-1970s when Valium became the most commonly prescribed drug of any kind, including antihypertensive, analgesic, and other mood-changing medications. In 1975, 62 million prescriptions were written for Valium, which, in Latin, means "to be strong and well." I remember a scene in the movie *Starting Over* in which someone in a crowd asks if anyone has some Valium, and everyone goes to their purses and pockets and produces a prescription bottle. Doctors were prescribing it for everything from aching backs to free-floating anxiety (Weiss, 1997).

Current studies of benzodiazepines demonstrate clearly that they produce tolerance and dependence in short- and long-term use (Miller & Gold, 1990). Patients can develop abuse and addiction to these drugs. However, confusion in diagnosis and treatment of abuse and addiction has clouded this issue. The lack of standards and monitoring permit physicians with good intentions to prescribe Valium even when it may not be needed, causing more damage from side effects, and from reduced productivity, than the benefits of being more relaxed might provide. But I am not a physician, so you will need to check with your physician. Get a second opinion before rushing to the pharmacy.

Nonprescription Substances for Relaxation

Kava: Kava (*Piper methysticum*) is a member of the pepper family indigenous to the Fiji Islands. Chewing or boiling the root to make tea produces a narcotic effect, and it has been used ceremonially in the South Pacific since antiquity. In northern Australia, kava was introduced by Western missionaries to replace alcohol. The Aborigines seemed to have a problem controlling alcohol use, similar to problems found in some Native Americans. The new use of kava was associated with less violence than caused by alcohol, but eventually many Aborigines developed habits of kava over-use, with attendant health problems. High doses (more than 300 grams, or 1.5 pounds of root per week) can cause puffy face, scaly rash, eye irritation, unhealthful weight loss and loss of body fat, blood in the urine, decreased platelet volume, shortness of breath, and possible pulmonary hypertension (Mathews et al., 1988). There is now a government campaign to reduce kava use (Cawte, 1985).

Kava is currently marketed in Western countries for its purported relaxing and mind-clearing effects. A German study found that it had an antianxiety effect (Kinzler et al., 1991). One group of 29 patients was given 300 milligrams per day of kava extract, another group of 29 was given placebo pills over four weeks. Anxiety scores decreased significantly more over the course of the study in the kava group. No adverse side effects were observed. Despite the dearth of scientific support, kava is being intensely marketed and may become extremely popular. My advice: wait until safety studies have been done by independent or government laboratories.

Valerian: Valerian consists of the roots and underground stems of *Valeriana officinale,* a perennial herb, native to Europe and Asia, which now also grows in North America. Valerian is Latin for "to be strong." Europeans fighting in World War I took valerian to calm down. There are a few studies showing that it may help promote relaxation and sleep.

In one study, each subject was given a placebo, valerian (400 milligrams) or a commercially available valerian product (Leathwood et al., 1982). Valerian produced a significant improvement in sleep quality in people who considered themselves to be poor or irregular sleepers. However, it also produced a feeling of drowsiness the next morning. The U.S. Pharmacopeial Convention has reviewed the scientific studies, and reports that claims for the effectiveness of valerian for insomnia cannot be supported (USP, 1998).

The drowsiness and sedative effects of valerian may be the result of a depression of the central nervous system. A study (Hendriks et al., 1985) of rats given valerian showed a decrease in their ability to move around; this is not a good side effect for humans who need to drive or be alert at work. Interestingly, valerian contains chemicals similar to catnip; if you want to act like a crazy cat, then perhaps valerian is for you. It's not for me.

Smelling Your Way to Relaxation: Aromatherapy

Pleasant odors have been used since the inventions of the nose and flowers to produce pleasant moods. Use of aromas may be needed even more today as technology inflicts us with automobile exhaust, factory smoke and effluvia, photocopy chemicals, and the dreaded redolence of new vinyl shower curtains (one of my most hated odors).

The time-tested aromas include: lavender, frankincense (olibanum oil), patchouli oil, rose, sandalwood, vanilla, lily of the valley, and ylang-ylang. There is not much scientific research on the effectiveness of these aromas, but aromatherapy falls into the category of ''if it works for me, I'll use it,'' so don't wait until a government panel determines that certain smells help people relax. Unless you are allergic to certain odors, there is little danger of harmful side effects.

One hospital study (Dunn et al., 1995) randomly assigned 122 patients in an intensive-care unit to one of three conditions: 1) massage; 2) aromatherapy using oil of lavender; or 3) a period of rest. Patients receiving the lavender odor reported significantly greater improvement in their mood and perceived levels of anxiety.

The cost of scented candles and oils is small; why not

have aromatic odors all the time in your home? Subdued lighting and aromas can significantly alter one's mood, although sometimes the mood turns from relaxation to romance, which ultimately can add to feelings of relaxation, after a brief exercise session.

Sounds Good to Me: Relaxing Sounds

One of my great desires is never to live within earshot of a freeway again. I want to live where I can hear a distant cricket, or the rumble of thunder from lightning on the horizon, or the gentle rustling of leaves as they flutter in a gentle breeze. Most of the time it seems that all we hear is the drone of traffic, the flow of air-conditioning, the blaring of electronic entertainment devices, or the whining of the younger and older generations. We need to pay attention to our sound environment. Here are some suggestions (see Resources to find most of these):

Sound machines: there are several brands of these which electronically generate soothing sounds of rain, waterfall, creek, crickets, birds, and surf.

Falling Rain chime box (Stressless): This little red box has tiny steel balls falling continuously on hand-cast temple bells, re-creating the gentle cadence of falling rain chimes.

Sound screens: These generate a steady "white" noise which can serve to mask distracting sounds. This may be the choice for those who would like to relax, but are distracted at work by more complex sounds.

Music: Of course, music hath powers to sooth the savage breast, and any recorded music store can offer a wide variety of such CDs.

Additional steps to take: Have others in your environment enjoy sounds via earphones. Work toward legislation prohibiting mega-power sound systems in cars, or the playing of loud music anywhere in public. Advise youth to sit at least 560 feet away from the band at any rock concert. Advise youth not to be a member of a rock band.

A Sight for Sore Eyes: Relaxing Your Visual Environment

Spend some time revamping your home environment. Do as the psychiatric hospitals do; they want patients and staff to remain as calm as possible. Paint your walls in dark, purple, or forest-green pastels. Or cover a whole wall with a forest photograph. This can be effective with a forest-sounds recording. Make general lighting subdued, with lamps for adequate reading light. Candles can be used to good effect, although this can be overdone, sometimes resulting in conflagration. Many people are stressed by clutter. Simplify your surroundings with lots of space. Do not make your living quarters look like a storeroom (see chapter 12 on Things, which will urge you to get rid of lots of stuff).

If you believe in Feng Shui, go for it. I don't. But certainly you should consider alternate ways of arranging furniture until you find a configuration that feels good. Small areas for relaxation or reading which are partitioned off by plants or screens can be cozy places to hide temporarily from the rigors of survival tasks.

Stress Management and Relaxation Products That I Think Might Be Helpful

To stimulate your creative thinking about altering your stressful environment, here is a list of products available through the resources listed at the end of this chapter.

Large hammock strung between two shade trees

Aroma-therapy pendant, so that the smell is right under your nose

Aroma diffusion devices, including one for use in the car

Zen garden: this is a little sandbox with a few rocks, which you can arrange and rake in a meditative way

Home sauna ($$)

Aromatic bath oils

Turbo spa to churn up the waters of your bath

Meditation pillows to sit on

Biofeedback equipment: finger temperature, galvanic skin response (GSR), breathing-rate feedback.

Relaxing the Body

There are many ways to relax the muscles of the body. All of them rely on paying attention to various parts of the body. Just paying attention to your feet, for example, can increase blood flow, making the feet feel warmer. (Focus on your feet right now for one minute. Stop reading this, and focus on your feet for one minute, to see what happens.) Remember, the stress response restricts blood flow to the surfaces of the body to prevent excessive bleeding during conflict. Relaxation does the opposite. As you focus on your feet, the muscles may relax as well. So pay attention to your body. Left to its own devices, it will tense up during the day, adding to feelings of stress.

A 15-to-20-minute relaxation practice should be done every day. Doing it right after exercising can be beneficial.

My Relaxation Induction Procedure

Here is the dialogue (below) I use to help people relax. It is a self-hypnosis procedure. You can practice reading it to each other in your support group. You can record it and play it back to yourself. Or you can have a loved one record it with heartfelt inflections. Or you can buy the tapes I recommend in the resources list. The advantage of listening to a recording or another's voice is that you are less likely to be distracted from the task of relaxation.

A Relaxation Induction Dialogue (*means pause for about 10 seconds)

Remove contact lenses, glasses, pagers. Get comfortable in a seated position in a chair with adequate back support. Let your hands rest in your lap, and put your feet flat on the floor. Be sure your environment is not too hot or cold, and that you will not be disturbed by noises or phones. Spend a few minutes getting relaxed, and focusing on the regularity of your breathing. After you feel comfortable, close your eyes, focus on your right foot. There are many muscles, tendons, ligaments, and blood vessels in your foot. Let all those parts relax. Sense how your foot feels on the floor, or how the sock and shoe feel in terms of pressure and temperature. Focus on letting your right foot be as relaxed as possible.

As you relax, continue to breathe regularly and normally. Now pay attention to your left foot. Feel a sense of relaxation flow slowly into your left foot.* Now experience feelings of relaxation and perhaps warmth in both feet. Imagine that they are both in a pool of warm, healing fluid which causes relaxation.* Let the feeling of relaxation flow up to your lower legs. There are muscles there, but these muscles are now at rest, and you can let them relax and feel good.* There is no tension in your knees; experience this lack of pressure, and let your knees and the muscles around them relax.*

Now, focus on your thighs. Here are the largest muscles of your body. But they are just sitting, doing nothing, so they can relax, too. Let the muscles around your pelvis become relaxed and at ease.* Allow your stomach muscles and lower-back muscles to feel comfortable, with just enough tension to keep you sitting upright, but in a state of peaceful balance.* Now focus on how your chest expands and contracts with each breath.* As you become aware of your breathing and the movement of your chest, let all the muscles there relax.*

Now focus on your hands. Again, there are many bones, muscles, and blood vessels in the hands, but as you pay attention to them, they become more relaxed. They become warmer as the blood flow increases with relaxation. Your hands are like limp rag dolls, completely without tension or troubles.* Let the feelings of limpness and relaxation flow up your arms. Your arms have muscles, but allow them to just hang down from your shoulders.* Let your shoulders relax. Let them fall a bit as gravity pulls them downward.*

Focus on all the parts of your body below your neck becoming more and more relaxed. Breathe in a bit more deeply, and as you breathe out, feel even more relaxation flowing through your body.*

Now focus on your neck muscles. Allow them to have just enough tension to hold your head upright, but in a state of relaxed balance. Let your jaw hang slack. Let your mouth open. Let all the muscles around your jaw relax.* Let your tongue lie limply in your mouth. Sense the coolness on your tongue as your inhale, and the warmth of your breath as your exhale.* Now let the muscles around your eyes relax. Let all the muscles in your face go limp, and enjoy the feelings of relaxation this brings. Let the muscles of your forehead relax.* Let a feeling of relaxed peace flow through your face,* your neck, your chest*, your arms and hands,* your legs*, and feet.*

With each breath, as you exhale, let your feelings of relaxation get deeper and more profound. Enjoy the feelings of tranquillity you can have by focusing on being relaxed.* Continue to feel relaxed. (Relaxation can continue for five minutes or more.)

Now, as I count to five, you can become more and more aware of your surroundings. As you begin to focus on the outside world, you can keep feeling as relaxed as you want. "One," you are very relaxed.* "Two," you are paying attention to the sounds and smells of this room.* "Three," your eyes are beginning to open slightly, and you become aware of your visual surroundings.* "Four," your eyes are open, but you still pay attention to your body being still and at peace.* "Five," you have returned to normal, but you can still enjoy a more relaxed state.

Progressive Relaxation

Progressive relaxation was developed by Edmund Jacobson in 1929 (Jacobson, 1974). This procedure involves tensing muscles for about five seconds, then relaxing them for thirty seconds. Try tensing your right hand in a fist as hard as you can for five seconds. Then let it relax. Notice that your right hand feels more relaxed than your left hand. Each muscle group is tensed and relaxed until it feels very relaxed; this may take up to five repetitions. After clenching your fists, tense your arms by bending the arm, and flexing the biceps. Relax. Tense your forehead, relax. Squint your eyes, relax. Then proceed in a like manner to your jaw, tongue pressed against the roof of your mouth, pursing the lips, tensing the buttocks, thighs, calves, stomach, and back muscles. Again, you should focus mentally on feelings of relaxation flowing throughout your body as you do this procedure.

I have had patients tell me they could not relax. I have them get as tense as possible, then stop, and repeat. After a while, they begin to notice the difference between tension and nontension. Nontension is labeled as relaxation.

Progressive relaxation can be helpful in getting to sleep. It has been used in countless studies with some benefits found for the amelioration of stress-related disorders. It needs to be practiced daily, until relaxation can be induced easily and quickly.

Autogenics: Autogenic training (AT) was developed about 100 years ago at the Berlin Institute by Oskar Vogt (Luthe, 1963). He found that a state of deep relaxation could be produced by asking patients to imagine their legs and arms being warm or heavy. The procedure involves saying to oneself, ''My right arm is heavy,'' or ''My right arm is warm.'' This is repeated for arms and legs. Other ideas include, ''My heartbeat is calm and regular,'' and ''My mind is quiet.'' The focus on body parts and paying attention to feelings of peace and relaxation is similar to other relaxation methods. I have been sensitive with overweight clients not to emphasize the ''my legs are heavy'' phrases.

Breathing Methods: The simplest breathing method for relaxation is simply to get comfortable, close eyes, and count each exhalation. The focus is on regular, relaxed breathing, which will slow down some during the procedure. The trick is not to be distracted. If distracted, start counting at "one" again. Instead of counting, a word or phrase (a mantra) may be said subvocally upon each exhalation. This could be a nonsense word that sounds relaxing, such as "Ahh," or words such as "peace," could be used. Whatever feels relaxing to you. I would not recommend mantras such as "The market is up and I am going to make a killing." There is no magic in relaxation. The trick is to remember to do the procedures, and not to be distracted by yourself or outside influences.

Abdominal breathing is another relaxation method. When lying down on your back, place your hands on your tummy, and focus on breathing regularly. Notice your hands rising and falling with each breath. This form of breathing is easier than if the entire chest musculature is involved, as might be the case during jogging.

A simple breathing method I recommend is called "747" breathing. Using a watch with a second hand, or by counting, you breathe in for a count of seven, hold the breath for a count of four, and breathe out for a count of seven. This should be repeated for several minutes, while focusing on letting the body relax. In this way, you are making yourself breathe in a way that might be achieved through meditation. It automatically slows down your thinking and relaxes the body.

There are many more breathing methods, not the least of which are included in yoga. At least one of them should be in your regular repertoire of relaxation methods. Breathing methods and how they are used in the treatment of stress disorders is described in a good book, *The Breath Connection* (Fried, 1990).

Note: If you have a medical problem (kidney disorder or diabetes) that causes rapid breathing, or involves impairment to your breathing function, do not attempt to alter your breathing without consulting your physician.

Biofeedback: Biofeedback means converting a body

function into a signal so that we can experience it as a visual or auditory stimulus. For example, a heart-rate monitor allows one to see heart rate. A thermometer allows us to see our body temperature. Scales tell us how much we weigh. For the purposes of relaxation, feedback of signals which indicate the body's state of tension or relaxation are converted to detectable forms.

The easiest form of biofeedback is the measurement of finger temperature. The stress response inhibits blood flow to the fingers, to prevent excessive bleeding. You might notice that some people have cold hands. This may be due to stress (businessmen are always on the lookout for cold hands, knowing that if their opponent is under stress, they have some psychological advantage). It may be due to intake of caffeine, or to Raynaud's disease. Your fingers fluctuate in temperature each day as a function of stress level.

An Interesting Story About Biofeedback

A famous professor once studied a group of Tibetan Buddhist monks. These monks were renowned for their disciplined use of meditation. Monks were said to achieve amazing feats through meditation, but only among those who had practiced diligently for decades. After days of rugged travel over mountain paths, the professor reached the monks. He found some who could, through meditation, raise their skin temperature enough to feel comfortable outside in the Himalayan winter. The increase in skin temperature was as much as 15 degrees F.

I once worked in a psychiatric hospital, using biofeedback to help young children learn to relax. I would attach temperature probes to their fingertips and have them lie down on the floor. Then I would play relaxing music and guide them through a relaxation procedure. Many of them reported feeling much more relaxed. They showed temperature increases of about 15 degrees F.

You can become a temperature biofeedback therapist for your own fingers. Go to Radio Shack and buy an indoor-outdoor digital thermometer (about $20). Attach the probe to the end of your third finger (opposite the nail) with transparent tape. Lie down in a comfortable position and practice some relaxation procedure. Have someone else monitor the increase in temperature. Under stress, a fingertip might be 80 degrees F. An excellent relaxation will bring it up to 96 degrees F. Your partner can call out your temperature as it changes, providing relaxing encouragement. As an experiment, try thinking about your worst stressors, or imagining something terrible happening to you. Watch the temperature drop.

I have often thought that everyone should wear a finger temperature probe at all times, with the temperature readout on a badgelike device worn so that others could read it. This might help in interpersonal relationships. You could tell how relaxing or stressful your interaction with another was by watching their thermometer.

Another biofeedback device popular in relaxation methods is GSR, or galvanic skin response. Under stress, the electrical conductivity of the skin changes. This can be detected as a change in resistance in a circuit that produces a tone, or moves a meter. GSR biofeedback devices are available for home use (see the Conscious Living Foundation catalog).

EMG (electromyographic) biofeedback allows one to sense small changes in muscle tension. These can be very effective in helping to relax the body. EMG units are somewhat expensive for home use. As the price comes down, they will become popular. I have a colleague who developed a biofeedback game involving a baseball computer game, called BioBall. The player has EMG electrodes attached to facial muscles. The more relaxation, the better the player does in terms of hits and home runs. A tense face will cause a strikeout. This game has been immensely popular and successful with troubled youth who need to learn to relax. (See BioBall under Resources for other biofeedback and relaxation computer-based games.) I can envision electromyographic biofeedback being incorporated into computer games for home use. Can you imagine your kids competing to see who can be the most relaxed?

While biofeedback can be fun, and certainly helps one focus on relaxation, it is not magic, and the results it produces for ordinary relaxation are not necessarily better than the relaxation produced by others methods, or by curling up in a comfy chair and reading a good novel.

Ways to Relax the Mind

If you practice muscular relaxation, the reduced tension should have a positive effect on mental tension. But mental relaxation methods can be very helpful in ways that muscular relaxation methods are not.

Mental tension could be defined as thinking at a rate which is too fast for comfort, or which produces confusion. Mental tension can be caused by allowing one's environmental stimuli to dictate brain behavior; there is no focus, so all stimuli vie for attention at the same time. Mental tension might also be due to excessive intake of caffeine or other stimulants. Mental relaxation methods are designed to limit mental focus to a simple stimulus, or to convert one's thought patterns to something pleasant and calming.

To a large extent, your mental state is something you can choose to modify. In Zen Buddhism, the story is told of a man walking in the rain forest. Suddenly a tiger jumps at him. The man runs, but ends up at a cliff. He climbs over the edge and holds on to a vine, where the tiger cannot reach him. The tiger lies down to wait. Then the man notices that the vine is slowly coming out of the earth. This will send him to his death far below. The man notices a strawberry on the vine, and thinks how lovely the colors of the berry are. Even in unfortunate circumstances, the mind has the power to control thinking, and emotions, by focusing on the positive.

Meditation

Meditation to achieve mental peace can be defined as any procedure that focuses the mind and that produces a sense of relaxation and a feeling that everything is okay. There are many forms and traditions of meditation, some connected with religions. You don't have to subscribe to any religious faith for meditation to work. One form is mental repetition, in which a word or phrase (mantra) is repeated silently. This could be "one," "peace," or "God is love." Behavioral repetition involves focusing on the repeating of a physical act. Breathing has been discussed above. Some do meditative jogging, repeating a mantra in rhythm to their strides. Another type of meditation involves focusing on an object, such as a candle or flower. ("Highway hypnosis" may be a form of involuntary meditation. The mind is led to focus on the repetitiveness of a straight highway, until a state of consciousness without awareness of what one is doing occurs. I have been on a freeway in the country, and suddenly realized that I have come to a stop sign at an intersection, totally unaware of having exited the freeway. Scary.)

Repetition makes the analytical part of the brain bored, and this may shift mental functioning from a state of "awareness-for-problem-solving-and-survival" to a state of intense but nonanalytical awareness of one sound, motion, or object. This is a shift from "left brain" to "right brain" functioning. Since left-brain functioning is associated with survival needs, some people have difficulty making the shift to right-brain work. Those who are anxious feel a need to remain in a vigilant mode, to avoid surprise attack from real or imaginary foes and forces. For meditation and any relaxation procedure, a sense of security about the meditative environment must be established. The basics for a meditation procedure are to be found in this box:

Meditation: How to Do It

Preparation for meditation includes:

1) No caffeine two hours before session.

2) No food one hour before.

3) Dim lighting.

4) Comfortable chair with good lower-back support, or cushion on floor.

5) Remove shoes, glasses, contact lenses, watches, tight clothing.

6) Get as comfortable as possible.

7) Arrange not to be disturbed in any way.

8) A kitchen timer can be used to let you know when the session time is over. Locate timer far enough away to avoid hearing its ticking.

The mental attitude for good meditation includes:

1) Don't worry about your mind drifting (in Zen temples, a monk will hit you on the shoulder with a bamboo stick, making a loud clap sound, to help you regain focus).

2) If you become aware of drifting off into left-brain thinking, such as stock-market trends, gently allow yourself to put those thoughts aside for later, then return to your original meditative focus.

3) Don't think of meditation as a task or job. It is a leisure-time, enjoyable activity.

4) There is no goal; do not be judgmental about how well you do.

5) Let the benefits of meditation come to you. Do not try to seek them.

Meditation

1) Begin saying your mantra (for example, "one") out loud with each exhalation.

2) Gradually get softer, ending up saying it to yourself silently.

3) Close your eyes, and continue "one" with each breath.

4) Continue for 20 minutes.

5) When done, open eyes very slowly. Remain in position for three minutes. Then get up very slowly.

Some people will have problems with meditation. Type-A people who are always feeling a need to keep on the go to remain ahead of the competition will not want to sit around being still. Control freaks may feel uneasy, since in meditation the point is to allow the left half of the brain to "let go," and get into a state of awareness without control-survival thoughts. Some people are just born fidgety; for them, perhaps a jogging meditation might be best. There are people who feel nervous when alone; they can meditate in a group situation. Those with rigid, puritanical person-alities, or who have very strict, non-Eastern religious faiths, may want to call their meditation "prayer." Somewhere in the Bible it advises one to be still before thy God.

Meditation may not be a good idea for those suffering from depression. This is because depressed people can ob-sess about their problems if they try to meditate. Talking with others and exercising might be better use of their time. There are rare cases of people having weird thoughts and images when meditating, some of which might come from suppressed memories of trauma. Seek professional help if these thoughts and images are disturbing.

Please remember that the point of meditation is to give your mind a rest. This may help it function more effectively in times of nonmeditation. Meditation also helps in physical relaxation. Do not expect miracles. Just enjoy the feeling of peace. Do not use meditation as an escape from reality. Regular meditation should help you see reality more clearly. If you find yourself meditating more than 20 minutes a day, examine why you are doing it.

Other, Meditationlike Awareness Exercises

There are many more methods to help your brain get focused away from the random bombardment of external stimuli. Here are some to try:

1) Sit still, close your eyes, and pay attention to all the sounds you can hear. Think about all the sensations coming from sources outside your body, such as temperature, air circulation, the feeling of contact with the chair, your skin in contact with clothing. Now pay attention to all your internal stimuli: can you feel your heart beating? Pay attention to your breathing as if you had to describe the feeling to an alien being that did not breathe. Are parts of your body warm or cold? Tense or relaxed?

2) Sit quietly with a pad and pen in your lap. When you become aware of the subject of your thoughts, write it down. Write down the main topics of your thought patterns as you let your mind drift wherever it might want to go, for 10 minutes. It can be revealing to find out how your brain works when you are recording its themes.

3) Go to where you can see trees, grass, and other plants.
   a) Observe how many different colors of green there are.
   b) Think about how many different life-forms there are.

4) Observe a freight train. How many colors can you see? This type of exercise may help you see the beauty of all things, which is in the eye of the beholder. This means that you have a choice whether or not to view aspects of your world as beautiful or not. This is also true of observing humans.

5) Lie down, look up. Imagine—no, realize that your line of vision extends out into the universe to infinity. Watch clouds form and change.

6) Visualize yourself in some other place, a place that is special to you. Imagine being there. Imagine the sights, sounds, smells. One of my special places is a small pond above a waterfall in Colorado, about 9,000 feet above sea level. Mountain bluebirds fly about, and the scent of pine bathes the air.

Yet Still More Relaxing Things to Try

1) Bubble bath, candles, Pachelbel CD

2) Take a stroll in a forest (take a friend for security).

3) Massage: hopefully by the hands of someone with whom you are in a love relationship. Or get a massage machine. Too many people these days go for weeks on end without ever stopping to relax and enjoy.

Journaling: Language allows us to put our thoughts into word symbols. Without language, we would be left only with images and emotions, which are not easily organized. However, language also allows a massive amount of information to be stored in our brains, and sometimes it feels like there is too much. Sometimes the hard drive crashes.

One way to download this information is to write it down. Several places in this book you are asked to write down your troubles, and stress responses, and habits. Writing down stressful experiences can have a therapeutic benefit for many people. Research has shown that writing down one's thoughts and feelings, as some do in a diary, can improve health and enhance the immune system (see Pennebaker & Francis, 1996). Writing is helpful when individuals examine their problems and emotions in depth, and then find insight and resolution of the problems.

Writing is a linear process; it puts thoughts into an order. With word processing, one can journal one's thoughts without worrying about order, and then go back and edit to see how the thoughts fall into a logical outline. Journaling produces its best results when the writing is later discussed with other support people, and when problem-solving methods are applied to the problems identified through writing.

In the next chapter, habits of regularly writing down tasks and goals can be construed as preventive journaling.

Homework

1. Try out all the methods. Get all the catalogs from the resources section. Buy some relaxation stuff such as candles, aromas. Make relaxing a hobby. It is better than making stress a hobby, as some people seem to do.

2. Pick some favorites which seem to work for you, and integrate them into your schedule.

3. Try to do a twenty-minute deep relaxation every day. You will see that practice can produce deeper states of relaxation. Relaxing before bedtime is not a bad idea, as you can use the relaxed state to enhance sleep.

4. Do a relaxation such as a breathing exercise before breakfast.

5. Try to remember that you can be relaxed throughout the day. Take relaxation breaks when possible. How-

ever, do not focus on physical relaxation at work. Use mental relaxation methods to keep your mind clear. For physical relaxation, take a brisk walk.

6. Alter your environment for relaxation.

7. Do your weekly diary, meet with your support group. Eat, exercise, sleep, relax.

Resources

Aveda Corporation, Blaine, Minnesota. 800-283-3224. www.aveda.com. ''The art and science of pure flower and plant essences.''

BioBall (Interactive electromyographic computer-based games): Creative Multimedia. www.flash.net/~bioball/. 800-707-7772.

California Fragrance Company. Huntington, NY. 800-424-0034. ''Essential oils, candles and home inhalations to surround you.''

Carrington, P. (1998). *The Book of Meditation: The Complete Guide to Modern Meditation.* Element Books.

Conscious Living Foundation. Drain, OR. 800-578-7377. www.cliving.org. Many stress and relaxation products, including biofeedback.

Davis, M., McKay, M., Eshelman, E. R. (1997). *The Relaxation and Stress Management Workbook.* Fine Communications.

Everly, G. S. (1989). *A Clinical Guide to the Treatment of the Human Stress Response.* New York: Plenum. Written for professionals, but the average educated person may find it very interesting and useful, especially as a resource to use in seeking therapy from health professionals about stress problems.

McKay, M., Davis, M., Fanning, P. (1998). *Thoughts and Feelings: Taking Control of Your Moods and Your Life* (2nd ed.) Richmond, CA: New Harbinger.

Stress Management Research Associates. Houston, Texas. www.stresscontrol.com. 281-890-8575. This is where to order the best stress management book: Charlesworth, E. A. & Nathan, R. *Stress Management: A Comprehensive Guide to Well-*

ness. They also have a set of audiocassette tapes, *The Relaxation and Stress Management Program*.

Stressless. 800-555-3783. www.stressless.com. "Your source for stress relief." Their catalog displays many kinds of stress and relaxation products.

References

Cawte, J. Psychoactive substances of the South Seas: betel, kava and pituri. *Australian and New Zealand Journal of Psychiatry* 1985, 19, 83–7.

Dunn, C., Sleep, J., Collett, D. (1995). Sensing an improvement: an experimental study to evaluate the use of aromatherapy, massage and periods of rest in an intensive care unit. *Journal of Advanced Nursing*, 21, 34–40.

Fried, R. (1990). *The Breath Connection: How to Reduce Psychosomatic and Stress-Related Disorders with Easy-to-Do Breathing Exercises*, New York: Plenum.

Hendriks, H., Bos, R., Woerdenbag, H. J., Koster, A. Sj. (1985) Central nervous depressant activity of valerenic acid in the mouse. *Planta Medica*, 1:28–31.

Jacobson, E. (1974). *Progressive Relaxation*. Chicago: University of Chicago Press, Midway Reprint.

Kinzler, E., Kromer, J., Lehmann, E. Effect of a special kava extract in patients with anxiety, tension, and excitation states of non-psychotic genesis. Double blind study with placebo over 4 weeks. *Arzneimittel-Forschung* 1991, 41, 584–88.

Leathwood, P. D., Chauffard, F., Heck, E., Muñoz-Box, R. Aqueous extract of valerian root (*Valeriana Officinalis L.*) improves sleep quality in man. *Pharmacology Biochemistry & Behavior*. 1982, 17, 65–71.

Luthe, W. (1963). Autogenic training: method, research, and applications in medicine. *American Journal of Psychotherapy*, 17, 174–95.

Matthews, J. D., Riley, M. D., Fejo, L., Muñoz, E., Milns, N. R., Gardner, I. D., Powers, J. R., Ganygulpa, E., Gununuwawuy, B. J. Effects of heavy usage of kava on physical health: summary of a pilot survey in an Aboriginal community. *Medical Journal of Australia* 1988, 148, 548–55.

Miller, N. S., Gold, M. S. (1990). Benzodiazepines: reconsidered. *Advances in Alcohol & Substance Abuse*, 8, (3-4), 67–84.

Pennebaker, J. W., Francis, M. E. (1996). Cognitive, emotional, and language processes in disclosure. *Cognition and Emotion*, 10, 601–26.

USP (1998). USP finds valerian evidence lacking. *The Standard*, (http://www.usp.org).

Weiss, M. J. (1997). The mother of all chill pills. In *You Shoulda Been There*. (http://discovery.com/area/shoulda/shoulda970616/shoulda.html). Discovery Communications.

9 | Attaining Peace: Personal and Work Organization

GOAL: To restructure life and work to enhance peace.

Now that you have energy from proper sleep, exercise, and nutrition, and your body and mind are relaxed, it's time to settle down and get your life organized and scheduled so that home and work responsibilities don't overwhelm the peace you have achieved so far. First, the organization of your personal life and home workstation or study can improve efficiency. Second, for those lucky enough to be gainfully employed, the office setup can be changed to help you do more work in less time, with less stress. The guidelines given herein are general. You can be flexible and adapt them to your own uses.

Life Organization at Home

Some people seem to get by with electric bills on the kitchen table, vacation plans on the TV, and reminders of the kids' doctors visits magnetically attached to the refrigerator. Here is what I recommend, based on my extensive experience as a human adult for thirty years:

1. Always use a personal organizer book, and keep it, or at least this week's schedule, with you at all times. Faithfully enter all activities. Each morning, review what will happen each day. Most people use an organizer for both work and personal schedules. Also each morning review the next seven days to make sure you are ready for them.

I use an actual paper and leather organizer, because I find that it is more convenient than having to access software organizers. Also, my schedule is not very complex. Others do well with products such as *Day-Timer Organizer 98* (available through Parsons catalog). Electronic organizers have many advantages, such as search functions, places for notes, drag-and-drop schedule changing which avoids erasures, and quick changes from daily, weekly, and monthly views. Of course, all needed phone numbers and E-mail addresses are listed in directories.

I also always carry a list of things I need to do, printed out in small font so that it will fit on a piece of 8½-by-11-inch paper when folded in half three times (then becoming pocket-size at 2.75 by 4.25 inches). The astute reader will immediately see that this folded sheet of paper can also be used to write on-the-run notes taken from thoughts, cell-phone calls, or pager messages.

2. For your personal life, keep a list of short- and long-term goals, with tentative schedules for completion of tasks for each goal. Discuss these goals with your spouse and support friends.

Goals Specification Table

Use something like this table for all your life goals. Update frequently. For this type of method, I use a word processor for ease of modifications. Don't worry about what your goals are at this time. I will tell you what they should be in forthcoming chapters.

SHORT-TERM GOALS	TASKS TO REACH GOAL	STATUS OF EACH TASK
1. Write chapter 7	1–1 research	done
	1–2 create clever fictional examples	need four more
	1–3 put in a lot of filler material	see what other self-help authors do
2.	2–1	
	2–2	
	2–3 etc.	
LONG-TERM GOALS	TASKS TO ACHIEVE GOAL	STATUS OF TASK
1. Nobel Prize, literature	1–1 Write good novel	Start next year
	1–2 Get chummy with Nobel Committee	Plan trip to Europe

To track the completion of tasks, and the achievement of goals, keep a poster of a 365-day calendar on the wall next to your desk. Or, use software such as APLANR (see Resources), which makes charts like this:

07/29/98   KEN 1998   PAGE 1

1998	Jul	Aug	Sep	Oct	Nov	Dec	Jan	Feb
1	Write book							
2		Vacation						
3		Go vegetarian						
4			Get job in Colo.					
5					Move to Colo.			

Figure 9.1. Scheduling Chart

The APLANR software is flexible in terms of time-frame expansion. Events can be moved around using mouse drag-and-drop.

3. I strongly urge you to set up a system of hanging files. These should hang in a desk drawer or filing module. No one should suffer from piles. You and I know that many people who have piles and piles of papers lying around their homes have no idea what is in them, or why they are keeping them, although they might not admit it, or even be aware of it. It's a sure thing that something extremely important is buried under one of those piles, and will never be found, except perhaps by archaeologists of the future.

The files should start, at the front, with a tickler file consisting of 31 numbered divisions representing the days of the current month, followed by 12 divisions representing the 12 months. This type of files is available at office supply stores. Bills that are due on the twenty-fifth can be placed in the division for the twentieth. Letters from Aunt Gertrude that you want to answer next weekend go in those divisions. July plans might go into May's place. And so forth. Of course, you have to check the tickler file daily to see what is in there.

After the tickler file should be, not necessarily in this order:

a) Accounts payable, if not in tickler file

b) Accounts receivable: statements about what others owe you, and what you have ordered

c) Health files for each family member, divided into medical statements, insurance claims filed, and statements of benefits received

d) Auto papers and maintenance records

e) Auto insurance

f) Home insurance

g) Life insurance

h) Loan records, credit-card statements (each in own file)

i) Inventory of household possessions, with receipts

j) Bank statements

k) Tax-deduction expense records

l) Income records for tax purposes

m) Lists of relatives and friends; records of correspondence

n) Lists of physicians, dentists, attorneys, clergy

o) Retirement-plan paperwork and statements

p) Family budget and savings plans and records

q) Survivor's file: List of all assets and liabilities, with policy/account numbers and addresses, wills, location of safe-deposit box where deeds are kept. This is for a surviving spouse or family member to figure out what to do if you become unable to handle your own affairs.

I am not going to teach you how to achieve financial success in this book, or even how to manage your financial affairs. The principles outlined, however, will certainly get you organized to take advantage of the resources I recommend for beginners. One is software, Quicken Estate Planner (available from Parsons) which helps one plan an estate. The other, aptly named for readers like me, is Joel Lerner's book, *Financial Planning for the Utterly Confused.* (See Resources.) Later in the book you may be delighted to discover that financial wealth is not necessary for happiness. However, financial irresponsibility is a no-no.

4. While I am writing about home-office organization, let me mention that a home answering machine is a must. Unless you are expecting a call, it is probably best to screen all calls with the machine before deciding to answer. This removes the irritation of unsolicited solicitors, and helps you develop a plan for responding to calls that have some value to you.

Important thought: Even though electronic communication technology allows the sending of messages at the speed of light, this doesn't mean we must have a sense of urgency when we receive an electronic message or call. In fact, some say interpersonal communication was better when people sent letters to each other. You can buy books that are collections of letters between famous people, but how many phone calls have you made that would be considered worthy of literary attention?

Life Organization at Work

After reading the above, you already have a personal organizer which you use to record all your appointments and daily tasks. For those of you who sit at your own desk at work, the following are recommended:

1) Hanging files, and everything needed for achieving projects in them. If piles exist in your office, either archive them in boxes out of sight if they could possibly be needed again, or dump them. In a file drawer in your desk or next to it, the first file is again the thirty-one day, twelve-month tickler file. The next file is a thin file of the actual work you are doing on Project A. This file could have attached to it a list of the tasks for the project, and notes on their achievement. Also included would be a list of things that need to be done soon, people that need to become involved, and resources that need to be acquired. The next file or two contain the materials needed for Proj-

ect A. Then Project B files, and so forth.

Somewhere else you should have a career-path development file, which contains plans and tasks about getting more training and education, as well as information on alternative careers, and alternative employers (see book *What Color Is Your Parachute?* in Resources).

2) I also have a wall covered with shelves, where additional materials are kept neatly stacked according to projects planned or in progress.

3) All phone numbers and other information needed for my job are within arm's reach. A shelf over the work space has all the books and dictionaries I may need. Of course, much information can be stored on the computer.

4) The desktop is kept totally bare except for the materials related to the task at hand.

5) A table of goals and tasks, and a planning chart (similar to personal-life methods above) are visible on a small bulletin board next to the desk. These are updated frequently.

6) When busy, I usually forward my telephone to a voice-mail system so that I don't even hear the incoming call. The message light lets me know to check messages later. I know some people who only get their voice-mail messages once a week. I sympathize with those of you whose jobs require instant telephone access for customers.

7) When logging calls, record them all in a spiral-bound notebook. The little message pads that let you tear off individual messages may work for some, but I

find them to be an invitation to play "Scatter the Messages Everywhere."

The columns in the notebook look like this:

*Ken's Telephone Message Recording
Notebook Format*

DATE/TIME	WHO CALLED, NUMBER	WHY THEY CALLED	WHAT I DID AND WHEN
7/10 9:00 A.M.	Boss 666-1000	re Project A	nothing
7/11 9:00 A.M.	Boss	re my job security	finished Project A, called him back to report

Periodically, I enter the phone information of people who have called into a database software that keeps names, addresses, phone numbers, and notes about each person. It also dials out.

Generally, when it comes to Post-it® yellow sticky notes, which are wonderful for marking pages in books and papers, I believe all notes should be consolidated into one spiral notebook, or software program. The software program can allow each note to be organized and stored according to whatever linkages you may want to make. However, you must remember to access the program in order to view your notes in a timely and as-needed fashion.

Time Management: In your personal planner, keep a log of what you do each hour. Attorneys and consultants record this for billing purposes. If you are not one of those types, pretend you are billing your employer for each hour you spend doing work for your company. Also record what you were doing when you were not working, or "on task." You may want to use a separate recording sheet for your time diary.

Categorize each activity as follows:

1) Definitely working up to my potential.

2) Working, but not very efficiently.

3) About half the time I was goofing off or distracted (for example, on the Web looking at pictures of comets impacting on Jupiter).

4) Out to lunch, literally or figuratively; spent most of this time period doing nonwork stuff such as reading a romance novel or planning my vacation.

Be honest. You can code your activity list with the above numbers so no one will know you did a lot of "4" stuff last week. Review at least five days to see how you spend your time. Most people realize they could get more work done, and feel better organized, by keeping and analyzing such records. I have sympathy for people such as the airline ticket reservationists, whose work is automatically tallied and analyzed for time efficiency by a computer. I assume the computer also automatically writes the termination notices for the slackers, so that the boss has only to sign them and then give them to the goons who go to transfer the targeted employees from their tiny carrels to the street.

Peace at Work

Even though you may get very well organized at work, and manage time well, you are at risk to suffer stress from a variety of sources. Here is a list of some of them, and what you might do to achieve greater peace. Even if you take no action to correct stressful situations, at least take the time to think of the reasons why you seem to have stress symptoms from work.

1. *Work overload: too much work.* In times of war or disaster, working extremely hard and heroically can have a positive effect on mental well-being. However, if you are asked to keep at maximum productivity to fulfill orders for relaxation cassettes, eventually your productivity will go down, and you will burn out. If you feel overworked and are suffering stress symptoms, it may be time to do something constructive. Compare the amount of work you do with your peers, or with the workload of others like you in different companies. If your workload seems excessive based on these comparisons, and you are not overpaid, some corrective action may need to be taken. (*Note:* I am not responsible for anyone getting fired for complaining of having too much work. Seek counseling through your company's Employee Assistance Program or other career/job counselors before confronting the boss!)

Arrange a calm, friendly meeting with your supervisor, pointing out the amount of work you do compared with others. Point out that over time, if everyone were to work as hard, the cost in stress and health effects would be greater than the added productivity of the excess work, and that productivity will decrease from stress. Your argument logically leads to the conclusion that the company would benefit if you did less work, and that perhaps another employee could be hired to fill in the productivity gap caused by your reduction in output. Or you could just suffer. It's up to you.

2. *Work overload: you are not adequately trained.* In this case, you are having trouble because you lack the training to do the work. This can be very stressful. But ultimately it is the company's responsibility to ensure that an employee gets the training needed to perform job tasks. Alternatively, you could be fired and replaced by someone

who has had the proper background and training. Ask for training. This shows initiative. Or ask if the company might not pay for part of your college tuition at night school.

3. *Work pressure*. This is the feeling the company is constantly pressuring you about your work. Few people like to be pushed around, even to get a salary. Productivity is usually higher when workers feel motivated to do good work because they have been helped to understand the company's goals, they have company T-shirts and hats, they sing the company song, play on the company softball team, and their supervisors have been trained to motivate using positive methods of rewards and recognition.

4. *Task clarity*. Not knowing exactly what you are supposed to be doing at work can be a cause for some stress. A principle of good management is that everyone has a job description which states what one is to do, what skills and supplies and equipment are needed to do the job, and some indication of productivity norms. Go to your supervisor and get a job description. Preface your request with an expression of your desire to do the best job you can for your supervisor and the company.

5. *Job control*. Some readers will remember the TV comedy *I Love Lucy*. One episode depicts Lucy at her new job putting pies into boxes as they come to her on a conveyor belt. Eventually, the number of pies coming down the belt exceeds her ability to put them into boxes. Pies begin to fall on the floor at the end of the belt. She cannot control the flow of pies.

Lack of control over one's job is one of the greatest causes of stress symptoms. One way to correct this is to implement participative management, in which the workers and supervisors meet as teams and develop ways that each worker can have some control over their function. The team also develops the best plan to improve productivity. Try to convince your superiors that productivity can be enhanced

if workers perceive that they have some control over how
they do their work, and how fast it is to be done. Participative management may be one of the reasons that Japanese
workers are about 12 percent more productive than U.S.
workers.

6. *Supervisor support.* Do you think of your supervisor
as fulfilling the role of "parent" in your work group "family"? Is s/he supportive, protective, instructive, and nurturing, the way parents used to be? Is s/he kind or mean? Does
s/he hover over you to make sure you do the job, or display
trust by leaving you alone? Generally, lower-level, less-
educated workers, such as ditchdiggers, need more supervision. However, most employees seem to be optimally
productive when supervision is consultative rather than dic-
tatorial. Someone once said that "management is the development of human potential." A boss should do what she
can to arrange work conditions to enable workers to do
their best with minimal stress.

I have consulted with numerous companies in which
workers are elevated to supervisory positions without any
training in how to motivate their subordinates. Due to ig-
norance, fear of insubordination, or sheer meanness, they
adopt the attitude of overseer, and crack their psychological
whips over the backs of the beleaguered workers. Many of
these supervisors learned techniques of intimidation from
their fathers and former supervisors. These types may be
tough nuts to crack. Passive or aggressive fighting back is
never the answer. Try to be friendly, even chummy. Take
the role of counselor, and think about what unfortunate
childhoods these supervisors must have had, and how un-
satisfied with their lives they must be to act so angrily and
impersonally. This may make you feel sorry for them
(good), or give you some feeling of satisfaction that they
are suffering, too (not so good). Do not be like the disgruntled workers at some government agencies where work

pressure from mean supervisors is an unwritten policy. Attempts at being friendly are almost always more effective in the long run than the use of automatic weapons.

7. *Peer support.* Do you feel that your fellow workers and you are part of the same team working cooperatively toward the same goal? Or is there a sense of hostile competition among you? Is everyone vying for promotion to one slot? A good supervisor will meet with his subordinates frequently to iron out interpersonal difficulties and to work on team building. You can help by striving to be as friendly and helpful as possible.

8. *Job insecurity.* Even if every aspect of your job is ideal, lack of job security is an extreme stressor. Decisions made in tall buildings in cities far away can put you out on the street without warning, even if your performance rating is top-notch. Keep an ''Alternative Career Path'' file active. This file should contain information about job opportunities for people like you, training programs for career enhancement, names and contact information on your network of friends, relatives, associates. An up-to-date résumé is in this file so that you can institute a job search immediately upon receiving your termination notification. And keep your copy of *What Color Is Your Parachute?* (Bolles, 1998) close by.

9. *Attention.* You get paid for the work you do. But humans being what they are, that is not enough. People like to be recognized for their good work, and often. Are you ignored, or taken for granted? If your company treats its employees like machines, have a talk with your supervisor to see what could be done to give respect through recognition to the workers. Remember to mention that recognition can improve morale and productivity as much as pay raises, if done correctly.

The Job Stress Evaluation Self-Survey Table

Make a table like this one, and fill it out periodically to keep track of your campaign to manage your job stress. Remember, putting your life and thoughts down on paper in an organized way can help clear up mental congestion, and restore free thinking within minutes.

Job Stress Area	Describe Problem	Action Plan and Progress Notes
Too much work (or too little)		
Not enough training		
Too much pressure		
I'm not sure what I'm supposed to do		
I can't control aspects of my job		
Supervisor is not supportive		
Coworkers are not supportive		
Lack of job security		
Lack of recognition for work		

Stress Symptoms: Job Related or Not?

Use this table to list the stress symptoms you have, and note whether you think they are job-related.

STRESS SYMPTOM	POSSIBLE JOB STRESS CAUSE	POSSIBLE NON-JOB CAUSE
Example: Headaches	Boss yells at me	Spouse yells at me

Job Stress and Disease

Surveys show that there is a strong association between work pressure, lack of job control, and increases in workers' blood pressure. Job strain overall is related strongly to heart-disease risk. These associations are as strong as the association between smoking and heart disease. Other stress-related disorders such as headaches, lower-back problems, depression, and increased colds and influenza contribute greatly to the increasing employee health-care costs faced by corporations. These companies are beginning to see that investing some money into stress management and job redesign may improve net profit by reducing health-care costs (Karasek & Theorell, 1990).

Summary thoughts: No one could possibly run a business without planning and paperwork, establishing goals, and keeping records. Your personal life and your career are as important as any business, at least to you. Get organized. Have a sense of clear direction. Write things down. Do something constructive about job stress.

Homework

1. Make as many of the suggested changes as possible.

2. Try to believe that it is worthwhile to spend about 15 minutes each morning going over your plans for the day.

3. Be persuaded that reviewing one's progress and goals each weekend for 15 minutes is a good way to spend time.

4. Review your whole life about twice a year.

5. Do at least one thing to manage work stress (keep it legal).

6. Keep a diary. Talk about this chapter with your support group.

Resources

APLANR: A project/event planner. Sapphire Software, Inc. 800-242-4775 (Product #11168) or www.pslweb.com.

Bolles, R. N., (1998). *What Color Is Your Parachute? A Practical Manual for Job and Career Changes.* Berkeley, CA: Ten Speed Press.

Davidson, J. (1995). *The Complete Idiot's Guide to Managing Your Time.* New Youk: Alpha Books. This book has many good tips and details on time management at work.

Davidson, J., (1997). *The Complete Idiot's Guide to Managing Stress.* New York: Alpha Books. Contains more suggestions on stress management at the workplace.

Lerner, J., (1991). *Financial Planning for the Utterly Confused*. New York: McGraw-Hill.

Parsons Technology software. www.parsonstech.com, 800-779-6000.

References

Karasek R., Theorell T. (1990). *Healthy Work: Stress, Productivity, and the Reconstruction of Working Life*. New York: Basic Books.

10

Your Life: Accident or on Purpose?

GOAL: This is the chapter where I help you answer these important questions:

1) What is the meaning of life?

2) What is the purpose of life?

3) How can happiness be attained?

4) Why do humans keep asking these tough questions?

All right. You are beginning to have more energy from better sleep, exercise and nutrition habits, and you have a sense of peace and calm because you are organized, you practice relaxation methods, and you have done what you can to arrange your environment for relaxation. You are beginning to attain the optimal state: calm energy. But is that all there is? No! You have become more energized, organized, and clear thinking, because you have taken care of yourself. Now that you are ready, you need to become a resource for others as well. Achieving feelings of energy and calm and comfort for yourself is good in and of itself, but too many people seem to stop there, using their new-found abilities to optimize their own hedonism. If you give too much credence to advertising, you would think the characteristics of an ideal life are to be strong, fit, un-stressed, wealthy, a driver of a BMW, to be a taker of tropical vacations, the possessor of nice clothing, and the keeper of a body with odorless breath and underarms.

But there is more to life, otherwise this book would end right here. The "more" has something to do with what people call "meaning" and "purpose" and "true happiness." People seem to seek after goals that have nothing to do with their immediate comfort, or their ability to buy stuff. Indeed, some of these activities make them uncomfortable, and cost them money and time away from television. What is it they are after?

Life's Meaning: Elusive or Yours for the Taking?

I am reminded of a comedy skit done by Monty Python (1989), the group of zany Brits who studied philosophy in college, then made millions, partly by mocking philosophers. In the skit, a philosopher is being interviewed. He says (this is from my memory of twenty years ago): "One purpose of philosophy is to understand the meaning of life."

The interviewer asks, "What do you mean when you say 'understand'? What do you mean when you say 'life'? What do you mean when you say 'meaning'? What do I mean when I say 'What is the meaning of the word meaning'?" And so on for several minutes.

This skit makes fun of the unfortunate habit of using words that are difficult to relate to reality, a style of language philosophers and psychologists use for two purposes:

1) To make themselves sound more knowledgeable than the average person.

2) To cover up for the fact that they are also confused
   about life.

This section will help clear up the confusion, or perhaps
add to it.

Normal people rarely stop to think about the meaning
of life, unless a tragedy strikes, someone dies, they are
stricken with cancer, or they are lost on an island without
TV. To help you think about the meaning of your life, fill
out the following table as best you can.

Table for Collecting and Evaluating Areas of My Life Which Have Meaning

LIFE AREA	THINGS I HAVE DONE WHICH WERE IMPORTANT TO ME (ACHIEVEMENTS)	WHY THEY WERE IMPORTANT
Relationships Example: Brought up child to be good adult		
Giving/charity Example: Helped at soup kitchen		
Religious Example: Helped others understand the love of God		
Creative/artistic Example: Made ceramic vases for friends		

LIFE AREA	THINGS I HAVE DONE WHICH WERE IMPORTANT TO ME (ACHIEVEMENTS)	WHY THEY WERE IMPORTANT
Personal Growth Learned meditation, told others how to do it		
Career Achievement Example: Wrote book useful for many		
Social Causes Example: Organized neighborhood to chase out gangs		

By filling out the table, I hope you developed a deeper understanding that life's meaning has something to do with achieving something, or making yourself, others, or some condition better. Imagine what would happen if large numbers of people regularly filled out such a table and made positive changes in their lives. This would be a nice alternative to the usual sleep-work-TV-sleep rut many of us find ourselves stuck in.

"Meaning of life," or "meaning *in* life," has been defined as a three-part phenomenon, which could be described as (Reker & Wong, 1988):

1. Cognitive (thought): A belief that one's life has order, the parts fit together, and a sense that there is a purpose in living—that there are worthy goals to be achieved.

2. Behavioral (action): Pursuing and attaining the goals.

3. Affective (emotional): A sense of accomplishment and fulfillment that the goals have been achieved.

Some goals could involve constant strivings which never end, such as the fight against war. The goal is to be involved continually in peace efforts.

The Signs of Meaning

How do you know your activities and behaviors are consistent with the purposes that give meaning to your life? Here are the signs (Waterman, 1993):

1. There is an unusually intense feeling of involvement in the activity.

2. There is a feeling of a special fit or meshing with an activity that is not the same as usual daily tasks.

3. There is a feeling of being intensely alive.

4. A feeling of being complete or fulfilled while engaged in the activity.

5. A sense that this is what you were meant to do with your life.

6. A sense that the activity expresses your true self.

How often recently have you felt this way about your life? Do you feel this way at work? You do? Good. Do you feel this way while viewing reruns of *Baywatch*? You do? Not good.

In striving to find meaning in life, the sense of accomplishment and fulfillment is independent of one's current pleasure or pain. The knowledge that one is participating in a worthy cause or action can bring fulfillment and joy, even if the action is helping others at a concentration camp, where the agony of starvation is punctuated by torture (Frankl, 1959). This has important implications for happiness, to be discussed later.

What the meaning of life really is could be illustrated by reflecting back to our childhoods. Imagine playing touch football with your friends. You are playing against the team for the adjoining neighborhood. It is a grudge match. You play well, and help your team surge to victory. This is meaningful. The game has order and rules, and a clear purpose. You act to attain the goals, and have a sense of fulfillment when you score a touchdown.

The opposite of a meaningful life is one of alienation. Imagine not playing with your neighborhood team. Imagine that you have no idea what the rules of football are, and you can make no sense as you watch from the sidelines. You can do nothing. You have no feeling of exultation as the team wins. You are alone, without a sense of purpose or fulfillment.

This analogy can elucidate why energy and peace, the ideal state, is not enough, and why hedonism, the pursuit of pleasure and security alone, is not enough to provide meaning to life. Imagine again you are a child. You have exercised, and have achieved a high level of fitness and skills for football. You have had a part-time job, and have been able to buy the best equipment for the game. Your ball is made of imported leather. But you choose not to play, because you have no desire to help the team. You have chosen alienation, which can never lead to fulfillment and meaning. Or perhaps, more realistically, you choose to play, but you do so only so that others will praise you for your skill; you play in order to get a scholarship and then a job as an NFL player, paying millions of $$. But without team spirit, you will not have fulfillment.

Viktor Frankl, the Austrian psychiatrist who endured the Holocaust, taught that meaning can be discovered by self-transcendence, by moving beyond concern for the self and focusing on other people and social and spiritual values. He pointed out that the direct focusing on pleasure to achieve happiness leads to an existential vacuum (not knowing who you are really sucks), while self-transcendence leads to fulfillment (Frankl, 1959). According to Frankl, life does not owe us pleasure, but it offers meaning. Our life goal should not be pleasure, or even equilibrium, but a healthy striving to travel from our current status toward the potential that we could become. As long as we know we are walking on that road, we should feel satisfied with our lives.

> Aristotle said it first: "The many, most vulgar, seemingly conceive the good and happiness as pleasure, and hence they also like the life of gratification. Here they appear completely slavish, since the life they decide on is a life for grazing animals."
> Aristotle believed that happiness "is an activity expressing virtue." Virtue was defined as the best in us, or excellence.

So it appears that meaning in life has something to do with working for a cause, rather than working only for one's own self-gratification. The figures tell the story:

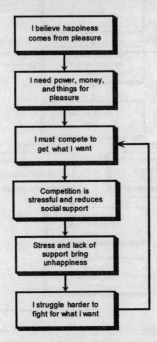

Figure 10.1. Selfish Orientation to Life

This diagram shows that the desire for pleasure involves a sense of competition with others for the resources and power needed to obtain it. The conflict with others is stressful, and others are less likely to provide support and comfort if they perceive selfishness. Eventually, the continuous sense of embattlement with others, and the alienation that goes along with this approach to life, result in unhappiness and despair.

If you can identify a purpose for living which involves the attainment of worthy goals (worthy in the sense of helping others as well as one self, e.g., not neo-Nazism), then one can draw a prettier picture.

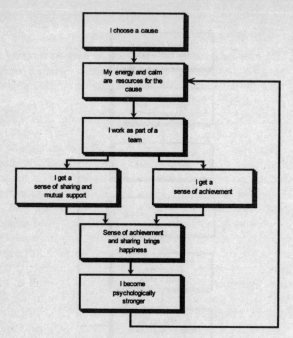

Figure 10.2. Cause Orientation to Life

In the case of working for a cause, you become a resource. The cause could be raising good kids, helping old
neighbors, supporting your employer in making useful
products, or saving the Dutch elm trees. You work with
others for the cause and feel that you are part of a team.
You give and receive emotional, informational, and material support. You feel you have accomplished a goal. You
get a sense of belonging and fulfillment, which leads to
happiness. Assuming that you take care of yourself to a
reasonable degree, then working for the cause makes you
stronger and more in touch with others. (There are those
who work so unnecessarily hard for a cause that they neglect themselves, burn out, and feel resentful when they are
not recognized as heroes. To these I would say, "Tough.")

George Bernard Shaw on Purpose

"This is the true joy in life—the being used for a purpose recognized by yourself as a mighty one; the being a force of nature instead of a feverish, selfish little clod of ailments and grievances, complaining that the world will not devote itself to making you happy."

Now that you have come to realize more clearly the importance of focusing on the meaning of life, it should come as no surprise that having meaning is good for you. Those with a sense of meaning in life seem to have better mental and physical health (Zika & Chamberlain, 1992). If they are involved in helping others through good relationships, they are more likely to get the support needed for psychological wellness. If they are involved in worthy causes, they are more likely to be able to withstand pressure. The stress that one may suffer as the result of hard work is less damaging if the work is for a worthy cause, a cause in which the person believes.

A review (O'Connor & Chamberlain, 1996) lists the following problems which have been associated with people who sense a lack of meaning in their lives:

- psychopathology (depression, anxiety, neuroses)

- reduced feeling of well-being

- substance abuse

- suicidal thoughts

It makes sense that a feeling that there is no order to life, and that there are no worthy goals to pursue, would lead to feelings of despair. It is also true that a mental disorder could make it difficult to achieve a sense of meaning.

Modern Problems and Existential Crises

Existentialists worry about the lack of meaning in life. They feel life lacks meaning because of several factors (Manfredi, 1997):

1. Mass media has created a common mind. We wear the same clothes, watch the same TV, eat the same food, etc. This leads to the destruction of the individual. Life can have meaning only if people feel that, as *individuals,* they are doing something worthwhile.

2. Science has led us to focus on objective, measurable events. People are viewed as nothing but the product of genetic inheritance and social training. Humans are viewed as organisms subject to these forces, without the ability to alter the direction of their lives. Without the ability to choose to do worthwhile activities, meaning cannot be achieved.

3. Humans usually act out of passion rather than from careful thinking, despite the emphasis in modern society on the value of being rational. This presents a sense of dissonance between the reality of human nature and our fantasies about what we might achieve to have meaning.

4. Because of human limitations, existentialists believe that nothing we can do can have meaning. From the perspective of the whole universe, our efforts to achieve meaning are absurd and insignificant. What meaning we get is that which we create for ourselves.

Go back and review these existential arguments. Have you ever thought along these lines? Sound discouraging? Go and give solace to a small child who has fallen and skinned his knee. Hold the hand of a terminal cancer patient. Organize a community group to check on the welfare of its elderly. Then ask yourself if life has meaning.

For a sense of meaning, life should be based on a formula or set of rules that allows you to put everything into an orderly plan. However, there can be confusion about this. Some people will tell you their goal is "to praise God and enjoy Him forever." This is good, but how does one translate that into specific behaviors? I don't think it means to spend all your time singing praise songs, and then going to heaven, although the behavior of some churchgoers might lead to that interpretation. I think it means to follow God's orders, which basically say to love one's neighbor as oneself. Love is expressed as helpful behavior. Identifying others' needs and helping them is a worthy cause that brings meaning.

Other people might organize their lives around the concept that the earth is deteriorating due to pollution, and they join the environmental salvation cause. This could be very meaningful. Certainly more meaningful than competing for the neighborhood "Yard of the Month" award for the achievement of the most tasteful display of horticulture.

Since having a meaningful life seems to be so important to psychological and physical health, it would make sense to help people find more meaningful lives. This is now called "meaning seeking." Meaning seeking (Wong, 1997) is becoming a form of psychotherapy; finding meaning implies finding purpose and developing a focus. This can help in some cases of depression. Depression can be caused by a learned perspective that one is not getting one's share of the goodies in life, such as a faithful spouse, or a decent amount of money. This *inward focus* on *what one is not getting* can be replaced by an *outward focus on helping others*. This is good for depression since working for a cause involves activity and social contact, two things generally lacking in the lives of the depressed.

According to Wong (1997), meaning-seeking-based therapy may help clients develop a deeper and more positive understanding of themselves and their life situations. The meaningful activities serve as inner resources for daily living and a buffer and distraction against stress and depression. Therapy involves helping clients develop meaningful goals so that they have a sense of purpose in their lives, and become less isolated. Having a purpose in life means developing a hope for the future, to replace the hopelessness of depression.

People can be helped to realize the meaning in their lives. Filling out tables such as the one above can help individuals organize their thoughts. This may help them see the order and principles that have directed their lives, the good they have done, and thus to feel more satisfied with life. Methods for teaching such critical thinking about one-self have been suggested as a way to help people glean meaning through transforming their perspective of life (Courtenay & Truluck, 1997). One way to instigate such thinking is to examine what happens when people are faced with experiences that challenge their basic assumptions about the world, and that require them to make meaning of the experiences from the perspective of their assumptions.

The Special Perspective of Mortality

Many people seem to be mentally asleep, traveling through life performing activities in a habitual way without critical thought. Sometimes life challenges force us to wake up from the slumber of our routine lives. Fill out the following table to wake up and discover what aspects of your life are all about.

What Would You Do If You Were Told You Had Only Six Months to Live?

What would I do regarding: My family?	
My friends?	
My Career?	
My Possessions?	
My Beliefs/Faith?	

Everyone will come to a point in life when they have only six months to live. Some will know in advance. Most will not. Should we struggle to make our lives meaningful through constructive activity? Some pessimistic people have been known to say, "What's the use? We're all going to die someday." I would rather say, "Until I am dead, I am alive. As long as I am alive, let me live a life of meaning." I have known cancer patients with only weeks to live and who are in great pain, yet they have been able to express love and concern for others. Their lives have meaning up until the end. Fortunately, when confronted by imminent death, patients change the criteria by which they evaluate their lives, and they usually gain a clearer perception of the meaning of life (Salmon, Manzi, & Valori, 1996).

Meaningful Therapy

I have used "meaning seeking" therapy with overweight women. In our culture, women are made to believe they should be thin. They get this belief from the admonitions of their mothers, and the values expressed by ladies' magazines, Hollywood, and weight-loss clinics and products. Managing weight is one of the top concerns of many women, perceived to be more important even than job, marriage, or family. They become obsessed with trying to lose weight. Most usually fail to attain slimness, and this leads to a continuing state of frustration and low self-esteem. I have tried to convince overweight patients that they should exercise more, eat more carefully, and accept the likelihood that they will never be thin (Foreyt & Goodrick, 1994).

I also try to convince them that they should focus their attention on doing something meaningful in their lives, instead of letting weight concerns cloud their whole existence. There are plenty of examples of very overweight people who lead meaningful lives, and stop complaining about their weight-control failures. This is the only way to happiness.

Finding Purpose

How do you find your purpose in life? Here are some steps to take:

1. Discover what you love to do (other than eating and sex).

2. Find out what you are naturally good at doing.

3. From the above list, ascertain what contribution you could make to the world.

4. When your passion and your contribution are the same, you have found your purpose. This may take many months. The trick is to find your purpose and still be able to pay the bills. (Ferguson, 1998; see also Bolles, 1998).

Cartoon

In this cartoon (drawn I think by Rodrigues), a guard with a whip is talking to his colleague in a dark dungeon. Upon the wall, hanging from their arms by chains, are two prisoners with whip scars all over their bodies. The guard says, "I'm so glad that, through therapy, I am finally able to channel my aggressive impulses into socially acceptable behavior."

Ralph's Idea of Success

"To laugh often and much; to win the respect of intelligent people and the affection of children; to earn the appreciation of honest critics and endure the betrayal of false friends; to appreciate beauty, to find the best in others; to leave the world a bit better, whether by a healthy child, a garden patch or a redeemed social condition; to know even one life has breathed easier because you have lived. This is to have succeeded."

RALPH WALDO EMERSON, 1987

What, Then, Should We Do? Part One: Management of Meaningful Time

A "meaningful" life appears to be a life involving a purpose that goes beyond self-gratification. The purpose is worthwhile activities. "Worthwhile" means helpful for survival, helpful in relationships, or helpful in creativity and art. Now that you understand these concepts, the question arises "Okay, how should I live my life?" This question (which I hope you have asked yourself before) can be answered in many ways. I am going to suggest two ways, which are related to each other.

The first way is to practice time management, paying careful attention to what activities you do during each day. A careful analysis will reveal that some behaviors are less useful than others in bringing meaning to your life. An analysis of how you spend your time might also reveal that you have more time to devote to worthwhile activities than you thought. For those of you who have two babies to take care of as well as a full-time job and a no-time spouse, please recognize that child rearing is one of the most meaningful activities there is. You don't have to save the world to have meaning in life. But most of us Americans can find an hour or two, or maybe even a whole weekend, to do meaningful stuff.

As usual, the path to self-awareness is to monitor your own behavior. Fill out this one-day diary by listing the activities you do during each time period. If the day is just beginning, start recording now and stop reading this book until you have a day's record. If it is late, do it tomorrow.

Leave the "Category" column blank until you have finished one day of activity recording.

Diary for Recording Your Activities over One Day

TIME	ACTIVITY	CATEGORY
6 A.M.		
7		
8		
9		
10		
11		
12		
1 P.M.		
2		
3		
4		
5		
6		
7		
8		
9		

Now that you have recorded daily activities, go back and categorize each one according to these categories:

Table of Activity Categories

Category/Code	Examples
Survival—SURV	Eating, hygiene, dressing, job, housework
Body Improvement—BODY	Exercise, relaxation
Mind Improvement—MIND	Education, meditation
Spirit Improvement—SPIR	Philosophical/religious study, prayer
Family—FAM	Sharing, mutual counseling/comforting in family
Friends—FREN	Sharing, mutual counseling/comforting with friends
Charitable—CHAR	Helping, comforting, without any payback
Creative—CREA	Inventing, writing, art
Self-Indulgence—SELF	Watching TV sitcoms or professional sports, playing video games, using recreational drugs, bonding with expensive cars and boats, reading romance novels
Other—OTHER	Anything not covered by above categories

Continue to record and categorize your activities for another six days. Add up the hours spent in each category. Circle the activities which you would like to reduce, such as TV. Put a "♡" next to the behaviors you would like to do more of. Make a list of things you would like to start doing, such as more volunteer work down at the soup kitchen. Millions of Americans will find, after recording their behavior over a week, that they spend little or no time doing anything worthwhile at all, except for the basic survival routines. (Of course, people who read self-improvement books do not belong to that crowd.) The idea is to become cognizant of how you are spending your time. At your birth, time was given to you to have a life, on average about 438,300 hours, not counting sleep. If you are about 35 years old, you have about 233,760 hours left. It's time to start living right, with meaning and purpose.

At this point I feel obligated to write more words about TV, since TV watching is the greatest hindrance to leading a meaningful life for most Americans, not only because of the preponderantly worthless content, but because it robs people of so much time they could be using to achieve something meaningful. The average American adult squanders about 21 hours a week in TV viewing. This represents about 50 percent of leisure time. Many people who sit around and watch TV will tell you that they deserve to be self-indulgent because they spend eight hours at work, and they need to unwind and to relieve stress. (They need to read the first part of this book, which describes more constructive ways to relieve stress, which take less than 30 minutes, rather than the several hours apparently required for TV to have a beneficial effect.) Having been a counselor for the chemically dependent, when I hear people say they have a right to watch silly TV programs because of stress, I am reminded of the alcoholics who used the same argument for self-intoxication. Does not TV viewing in some way toxify the brain? Computer people say, "Garbage in, garbage out."

Television: The New Opiate of the Masses

The great playwright George Bernard Shaw once wrote, "Chess is a foolish expedient for making idle people believe they are doing something very clever when they are only wasting their time" (Bryan & Mieder, 1994). I do not know what he said about TV, if anything. I am sure it would not have been complimentary. Even addicted TV viewers would not try to convince someone that what they were doing was "clever."

But as unclever as it is, TV watching has become the dominant activity in the U.S., so much so that not watching TV is a severe handicap to effective socializing. When I am with a group of typical Americans, conversation often turns to relating the details of televised situation comedies, of which I have never seen even one episode. For example, the whole nation becomes transfixed upon the occasion of the last episode of *Seinfeld,* which I totally missed. Sure, a good laugh is a blessing to the soul, but not for hours every day.

The main purpose of TV is to keep "consumer lust" burning at a high level (Berger, 1981). The purpose of most television programs is to provide something attention-grabbing enough that the viewer will stay tuned to see the advertising. In third-world countries, the first thing the government does to stimulate the economy and the people's drive to better themselves is to put a television in every little village. Only then do the people realize that they do not have cars, refrigerators, fancy clothing, and TVs. This feeling of deprivation thereby engendered drives the people to accept education and economic development.

There is a good side and a bad side to television (Berger, 1981):

1) It can be informative.

2) Most dramas are moralistic in the sense that good triumphs over evil.

3) It can raise people's consciousness about social issues, such as racism and political parties.

4) It unifies the culture by providing a common framework for discussion.

5) It serves as entertainment, which can be part of a healthful life.

The bad side is:

1) It is a narcotic, in the sense that it soothes people even when they neglect their own problems and those of others; it fosters escapism and isolation.

2) It can be addictive, in the sense that even though the viewer knows he should be doing something more meaningful, he cannot turn the set off.

3) It appeals to the lowest common denominator. Remember that the average IQ is 100, somewhat lower than the average IQ of self-improvement-book readers. This makes TV rather silly for the most part.

4) It exploits violence and sexuality to get people to watch.

5) It overstimulates us, but rather than helping us to take action to cope, it promotes a state of passivity.

In order to study the effects of television in your own life, unplug all your sets for one week. See what happens. I dare you. And before you plug it back in, ask yourself, "What is it about the program I am about to watch that is good for me?"

When you have categorized your activities for a week, you can begin to set for yourself some goals about time resource allocation. Table 3 in chapter 4 showed a day's time well spent. Here it is again, slightly modified:

Time Management for Optimal Living: Comparison to Current Schedule

Activity	Time	My Current Schedule for Activity
Awakening ritual	5:30–6 A.M.	
Bath, breakfast	6–7:30 A.M.	
Commute	7:30–8 A.M.	
Work	8–5 P.M.	
Commute	5–5:30 P.M.	
Exercise	5:30–6:30 P.M.	

ACTIVITY	TIME	MY CURRENT SCHEDULE FOR ACTIVITY
Supper	6:30–7 P.M.	
Family/friends	7–8 P.M.	
Self/spouse	8–9 P.M.	
Presleep ritual	9–9:30 P.M.	
Sleep	9:30–5:30 A.M.	
Television	Meaningful TV only	

Fill in the table according to the time you now spend in each activity. Make goals to add time for meaningful activities, and to subtract time from the less meaningful activities.

You can then define your purpose in life as spending a certain amount of time for the various categories. For example, "My purpose in life is to spend 30 percent of my free time helping the less fortunate at a charity organization, 40 percent volunteering at my church, 20 percent pursuing my hobby in ceramics, and 10 percent taking bubble baths." Remember, you should spend enough time for self-care to maintain energy and calm. The rest of your discretionary time should involve other care, or artistic/creative expression which has aesthetic value to others.

What, Then, Should We Do? Part Two: Focusing on Happiness.

Some poets have expressed the idea that they feel fully alive only when experiencing extreme pathos. It is true that when we are faced with death or suffering, we are forced to get serious about life, and it may have a more intense meaning. When everything is going right, we lose an emotional edge, and life may seem humdrum. Of course, it is the instability of life, the continual fluctuation between the highs and lows, which make life interesting and challenging. There are "thrill seekers" who jump off bridges attached to bungee cords to add an artificial death threat to their lives.

Other than for these odd types, most people want to be as happy as possible. There are two views on happiness. One is that happiness is an outcome of everything going your way, and you having everything you want. (Go back and look at Figure 10.1). This is the incorrect view, and causes much unhappiness for those who believe in it. The other, correct view is that happiness comes from feeling that one is involved in a worthwhile purpose (Figure 10.2). Happiness is the emotion one gets from leading a meaningful life. I suppose there are some people who could feel happy without leading meaningful lives, if they were mentally detached from reality.

Since happiness is the outcome of a meaningful life, then if we aim for true happiness, we will necessarily find purpose in a meaningful life. An examination of happiness research will shed light on the ideas of "purpose" and "meaning." If you are interested in this happiness research, you will need to start with a good book on the topic by psychologist David Myers (Myers, 1992). His review of the scientific literature found that:

1) Happiness and wealth are not very well related to each other. You can be happy and poor.

2) Happiness in part depends on our comparisons with your own past, and comparisons with others.

3) The happiest people are those who have realistic goals and expectations about what they can do and have in life.

4) Happiness doesn't change with age, and is equal between genders.

5) High self-esteem is correlated with higher happiness. This makes sense if self-esteem is based on a self-judgment of how meaningful one's life is in terms of achieving worthwhile goals.

6) Happy people feel they are in control of their lives, are optimistic, and outgoing.

7) Happy people have better friendships.

8) A good, intimate marriage seems to help.

9) Happiness is enhanced through having a faith involving communal support, purpose, acceptance, outward focus, and hope.

Happiness: An Often Neglected Mental Disorder

Happiness is clearly a psychiatric disorder (Bentall, 1992). This becomes apparent when one examines the facts about happiness:

1) It is statistically abnormal.

2) Happy people, compared with miserable people, have difficulty remembering negative events from long-term memory.

3) Happy people, compared with miserable people, tend to make unrealistically positive assessments of their lives and the world.

4) Happy people, compared with the miserable, have an optimistic view of the future which is not based on reality, since the future has not yet occurred.

There is obviously an urgent need to develop treatment programs for the happy, who clearly fail to see the reality of modern life. There is a critical need to develop drugs to alleviate the symptoms.

Pierre Teilhard de Chardin, the visionary Jesuit philosopher, examined the nature of happiness 50 years ago (Chardin, 1966). He tells the story of a group of people climbing a mountain. Some, the pessimists, decide they are too tired to climb, and give up early. Another few, the hedonists, get halfway up, and decide it is a beautiful place for a picnic. So they stop and eat. The remaining climbers feel the need to attain the summit; they conquer the peak. These are the enthusiasts.

These three groups illustrate different happinesses. There is the happiness of tranquillity, which involves a reduced life of passivity and avoidance. Television addicts might fit into this category. Others experience a happiness of working to seek pleasure; these are the hedonists. The highest level of happiness is experienced by those who seek growth, and who are willing to suffer for a cause.

In this growth, there are three components. The first is of *being*, and involves constant self-development. The second is of *love,* and involves uniting with others in sharing relationships and a shared consciousness. The third component is *worship*. Worship involves subordinating ourselves to, and incorporating ourselves in, the organistic totality of mankind, recognizing that what connects us all is an overriding love, known to some as God. I think by "organistic totality," Chardin meant the totality of living things, which find optimal existence and happiness when behavior is dominated by a spirit of love. At least, this seems to work when everyone belongs to the same species.

Chardin concluded that in order to be happy:

1) Don't follow the easiest path, but work for self-improvement.

2) React against selfishness: your own and that of others.

3) Transfer the ultimate interests of our lives to the advancement and success of the world and all that lives upon it.

This last suggestion has made Chardin a posthumous darling of the environmental movement. I see his teachings as consistent with the "meaning of life" route to happiness discussed previously.

Can Happiness Be Taught?

The ability to feel happy may, in part, be determined by your inheritance. David Lykken, a behavioral geneticist at the University of Minnesota, studied 1,500 pairs of identical (they share the same genetic inheritance) and fraternal (they have different genetic inheritance) twins who were raised together. When they rated their feelings of well-being, results showed that genes accounted for about half the variation in well-being (Lykken, 1996). This indicates that a large portion of the ability to be happy may be inherited. Thanks a lot, Mom and Dad. But it is still a good research question, "How many people who report feeling not too happy can be changed for the better through teaching them lifestyle change?" If you have been chronically unhappy, don't give up hope!

A psychologist in Ft. Myers, Florida, Michael Fordyce, has done preliminary work in this area. He studied people who said they were happier than the average person. He discovered that these happy people had certain characteristic behaviors and attitudes. Then he took a group of not-so-happy people, and taught them how to think and act like happy people. After the course, many of the participants reported feeling happier (Fordyce, 1977, 1983).

I recommend his book, *Psychology of Happiness* (1993). It will provide the basis of some good discussion in your support group. The book covers 14 "fundamentals" for happiness, which are (with my comments):

1) Be more active. (Here we see the theme common to all paths to meaning and happiness. Turn off the TV. Get off your duff.)

2. Spend more time socializing. (People do much better with social support and sharing.)

3. Be productive at meaningful work. (Meaningful work is part of happiness. See chapter 13.)

4. Get better organized and plan things out (See chapter 9).

5. Stop worrying. (This can be a tough one to stop. Get opinions from others about how much you should worry about something. Worry never changed anything for the better.)

6. Lower your expectations and aspirations. (I would say to have realistic goals.)

7. Develop positive, optimistic thinking. (This may take some training.)

8. Get present-oriented. (Don't dwell on the past, or think about the future so much that the present is ignored and not enjoyed.)

9. Work on a healthy personality. (Fordyce advises having high self-esteem, and caring for oneself.)

10. Develop an outgoing, social personality. (Important for number two above. See chapter 11.)

11. Be yourself. (Don't assume a role, or conform, to try to attract people.)

12. Eliminate negative feelings and problems. (Fordyce recommends talking with others to vent feelings, and to get help from others.)

13. Close relationships are the number-one source of happiness. (The ultimate source of support.)

14. Think always about happiness and how to get it.

Studying happy people and teaching the not-so-happy to be like them seems a very sensible approach. Happiness research is not very popular, however, since research requires money, and research funding tends to go toward the squeaky wheel, which is disease. You can get money to research depression, drug abuse, diabetes, and dystrophies, and these diseases deserve research for better treatment and cures. But it is difficult to get a substantial amount of research money to study "happiness" or "the meaning of life."

Summary

For life to have meaning, one should work for a purpose that involves achieving goals which are worthwhile in terms of helping people (emotionally, materially, physically, professionally, or aesthetically through art). One of the people you help is yourself. Happiness can be enhanced through meaningful work and good relationships. Self-awareness through keeping a diary of time use, and thinking about goals, can help put a person on the right path.

Go back to chapter 1 and meditate on the meaning of Figure 1.3.

Homework

1. Go one week without TV. Write down your experiences.

2. Define your life purpose in terms of *the percent discretionary time* spent in meaningful activities. Use a table like this one:

My Life Purpose: Tabular Version: One Week

ACTIVITY (DESCRIBE)	DAY AND TIMES	PERCENT OF TIME SPENT (OF 35 HOURS OF FREE TIME PER WEEK)
Self-care:		
Helping others:		
Creative/artistic:		

3. Ask several people what their purpose is in life, what they are doing to achieve it, and why? Get them to tell you specific activities, not general principles.

4. Ask yourself: What major changes have you made in life. Why? Have these changes led to more or less meaning in life?

5. Does your life show progress in at least some areas besides aging?

6. Does your need for financial security, or your fear of change, keep you stuck in a life that has little meaning?

7. Keep up with your diary, and meeting with your support people.

References

Aristotle (1985). *Nichomachean Ethics*. (T. Irwin, trans.). Indianapolis: Hackett.

Bentall, R. P. (1992). A proposal to classify happiness as a psychiatric disorder. *Journal of Medical Ethics,* 18, 94–98.

Berger, A. A. (1981). Too much television. In S. J. Mulé (ed.). *Behavior in Excess: An Examination of the Volitional Disorders.* New York: Free Press.

Bolles, R. N. (1998). *What Color Is Your Parachute? A Practical Manual for Job-Hunters and Career-Changers.* Berkeley, CA: Ten Speed Press.

Bryan, G. B., Mieder, W. (1994). *The Proverbial Bernard Shaw.* Westport, CT: Greenwood Press.

Chardin, P. T. de (1966). *On Happiness* (trans. René Hague, from a lecture given in 1948). New York: Harper & Row.

Courtenay, B. C., Truluck, J. (1997). The meaning of life and older learners—addressing the fundamental issue through critical thinking and teaching. *Educational Gerontology,* 23, 175–95.

Emerson, R. W., Ferguson, A. R., Carr, J. F. (1987). *The Essays of Ralph Waldo Emerson.* Cambridge, MA: Belknap Press.

Ferguson, B. (1998). *Miracles Are Guaranteed.* Return to the Heart Press. http://www.billferguson.com.

Fordyce, M. W. (1983). A program to increase happiness: further studies. *Journal of Counseling Psychology,* 30, 483–98.

Fordyce, M. W. (1977). Development of a program to increase personal happiness. *Journal of Counseling Psychology,* 24, 511–21.

Fordyce, M. W. (1993). *Psychology of Happiness.* Ft. Myers, FL: Cypress Lake Media. Available through www.amazon.com.

Foreyt, J. P., Goodrick, G. K. (1994). *Living Without Dieting.* New York: Warner.

Frankl, V. (1959). *Man's Search for Meaning.* London: Hodder & Stoughton.

Lykken, D., Tellegen, A. (1996). Happiness is a stochastic phenomenon. *Psychological Science,* 7, 186–89.

Manfredi, P. A. (1997). *Introduction to Philosophy: The Meaning of Life.* Lecture outline. Carbondale, IL: Southern Illinois University.

Monty Python (1989). *The Complete Monty Python's Flying Circus: All the Words Vol. 1*. New York: Pantheon Books.

Myers, D. G. (1992), *The Pursuit of Happiness: Who Is Happy—and Why*. New York: William Morrow.

O'Connor, K., Chamberlain, K. (1996). Dimensions of life meaning: a quantitative investigation at mid-life. *British Journal of Psychology,* 87, 461–77.

Reker, G. T., Wong, P. T. (1988). Aging as an individual process: toward a theory of personal meaning. In J. E. Birren, V. L. Bengston (eds.), *Emergent Theories of Aging,* pp. 214–48. New York: Springer.

Salmon, P., Manzi, F., Valori, R. M. (1996). Measuring the meaning of life for patients with incurable cancer: the life evaluation questionnaire (LEQ). *European Journal of Cancer*, 32A, 755–60.

Waterman, A. S. (1993). Two conceptions of happiness: contrasts of personal expressiveness (Eudaimonia) and hedonic enjoyment. *Journal of Personality and Social Psychology*, 64, 678–91.

Wong, P. T. (1997). Charting the course of research on meaning seeking. Paper presented at the Eighth World Congress on Logotherapy, Dallas, TX, June 1997.

Zika, S., Chamberlain, K. (1992). On the relation between meaning in life and psychological well-being. *British Journal of Psychology,* 83, 133–45.

11 | Your Purpose in Life: Meaningful Interpersonal Relationships

GOAL: There are two main components of a life of optimal happiness and meaningful purpose: loving relationships and meaningful (doing something worthwhile) work. This chapter will help you establish meaningful relationships.

What Are Meaningful Relationships?

Definition: In the context of this book, a *meaningful relationship* is one designed for the purpose of nurturing another human being (or dog, cat, or horse, etc.). This is done, usually with the expectation that the other being returns the nurturing. However, the best relationships are formed on the assumption that one gives of oneself without expectation of a return. (Assuming that oneself is strong due to self-care.) This is referred to as *love*. Not "falling in love," but love as caring.

To find your identity, to discover who you are, you need to ask the question "What are your relationships with others like?" Descriptive terms such as "high self-esteem," "brave," "trustworthy" have no meaning if you are living alone in the forest. You are what your relationships with other people are.

I am suggesting to you in this chapter that a careful study of what makes for good and bad relationships may shed light on your particular interpersonal situation. A sense of meaningful, constructive purpose in life necessitates skills in relationship building. So first, there will be a discussion of relationship qualities and behaviors. Then I will propose to you that the best strategy for relationships is to take on the role of counselor.

The qualities of good relationships can be construed to be rules for good behavior, or moral behavior. There is controversy about morality in our society. What is moral? What is immoral? Should morality be taught in the schools? Is the president's behavior immoral? But I want to remind you that "moral" means ethical, honorable, meritorious, principled, proper, chaste, pure, or virtuous. (These synonyms come straight from the *WordPerfect*© v.6.1 thesaurus.) There may be confusion about where to draw the line between morality and immorality, but generally, moral principles are based on the notion that immorality hurts someone. Moral principles are a set of guidelines for making choices that have genuine happiness or emotional well-being as their effect (Ramm, 1996). Let's look at these rules. Be thinking about yourself and others in your life, and ask yourself, "How well do I and others follow these rules?"

Rules for Relationships: Biblical

Throughout history, man has been concerned with how people should relate to one another. Examples of relationship advice come from many sources, including religion and philosophy. The early Christian Paul wrote to a church in Galatia, advising them on good-relationship principles, noting the difference between those relations based on the "Spirit" and those based on the "flesh." "Spirit" could be interpreted by nonbelievers as the overriding life principle that love is the best basis for relationships. People motivated by the Spirit are working for the cause of caring (self and others), sharing, and nurturance. Such relationships are characterized by joy, peace, patience, gentleness, goodness, trust, meekness, and temperance.

"Flesh" can be interpreted as a focus on meeting one's selfish needs for pleasure; the cause one works for is self-gratification. Relationships motivated by the flesh are characterized by selfishness, hate, jealousy, anger, dissension, envy, drunkenness, carousing, promiscuity, and fornication, to name a few that Paul listed. Based on the evidence from the behavior of some children who have been raised without the benefit of good parenting (and by observation of some college fraternities and many politicians), it would seem that man's natural relationship style is motivated by the "flesh." Unless children are carefully inculcated with the values of love (helping others), and have learned to work for a worthwhile cause rather than self, then we can expect to see more flesh-type behavior in our society.

Paul also gave an outline of the ideal relationship, which describes characteristics of perfect love. Of course, no one can ever achieve this ideal, but it is a good idea to have an ultimate standard to help us know in what direction we should be striving. Here are the guidelines:

Love is patient

Love is kind

Love is not jealous or boastful

Love is not arrogant or rude

Love does not insist on its own way

Love is not irritable

Love is not resentful

Love does not rejoice at wrong, or at another's pain

Love rejoices in the right

Love bears all things

Love believes all things

Love hopes all things

Love endures all things

Love never ends

The "love" in this passage is not describing the emotional feeling or sentimental state that is meant by the expression "I am in love with so-and-so." The original version uses the Greek word *agape,* which refers to the kind of love that is an act of will directed at helping and caring for someone.

I have counseled couples who claimed to be Christians, who, when presented with the above list, began to see many areas in which they had deficiencies. Whenever a patient said that their spouse "loved" them, I would always ask, "How do you know? What is the evidence?" The answer I usually got back was, "Well, he says he loves me." Or, "He's always bringing me flowers and such."

I would then talk about how "love" meant caring for someone, helping them, and nurturing them. I would ask, "What *behaviors* does your spouse do that indicate love?" At that point, many patients would be at a loss, since they realized their spouses really didn't show any caring behaviors.

Note: These rules come from what Christians call the New Testament part of the Bible. There are similar suggestions in the other major religions.

Rules for Relationships: Boy Scouts

I spent a few years of my boyhood in the Boy Scouts. I had good parents, so I probably would have grown up to be a nice person without scouting, but I think it helped. Learning oaths and laws at least made me think about purpose in life and how to relate to people. *Boy's Life* magazine came every month replete with examples of heroism and community service. We had a lot of fun camping. Almost everyone I know who was a Scout tells me some of their happiest memories are of scouting.

This is what we learned in scouting:

Scouts' Oath: On my honor, I will do my best to do my duty to God and my country, and to obey the Scout Law. To help other people at all times, to keep myself physically strong, mentally awake, and morally straight.

Boy Scout Law: A Scout is trustworthy, loyal, helpful, friendly, courteous, kind, obedient, cheerful, thrifty, brave, clean, and reverent.

Today, how many kids are getting any instruction in how to live a purposeful life? Is it taught in school? Places of worship? What values do music-video cable-TV channels teach? What values do Mortal Kombat video games teach? How many parents schedule a weekly time to sit down with their kids and help them to establish values? How many parents have values worth transmitting to their offspring? The transmission of values to the next generation is not achieved genetically. Let me reiterate an important point: unless youth are inculcated with values of morality (interpersonal niceness) and of service (to company and country), the legacy of civilization built up over thousands of years will go down the tubes.

By the way, I should mention that I still adhere to the Boy Scout Oath and Law.

Rules for Relationships: Cultural Virtues

Within any culture, there is a set of rules for constructive interpersonal relating. These rules are reflected in the songs, stories, and dramas of the culture. The rules prescribe behavior that conforms to virtues. ''Virtue'' means goodness and morality. Fearing that virtues are not being adequately taught to today's youth, William Bennett has spearheaded a drive to preserve them, and to ensure that children will have a chance to learn about virtuous behavior. In addition to leadership in Empower America, he has edited a compendium of great moral stories, *The Book of Virtues*, suitable for the education of children, as well as for the many adults who may have missed out on this important aspect of upbringing. You really ought to have a copy at home, and refer to it frequently.

To help you become aware of how well you have learned the virtues, here they are in tabular form, with an opportunity for you to ponder how well your behavior reflects them. Fill out this table, then have your support people do the same. Sit in your group and discuss the results at great length. How well do you do compare with the average person you know? Discuss celebrities and famous people who may serve as positive and negative examples of each virtue. Talk about how people who read and discuss self-improvement books are so superior to the massed rabble.

Table for Virtues Awareness Enhancement
(A = very good; B = above average; C = average;
D = below average; F = really bad)

Virtue	My Grade	Evidence
Self-control: I control my appetites and passions.	A B C D F	*Example:* I never overeat, nor do I attack those whose presence inspires my libido.
Compassion: I comfort those in need.	A B C D F	
Responsibility: I do my part in everything.	A B C D F	
Friendship: I am in good, sharing relationships.	A B C D F	
Work: I do the best I can, without resentment.	A B C D F	
Courage: I do what needs to be done, without fear for myself.	A B C D F	
Perseverance: I stick to a task until it is done.	A B C D F	
Honesty: I tell the truth, even if it hurts me.	A B C D F	
Loyalty: Others can trust that I will continue to be on their side.	A B C D F	
Faith: I follow a plan based on love which overrides materialism.	A B C D F	

In case you scored yourself rather highly on these virtues, I add one more:

Humility: I judge myself to be no better than others.	A B C D F	

It is clear that adherence to these virtues is critical to the maintenance of good relationships.

Rules for Relationships: How to Be Nasty Through Narcissism

To learn more about relationships, a negative example can be instructive. Some people seem motivated only to help themselves. Their exclusive self-concern directs them to do whatever they can to get what they want, regardless of the cost and hurt done to others. As Paul noted, the works of the flesh involve selfishness, anger, envy, and jealousness.

Narcissism, egomania, or self-loving me-firstism may be caused by failing to learn in childhood the advantages of loving relationships. This could be due to the lack of such relationships in families of origin. Children in dysfunctional families may learn that the only way to survive is to assume that everyone else is out to get their share, so they assume that they have to fight to get what they can.

Narcissism has been declared a psychiatric disorder by the American Psychiatric Association (1994). The symptoms include:

1) A grandiose sense of self-importance

2 A preoccupation with fantasies of unlimited success, power, and brilliance

3 A need for excessive admiration

4 Unreasonable expectations of especially favorable treatment; the expectation that everyone will comply with his/her wishes

5 Taking advantage of others to achieve his or her own ends

6 A lack of empathy: unwilling to recognize or identify with the feelings and needs of others

7 Envy of others or the belief that others are envious

8 Arrogance and haughtiness

If you recognize yourself in this symptom profile, seek help. If you see these symptoms in others, do not try to refer them to therapy. They won't appreciate your efforts. I predict that narcissism will someday be viewed as a tragic disease, and that the National Association for the Advancement of Narcissism Acceptance will lobby for legislative protection from discrimination in employment.

Psychiatrist M. Scott Peck has made an association between narcissistic personality disorder and what most people would call evil. Evil behavior is designed to help the self at the expense of the other (without some overriding cause, such as protecting one's country). Some would say that the so-called Generation X, which is concerned with material success, displays some narcissistic traits.

Narcissistic people care about being superior to others, but they are not convinced they have achieved superiority. In fact, the drive to be superior may be a defense against the underlying realization that one is not very superior at all. In a study using undergraduate students (Bushman et al., 1998), narcissism was measured, and then the subjects were given an opportunity to act aggressively toward people in three interaction situations: a) people who insulted them; b) people who had praised them; or, c) a neutral person. The most aggressive subjects were the narcissists who were attacking someone who had given them a bad evaluation. This aggression may be a response to a perceived threat to their inflated but fragile egos.

Narcissism can serve as a negative example for good relationships. In good *relationshipping*, concern for others is equal to or greater than self-concern. The purpose is to work for a cause greater than oneself. Threats to self-esteem or ego are not important. As long as you are sure that you are doing something worthwhile for a good cause, then personal attacks have no meaning to you. If the tone of your emotional life is based on your self-evaluation, you will discover that there are plenty of people in the world willing to pop your ego bubble. Worry about the success of worthy causes, not about what other people think of you.

Of course, most advertising messages appeal to the narcissist within us all. "You are important! You deserve our product! Think how important and cool you will be flaunting the new Z-88 convertible European sports car through your neighborhood, as neighbors jealously wave. Leave others in the dust as the superior power of the V-12 engine's turbocharger kicks in with a mighty roar . . . etc."

Be a Counselor

Other self-improvement books may promise to make you more powerful, richer, sexier, or more popular. This is how people who write books make money. They appeal to the narcissistic desires of the masses of people who feel inadequate, and who believe they are not getting their fair share of the goodies in life. Sorry to disappoint you, but this book, in case you haven't already guessed, isn't providing the secret keys to wealth, power, and influence. It is directing you toward a lifestyle that will improve energy, induce calm, and give you a sense of purpose.

Getting a sense of purpose in relationships means learning to be helpful and kind. You may improve your influence over others through helpfulness and kindness. Your business dealings may be more successful because of your reputation for helpfulness and kindness. But even if you don't get anything out of being helpful and kind, you will at least know that you have done some good. This is far better than being powerful and rich, realizing that you have hurt people to achieve your status.

The model for a helpful and kind person is that of counselor. Religious faiths talk about their gods as being counselors. People turn to them for comfort and guidance. So instead of teaching you skills designed to help you get your way (there are other books for that: see McKay, Davis, & Fanning, 1995), I will give you a brief lesson in how to be a counselor. Of course, if you are currently beset with many personal problems, and are having difficulty coping, you will need to seek therapy first. Being an amateur counselor requires at least a small amount of composure and mental strength, because part of counseling is giving a sense of assurance. However, if you have come this far in this book, you have strength, you are organized, and you are calm. You are a good resource for your friends who have not learned these skills. Here are some guidelines for taking on the role of counselor.

Talk About Life

Our society is bombarded by so many modalities of news and entertainment media that conversations tend to focus on gossip about the president, professional sports, movies, and TV sitcoms. It is easier to communicate about things that have no importance to our personal lives, because everyone has the same knowledge base, and because this avoids the potential pain of confronting our own problems. The potential for real interacting, for loving relationships, is replaced by the drivel of the masses. Men are worse than women in this respect. Talk about the reality of your own lives.

I suggest that you schedule regular times each week to have counseling sessions with family and friends. Spend an hour with your spouse: you counsel your partner, then reverse roles. With children the session length may need to be no longer in minutes than the age of the kid. Meet with your close friends (your support group) and pass around a symbolic feather (after the Native American custom). The holder of the feather is the "counselee," and the others, as counselors, focus on his/her problems for 15 minutes, or longer if special problems arise. Take turns making gourmet (low-fat!) food to share. Avoid alcohol and other drugs; use of these is not conducive to good communication. Use the support-group ideas listed in chapter 2.

Strive to make your interactions with others into brief counseling sessions whenever you have the opportunity to be helpful. When you meet someone, and you ask each other "So how's it going?" and the other person answers, "Oh, fine," you can probe through this obvious mask of deceit by asking questions such as "How are the kids? How is the job going?" People like to talk about themselves. If they know you as a nice person, you may be able to get them to talk.

Counseling Process: How to Do It

Here are some guidelines of basic counseling methods. The goal is to get people to talk about their problems, and help them to develop an approach to solving or coping with their predicament.

Note: If, in the course of conversation, you realize that the person you are talking with cannot think straight, or has ideas which are really divorced from reality, consider getting professional help. You may need to call a therapist and talk about the person to get some tips on how to get the person engaged in a treatment program. The kind of amateur counseling I am outlining here is for ordinary problems of everyday living. It is not for depression, anxiety attacks, hearing voices, and so forth.

A) Getting them to talk. I am not talking about police interrogation methods here. All you need is to establish the understanding with the other person that you want to be there as another human being to provide whatever support may be needed. Just let the person talk. If you are a trustworthy person who will not gossip about what you hear, and you express a genuine concern for the other's emotional health, then you have set the stage.

   If you are quiet and listen without interrupting, you will become a valuable helper. I have sat and listened to many people in crisis unload all their fears, frustrations, and confusions. Often, I just sat there looking knowledgeable, nodding from time to time, and making comments such as "That must be really difficult for you." Just providing an opportunity for another person to get all their troubles out can be very therapeutic. You don't have to be a trained counselor, just a person who is willing to listen and be nonjudgmental.

B) Help them relax. Use relaxation methods described in this book.

C) If they appear tired, make sure they are taking care of themselves in terms of eating and sleeping.

D) Help them organize their thoughts. Have them write out the components of their problems on paper.

E) Get them to talk about their emotions related to the problem.

F) Assure them from time to time that you will do whatever you can to help, but you are not their therapist. Your job is to provide a friendly ear, and to help the person sort out their thoughts, and to give feedback from another person's perspective.

G) Help them list possible solutions. Discuss the pros and cons of each one in a step-by-step way.

H) Don't be judgmental. If the person appears to have a really bad idea about how to proceed, don't say, "That's ridiculous!" Instead, use comments like, "You know, that's an interesting thought, but let me suggest another approach which might work. What if you did . . . ?" If the person appears to be heading in a good direction, reinforce his comments with praise, such as "I like your idea. Let's talk about how your plan might work."

H) Don't ever tell a person what to do. Use questions, such as "Have you thought about trying to do such and such?" "What do you think would happen if you did that?"

I) Indicate that you understand what the person is saying by summarizing what he has said from time to time. "Okay, let me get this straight. What you are telling me is . . ."

J) Remember, it is not your job to solve the other person's problem, or to treat him for, or cure him of any disorder. You are a valuable friend, but just a friend. You can offer information, share what you have done in similar circumstances, direct the person to resources, and listen.

This type of informal counseling can be learned by the average person. It can be a very precious resource for those in your support group. Imagine having a group of friends that meets regularly, and really gets down to serious life issues by guiding each other through a counseling process.

Practice counseling skills with each other in your support group. Practice not talking so much about sports and recipes. Think about the role of counselor when relating to your spouse, children, friends, coworkers, and subordinates. You will gain admiration and respect, and possibly someone will return the favor when it's your turn to have a crisis.

How to Win Friends and Influence People

A chapter on relationships would be incomplete without reference to the work of Dale Carnegie, who gathered his personal experience and the wisdom of the ages into some remarkable books (Carnegie, 1970). His advice in relationships (with my comments):

1) Never criticize anyone. It puts people on the defensive and causes resentment. Listen to their interests and needs. Show respect for their opinions. (This goes along with the counseling principle never to be judgmental.) "When dealing with people, let us remember we are not dealing with creatures of logic. We are dealing with creatures of emotion, creatures bristling with prejudice and motivated by pride and vanity" (Carnegie, 1970).

2) Make people feel important. Let them know you appreciate them. Encourage them. Once you have demonstrated to them that you are going to build them up, then you can start to influence them (hopefully in a positive direction).

3) To have influence, talk about what interests others, and what their desires are. (This is basic to the counseling role.)

Carnegie's books are filled with interesting examples and stories that illustrate the main principles. Look for Dale Carnegie training courses in major cities.

Are You Lonely Tonight?

Loneliness is an increasing problem which may increasingly damage psychological and physical health. Psychologists are beginning to examine ways to help the lonely through individual counseling and by changing the structure of our society (Rook, 1984). Surveys find that one in every six Americans does not have a friend in whom he or she can confide personal problems (Campbell, 1981). That's millions and millions of people. Loneliness may be linked to depression, drug abuse, aggressiveness, and suicide. Over the last forty years, the U.S. has seen increasing divorce, more people living alone, and a rapid growth in the singles industry (for example, frozen gourmet dinners for one). Modern social interactions seem to be getting more superficial and transitory, possibly due to the breakdown of the family and an increase in narcissism.

Two hundred years ago people were constrained to interact in the sharing of survival tasks. Now it is possible to live one's life without ever having a meaningful relationship. For example, some people lead lives such as this: Go to work, develop software for video games, go home, play video games, go to sleep. Repeat. Some people have difficulty relating because they were abused as children. Others have chemical imbalances in their brains which make them more paranoid. These people need treatment. Other people just never learned social skills, which can be taught to adults.

At the community level, neighborhoods could be designed to facilitate contact. In the old days in Houston, before air-conditioning and television, people would sit on their large front porches in the evening and chat with their neighbors. Now everyone is hidden inside with their faces glued to the tube. A security system protects them from other citizens.

I have thought that new housing could be designed so that private residences surrounded a common center which would include exercise, crafts, and communal dining facilities. Of course, potential property owners would have to be carefully screened, because you wouldn't want any_____(fill in this blank with whatever groups you have prejudices against) living in *your* neighborhood. I have visited kibbutz, or communal farms, in Israel. Child care, dining, and other functions are done communally. For the most part, I think they have been a social success, and I would guess that loneliness is not a big problem.

Lack of Forgiveness As a Barrier to Meaningful Relationships

In my counseling experience, I have seen that the atmosphere of unforgiveness casts a dark cloud over a great many lives. Relationships become a source of hate and guilt, rather than of nurturing. Everybody has been emotionally hurt by someone, and everybody has hurt another. This is normal life for humans, who are likely to strike out at others, as other animals do, when subject to fits of selfishness and anger. The natural animal instinct when harmed is to feel resentment, and to avoid a relationship with the perpetrator. The problem is that carrying resentment on the one hand, and guilt on the other, will cause psychophysiological harm.

Forgiving is not easy. The average person feels that revenge or payback is needed to make things right again. Not forgiving allows us to place the guilty party into a state of continuing shame. We continue to have feelings of hate, which gnaw at our innards even if the target of our hate is unaware of our feelings.

How do we deal with this situation? There are several steps recommended by therapists (for example, Smedes, 1984). (*Note:* if you are forgiving something serious such as incest, seek help from a therapist before proceeding.)

1) First, think about and feel the hurt you suffered. Write it down.

2) Confront the perpetrator and, in a calm way, say that you feel hurt by his/her actions.

3) Focus on the bad behavior, not the person. Assume that the person is not totally evil, that he has some good qualities, and that everyone has moments of hurting that they wish they could take back.

4) Realize that the act of forgiving is a way of devel-

oping a new attitude toward the perpetrator, switching from hate/revenge to forgiveness/let's get on with life and be friends.

5) Let the emotions generated by past mistakes be put to rest.

6) If the other person responds positively, then there is a victory for love over hate. If the other person remains unrepentant, then you can terminate any relationship and move on with your life without rancor weighing you down.

Asking for forgiveness is not easy either. But letting your wrongs go without taking some corrective action is more painful. The steps for seeking forgiveness might include:

1) Thinking about how it was that you hurt someone. Write it down. Think about your feelings, and those of the victim.

2) Go to the person and ask for forgiveness. Say that you were wrong in doing what you did. If seeing the person is not possible, write a letter. (Consult your attorney before making admissions in writing, or use general terms.)

3) Offer to make up for the damage done. You are not free of the guilt until you have made such an offer. And you should follow through with your offer.

I have seen some major emotional healing in cases in which I was able to motivate people to get involved in the forgiveness process. I remember a middle-aged woman whose entire life was a mess, due apparently to her father sexually abusing her from age 10 to 16. Even thirty years later, she was still obsessed with hate. Needless to say, she had not been able to form any satisfying relationships with men. I convinced her to visit him and forgive him. She had not seen him in 25 years. She found him to be a broken man, in spirit and health. They had a long talk, and she forgave him for the past. Her hatred is dissolving, and the old man has a daughter who visits him in his declining years.

In my rampant young adulthood, I was not as understanding to others as I think I am now. Twenty years later, I began to meditate on what I had done. I wrote letters asking for forgiveness. The response I got was very positive; they said I wasn't as bad as I thought I was. It is nice to clean up the clutter of the past.

Ophthalmological and Dental Aspects of Forgiveness

"If we practice an eye for an eye and a tooth for a tooth, soon the whole world will be blind and toothless."

Mahatma Gandhi

Anger: Don't You Just Hate It?

Along with forgiveness, dealing with anger can have beneficial effects on establishing meaningful relationships. I know some people who are educated, and really nice most of the time, but their periodic hotheadedness seriously interferes with relationships. Cynical hostility is thought to cause health problems, notably cardiovascular disease, through the violent shifts in physiological reactivity. Health is also impaired because angry people tend to have poor social support networks, for obvious reasons.

The way to help yourself deal with anger is to recognize that anger is never useful in helping you get what you want out of life. Perhaps, in caveman times, anger and the display that goes with it were helpful in establishing dominance over the others in groups. This allowed one to have the best mate, and the choicest pieces of mammoth meat.

Now friendly cooperation is the mode. Here are some anger-control tips:

1) Write down what is making you angry. Examine each thought you may have, to see if it is realistic, based on fact, or if it is really a distortion based on your attitude.

2) Ask others for their opinion.

3) Write down the argument of your opposition.

4) Practice relaxation. It is difficult to be angry and re- laxed at the same time. (People should wear biofeed- back devices to signal their stress level so that others could be forewarned of increasing stress reactions in confrontational situations, and also to remind one to relax.)

5) Meet as soon as possible with your adversary. Plan to be relaxed, and be willing to hear both sides. Ar- range for a neutral arbitrator to attend the meeting. It is human nature for anger to escalate between foes. We are physiologically designed to escalate to the point of violence. Strive to heal relationships; avoid injury or prison.

6) When dealing with angry persons, let them vent their anger verbally while you patiently listen. This can defuse hostility.

Why Revenge Is Not Needed

"If we could read the secret history of our enemies, we should find in each man's life sorrow and suffering enough to disarm any hostility."
                                                    Henry Wadsworth Longfellow

Homework

1. To get into the practice of taking on the role of counselor in your relationships, use the following lists to structure an initial interview. Start with your own family (or significant others) first. Schedule regular meetings with spouse and family. Meetings with spouse and kids (after age 11) should be reciprocal: they take a turn acting as counselor to you. Families are supposed to serve as one's core support team. Before the initial "counseling" sessions, explain that the ultimate goal is to develop ongoing interactions to other areas such as discussion of spending too much time in the bathroom, or who gets to hold the TV remote-control unit.

List for Spousal Counseling (Schedule Weekly)

How are you coping/feeling in these areas? (Remember, don't be judgmental!)

1. Physical/medical and mental state: what symptoms do you have?

2. Household chore management.

3. Self-care and recreation, hobbies.

4. Getting enough affection from me, the kids?

5. How are your friendships going?

6. Dealing with parents and in-laws.

7. Activities with me (enjoyable, enough time together)?

8. Sexual satisfaction: any changes you would like to see?

9. Your work.

10. Your religious/spiritual situation.

11. Relationship with the kids.

List for Counseling with Your Children (Weekly or Biweekly)

As soon as they can talk, communicate with your children often; get them to talk about their life. Have formal, mutual counseling sessions scheduled starting at about age 11.

How are you doing in these areas?

1. School.

2. Friends.

3. Recreation/sports/TV.

4. Emotional/physical problems. Feelings of energy.

5. Self-care: eating, exercise, sleep.

6. Opinions about parents and their parenting.

7. Relations with siblings.

8. What they want to be when they grow up.

9. What they think about community, world events.

10. Spiritual/religious thoughts.

When children become teenagers, give them a copy of this book, and discuss it with them.

Counseling Friends

Helping friends and establishing good relationships by playing the role of informal counselor is not something you schedule or announce to the public. It involves an effort to move conversation to important topics about life. If you are genuinely a nice person interested in other people's well-being, they will sense this and be willing to talk about themselves. In fact, people like to talk about themselves if given the chance. Practice the counseling role in your support group. Then go out and be helpful.

When encountering a friend, after the usual, meaningless introductory remarks, such as "Pretty hot today, isn't it?" or "How about them Bulls?", you should ask, "So how are your kids/job/spouse?" The secret is to ask enough questions to get into some details about the other person's life so that problems come up, and you can help explore the potential solutions or coping methods. The temptation is to start talking about yourself. Save talking about yourself for when you are in a crisis.

2. Practice being a warm, helpful kind of person. One way to make yourself aware of your warmth behaviors is to wear a golf counter. For nonduffers, this is a product that looks like a wristwatch. Press a button on the side, and the number in the little window goes up. Each time you say something genuinely complimentary or helpful or empathetic, record the event. See if your count increases over time.

3. Make a list of all the people who may ever have hurt you. Write each a letter stating:

a) Why you feel hurt: what they did.

b) Your willingness to forgive, and let bygones be bygones.

c) Your hope that you can be friends (unless you consider the person to be dangerous, unremorseful and unrepentant).

d) Your hope that the person can find happiness whether an offer of friendship is accepted or not.

4. Make a list of all the people you have hurt. For each of your victims, describe why you did it and how you feel

about your actions now. Assuming that you feel some remorse, and your guilt is painful, write a letter to each one asking for forgiveness. (Consult an attorney if there are legal implications of documenting wrongdoing.) This is usually easier than confronting them personally, or telephoning. But say that you would like to talk to them about it, and ask them to call (collect if needed). Ask how you can make it up to them.

See the book by Smedes (1996) for more detail on forgiving.

5. Think about what makes you really angry. For me, it is people driving dangerously or stupidly. I have made a good effort to let them go first, and not worry about them cutting in front of me. I try to relax, feel good about helping them get ahead, and to be comfortable in the knowledge that their hurrying and hostility will lead to an early grave. But seriously, folks, try relaxation the next time you feel angry. It's the old "count to ten" method, with muscular calming added. When conflict appears imminent, all parties should take a ten-minute time-out from interaction. See also the book by Rubin (1998) for dealing with anger.

References

American Psychiatric Association (1994). *Diagnostic Criteria from DSM-IV.* Washington, DC: American Psychiatric Association.

Bennett, W. J. (ed.) (1993). *The Book of Virtues: A Treasury of Great Moral Stories.* New York: Simon & Schuster.

Bushman, B. J., Baumeister, R. F. (1998). Threatened egotism, narcissism, self-esteem, and direct and misplaced aggression: Does self-love or self-hate lead to violence? *Journal of Personality and Social Psychology,* 75, in press.

Campbell, A. (1981). *The Sense of Well-Being in America.* New York: McGraw-Hill.

Carnegie, D. (1970). *How to Enjoy Your Life and Your Job: Selections from How to Win Friends and Influence People (1936)* and *How to Stop Worrying and Start Living* (1944). New York: Pocket Books.

McKay, M., Davis, M., Fanning, P. (1995). *Messages: The Communication Skills Book*. 2nd ed. Richmond, CA: New Harbinger.

Peck, M. S. (1997), *People of the Lie: The Hope for Healing Human Evil*. New York: Simon & Schuster.

Ramm, D. R. (1996). Clinically formulated principles of morality. *New Ideas in Psychology,* 14, 237–56.

Rook, K. S. (1984). Promoting social bonding: strategies for helping the lonely and socially isolated. *American Psychologist,* 39, 1389–407.

Rubin, T.I. (1998). *The Angry Book.* Touchstone Books.

Smedes, L. B. (1996). *Art of Forgiving: When You Need to Forgive and Don't Know How*. New York: Ballantine.

12 | These Are a Few of My Favorite Things

GOAL: To learn that people are more important than things.

Have We Been "Malled"?

The title of this chapter comes from *The Sound of Music*. The "things" Maria is singing about include raindrops on roses, whiskers on kittens, bright copper kettles, warm woolen mittens, and brown paper packages tied up with string. As for me, I also like sunrises and sunsets, a good thunderstorm, watching animals in their natural habitats, hiking in the mountains, and other such stuff which I can share with my loved ones.

In our society, there is a great temptation to buy an awful lot of stuff. We spend time fussing over stuff, or using it to entertain ourselves, or to impress others. In these ways, possessions can be a barrier to relationships and happiness.

The purpose of this chapter is to have you focus on your possessions. A careful examination of all of your stuff, and the motivations you have to buy and keep it, may help you to purge yourself of things that get in the way of happiness.

In a competitive society such as ours, some groups are more susceptible to the notion that possessions can bring power, influence, and happiness. For example, those raised in poor families may as adults put an abnormal emphasis on financial success and the material trappings that go along with it. Men of short stature may be more likely to drive powerful sports cars to compensate for ''heightism.'' Some people with sexist attitudes think that women are materialistic because they feel a need to compensate for all the subjugation they experience from men, and because they have been denied access to the normal avenues to power and influence.

It's the Real Thing

In the hilarious movie *The Gods Must Be Crazy* (directed by J. Uys. 1981), a bush pilot flying over South Africa drops a Coca-Cola bottle out the window of his plane. It lands next to a peaceful little village which has been isolated from the outside world. In this village, the people have been living in complete harmony with nature. All their needs are supplied in abundance from the streams and plants. There is no conflict over possessions, since "possessions" are available free from the surrounding jungle.

The Coke bottle discovery causes quite a stir; no one has ever seen anything like it. Light shines through it. It has a mysterious shape. Many find it quite beautiful. Some of the women find it is useful for pounding grain into flour. The kids want to play with it as a toy.

Soon arguments arise about who gets to possess the bottle and for what purpose. In one of these arguments, someone discovers that the bottle is useful for hitting his opponent on the head. This outburst of hostility and aggression is unheard of. The elders decide the bottle must have come from evil forces. They assign an elder to take the bottle to the end of the earth (a high cliff), where he tosses it into a seemingly bottomless chasm. Normalcy is restored.

In the modern Western world, we do not live in harmony with nature. Most of us could survive only a few days without all the things we take for granted: grocery stores, electricity, running water, flush toilets, air-conditioning, wrinkle-free clothing. The more advanced our society becomes, the more things we seem to need. Because businesses need to sell more products, they bombard us with advertising designed to make us feel inadequate if we do not run out and buy their latest gadget. For example, someone in the United States today probably bought a Belgian waffle iron, feeling that his regular waffle iron was not quite good enough. Most citizens buy into the idea that possessions, and especially display of possessions, are a valid measure of "success" not only in the sense of financial success, but also in terms of "worthiness" or adequacy as a human being.

Thus, we all feel pressures to buy, possess, and display things. All this is done without careful examination of *what is going on here, anyway?* Few people are asking important questions like, "Is amassing a great quantity of things what I really should be doing with my money resources?" and "Is it possible that too many possessions can interfere with what's important in life?" and "Is there something more important than STUFF?"

To Have or to Be

The late psychiatrist Erich Fromm (1976) had a clear vision of the problems of modern man's focus on things. The industrial revolution was supposed to bring progress and greater freedom from work; yet many people ended up as cogs in the machinery of an increasingly complex society. As a result, well-being declined and ecological problems grew. Fromm saw two reasons for the failure of technological advances to have an overall positive effect on mankind. One was the faulty premise that the aim of life was to achieve happiness defined as satisfaction of any desire or need. The other dubious notion was that egotism, selfishness, and greed all work together in an economic system to raise productivity to a level where there are enough goods for all, and that this provision to the masses would result in greater social harmony.

Even though ancient philosophers and religions have pointed out that well-being does not come from the satisfaction of transitory needs, humans have a tendency to forget universal truths. In the sixteenth and seventeenth centuries, happiness was construed to be the fulfillment of every human desire. According to Fromm, this type of thinking has led to a "passion for having," which leads to a never-ending class war. Fromm felt that world destruction would result unless there was a radical change of heart, from a focus on what is good for the self to what is good for the world.

The focus on things and possessiveness has been reflected in language. People are more likely to say, "I have a problem," than they are to say, "I am troubled." This may reflect an attempt to distance themselves from emotions. Indeed, Fromm noted that our very identity had switched from notions of character and relationships to concepts of possessions and net worth. Thorstein Veblen (1857–1929) noted early in this century that "conspicuous consumption," or the display of wealth, especially wasteful uses of money, was a way the rich could elevate themselves in the social hierarchy. In contrast to ostentatious displays of wealth is the Jewish *Shabat*, which is supposed to be a time of focusing on being and relation to God; participating in material endeavors is avoided (Laufman, 1998). In Christianity, there is a strong emphasis on avoiding cravings for possessions. Followers are urged to focus on spiritual rather than material treasures. In Buddhism, the cause of all suffering is thought to come from wanting things.

Current social values are influenced by wealth. The wealthy are celebrated and their lifestyles are emulated. Those who are poor are thought to be unworthy, suspect, and dangerous. The only poor people we trust are priests.

Fromm pointed out that in a system of human interaction (society) based on "having," sin is defined as disobedience to the rules of possession. Virtually all of our laws fall into this arena. In systems of human interaction based on "being," sin is defined as a cause of estrangement in relationships. Fromm's advice to the world was to reduce greed and narcissism, and to establish a society in which giving and sharing were the norm. In his utopia, loving character would be more important that material wealth. Good luck to anyone working toward these ends.

This chapter is designed to help the reader gain a perspective on the rampant materialism of our culture, to look at his/her own acquisitiveness and possessions, and to make changes to enhance happiness. I report evidence to see whether having STUFF leads to greater or lesser happiness. I will boldly suggest that reducing one's possessions might yield some benefits, even though the neighbors may think you are weird. But to help you feel superior to your possession-laden friends and neighbors, I will discuss the psychology of *things* so that you can feel sorry for those who depend on STUFF to find meaning and happiness in life.

Evidence That Getting a Lot of Stuff Might Not Be a Good Idea

Americans have a lot more stuff now than ever before. Are they happier? Social psychologist David Myers has reviewed the research on the relationship between material wealth and happiness in his excellent book *The Pursuit of Happiness* (1992). There has been a trend away from traditional values of marriage, family, friendships, and community togetherness. People seem more interested in being financially successful. But happiness comes from good, sharing relationships with others; material wealth does not help in relationship building. In fact, material abundance can interfere with relationships.

Factoids:

1. Per capita consumption of material goods has gone up 45 percent in the last 20 years, but happiness has not increased (During, 1992).

2. Banks are now urging people to take out loans to buy luxuries such as home entertainment systems. The typical American household carries $9,000 of nonmortgage debt (Granfield, 1991).

3. Only 2 percent of American workers believe that "keeping up with the Joneses" does anything positive for them (Harris & Yankelovich, 1989).

Evidence That Our Society Has Unhealthful Priorities

(Perhaps you have them, too?)

1. Ninety-three percent of teenage girls say that store-hopping (malling) is a favorite activity (Shames, 1989).

2. The average American spends six hours shopping each week, but only 40 minutes playing with the kids (Morris, 1987).

3. A report commissioned by the Merck Family Fund and prepared by the Harwood Group found that Americans believe their priorities are out of whack. They believe materialism, greed, and selfishness increasingly dominate American life, threatening the values centered on family, responsibility, and community. They feel the material aspect of the American Dream is spinning out of control, with increasing pressure to buy more and more. They feel confusion about trying to keep ahead in the race for success and materialism, but they yearn to focus on more spiritual concerns. They yearn for things that money and possessions cannot bring: more time, less stress, and a sense of balance in life. They feel that even though they gain higher levels of wealth and possessions, they are losing ground, since everyone is getting wealthier but at the cost of increased stress (Harwood Group, 1995).

4. One of the fastest-growing industries in America is self-storage for those who have run out of space to store their things at home.

5. Technology and increased competition have created a flood of products. Exposed to relentless advertising and a constantly rising standard of living, people are thrown into a cycle of perpetual consumption. Everyone is expected to want more. Americans tend to use money and possessions as a substitute for faith and a sense of community. The security and power people feel when they stock their homes with new things are short-lived, and create a fruitless cycle. As the novelty of new things wears off, boredom and loneliness set in, and *more* STUFF is needed to alleviate the pain (Wachtel, 1989).

The Ring's the Thing

A few decades ago, no young men in Japan ever presented their sweethearts with a diamond engagement ring. This came to the notice of the owners of the de Beers diamond mines. They launched a massive marketing scheme to convince the Japanese that everyone in the Western world gave their women diamond rings, and if the Japanese men wanted to feel adequate, they must do likewise. The campaign worked. I'm not sure that Japanese society benefited, or that Japanese marriages were made more solid by this adoption of a totally unnecessary and expensive symbolic act.

The Psychology of Wanting Stuff

How did STUFF get to be so important in our culture? There are two reasons. One is that useful STUFF is important to survival, but we have come to confuse stuff we really need for survival and happiness with stuff that is unnecessary and perhaps even destructive of our happiness potential. Everyone trying to make a buck by selling *stuff* expends an awful lot of energy, creativity, and money trying to convince us all that what he is selling is *necessary* in some way. Individuals exposed from infancy to television and other media come to believe these advertising messages, and have trouble distinguishing between stuff they need for survival and happiness, and the rest of the junk they accumulate. Research shows that there is a positive association between attitude toward advertising and materialism. The more materialistic a person is, the more likely he is to believe advertising.

This belief that advertising messages are truthful and full of wisdom must provide a partial explanation for the growth of television channels devoted exclusively to advertising and "home shopping." Now one can sit at home with a TV remote controller, a phone, and a credit-card number waiting for opportunities to satisfy an emotional

longing to possess stuff which a more secure person would
be able to avoid. Viewers are apparently bedazzled by the
endless display of jewelry rotating on little turntables so
that the beams of light directed at them are reflected via
television into the deeper and less rational depths of their
brains, causing impulsive purchases. The existence of these
TV channels cannot be very therapeutic for shopaholics,
who seem compelled to buy, buy, buy in order to feel good,
or to escape some repressed negative emotion.

At the dawn of civilization, people who possessed more
of the stuff needed for survival found they had an advantage over others. For example, a man with many fine spears,
or many goats, held a position of greater power in a village
because he, along with his possessions, was potentially
more valuable to his fellow citizens than the person with
nothing. There was a relationship between the number of
possessions a man had and the work he performed to attain
it. This was well and good when work and the things that
work produced were obviously needed for survival. No one
questioned the value of these things. Perhaps a visit to an
Amish town would reveal a culture in which a person's
worth depended on his work achievements in terms of farm
size and productivity, the quality of his furniture, and the
health and happiness of his family.

An Amish farmer presents quite a contrast to the modern
urbanite struggling to survive in a world of one-upmanship
defined in terms of symbols of wealth. We feel compelled
to acquire things that have little to do with survival. We
buy things now because of their value as status symbols,
in order to impress others and give ourselves greater influence and power, or at least the perception of this. Advertising has taught us that possession of the best, most costly
products translates into a higher level of perceived worthiness. Who among us would not assume that the owner of
a new BMW 7.30 is not superior in some way to the driver
of a beat-up 1988 Pontiac 6000? But what about Sam Wal-
ton, zillionaire founder of WalMart and Sam's Clubs? He

enjoyed his old pickup, apparently feeling that a luxury car or chauffeur was not needed to bolster his ego.

The relentless struggle to enhance feelings of worthiness through possessions can be compared to the psychiatric disorder known as hoarding. Hoarding is an abnormal concern about maintaining control over possessions, with a greater emotional attachment to them. Hoarders seem to rely on possessions for emotional comfort. If children are raised in abusive or neglectful families, their self-esteem may be damaged, and they may have difficulty forming meaningful relationships. To compensate for feelings of low self-esteem, they may acquire a great number of possessions in an attempt, conscious or unconscious, to show the world that they are worthwhile. ("I have twelve cashmere sweaters, therefore I must be an okay person.") Or consider the child who was given toys as a substitute for attention and love. Such a person might also have difficulty in forming satisfying relationships; possessions might become more important as a substitute source of comfort.

It is unclear where the normal need to satisfy basic needs ends and the disorder of hoarding begins. People identified as suffering from compulsive hoarding have trouble forming emotional attachments with others, tend to avoid others, and have erroneous beliefs about possessions. These beliefs tend to reinforce the idea that possessions are good and comforting, and can enhance happiness. Hoarders tend to buy extra things in order not to be caught without a needed item. Hoarders tend to be insecure about making decisions; they avoid the decision to throw something away by keeping it. They also thus avoid the sad emotional reactions that accompany parting with cherished items. The more items they possess, the more they feel in control of their surroundings.

A good psychologist should be able to spot hoarding that is so bad that therapy is needed. But who among us does not share to some degree the symptoms of hoarding? How easy is it for us to go through our entire inventory of possessions, and get rid of everything that we really don't need for work or happiness? Some people enjoy the feeling of cleansing and simplification they get from such a purging. Others can't bear the thought of losing something; indeed, you may see them lurking around your house during your purge, hoping to rescue some wonderful THING they know needs a new home.

Hoarding Self-Evaluation

You may have a problem if you say "True" to two or more:

1. Do you have more STUFF than the average person?

2. Do you have possessions you couldn't think of parting with, even though you don't need them for work, and they don't help your family life or friendship?

3. Do you go to garage sales and stores without even the faintest notion of what you might be needing?

4. Do you have special container systems in your house to store stuff that most people would find useless?

The Importance of *Things* in the Establishment of the *Pecking* Order

In man, as well as among most animals, a pecking order is established through real or symbolic fighting to prove who is the most powerful. The most powerful males get the most chances to reproduce. This is good for the species, since it increases the probability that genetic inheritance favoring strength will predominate. In our society, the pecking order is confused, since we are so crowded together, and since we are supposed to operate under a system of equal opportunity. We symbolically try to achieve superiority over others through displays of possessions. For men this works in mate selection as long as women are fooled into believing that a large number of possessions predicts a good husband. Unfortunately, a focus on material wealth is not the best basis for mate selection or happy marriage.

As for establishing a pecking order in our society, I think what has happened is that there is a relatively small number of rich people (the "peckers") who become wealthy by convincing us (the "peckees") to buy many products, many of which we really don't need. What a sense of freedom can be achieved when one finally realizes that happiness can be achieved without a home-theater entertainment system with an 40-inch television and wraparound Dolby sound.

Wisdom of the Gods

(translated into modern American English)

Jesus: "Don't try to gather a lot of materialistic treasures. Focus instead on spiritual values. Your heart should be concerned with other people, not things."

Buddha: "Unhappiness comes from desires. Reduce desires by not wanting. Be happy with what is given you."

American*, 1996: "My BMW is bigger than yours."

*(In a humanistic society, everyone is a god)

Note: It may be worthwhile to note that among the Seven Deadly Sins are *greed* and *envy*.

Industries That Would Be in Trouble If Everyone Lived Like Me

Some of the products I generally do not buy: TVs over 11 inches diagonal, home-theater systems, CDs, fancy cars or raised-up trucks with "elephantire-sis," car accessories, cologne, jewelry, watches costing over $35 (I used to wear

Wisdom of an Ancient King

(translated into American English)

"Look—you bust your ass all your life, you earn some money, you buy some things. Does it make you happy? No! All you do is worry about working and getting stuff!

"Look at me. I'm a king and have more stuff than anybody. I'm still not happy. What really gets me is that all this stuff I possess is going to be inherited by some idiots who won't appreciate it. The way I see it, you need to stop working so much, and stop worrying about having so much stuff. Enjoy your work, enjoy your spouse and family, enjoy good food. He who trusts in his riches will wither." Solomon, King of Israel

an expensive-looking Rolex-type watch, but too many people are killed by Rolex bandits, so now I wear a black Timex), pens costing over $5, video games (which account for over 15 percent of the U.S.-Japan trade deficit each year), movies on video, clothes costing more than those found at Sears, liquor, tobacco, high-fat foods, pain and digestion remedies, sleeping pills, "nutritional supplements," and romance novels.

IMPORTANT NOTE: If you decide to reduce your materialism as suggested in this chapter, do not urge others to do so. This could start a trend that would destroy the economy of the industrialized nations and put us in a deep economic depression.

Review: What Are the Purposes of Possessions?

There are many reasons why we have possessions. Think about what stuff you have and why you have it.

1. Sensory/entertainment value: Some things (TV, stereos) are used for sensory pleasures. Some sensory pleasure is a good thing, but one's life should not be directed at feeling good through sensory stimulation. Other things (e.g., a 42-foot yacht) are merely expensive toys, used for temporary diversion and relaxation, but otherwise serving no useful purpose for a mature adult.

2. Symbolic expression of superiority over neighbors: What is the value of trying to make others think you are really wealthy? Does this improve or hinder good relationships? Also, a display of nice possessions invites attack from heavily armed criminals who want your stuff so they can sell it to others who suffer from the delusion, promoted by modern marketing methods, that purchasing expensive stuff is the secret to happiness. (*Note:* In Australia, robbery statistics have been rising since 1980. Since the assault rate did not go up, criminologists conclude that the increasing prevalence of robbery reflects an increase in acquisitiveness rather than aggressiveness [Indermaur, 1995].) In the U.S., many children are raised more by the values they learn from television rather than from their parents. Is it any wonder then that some of these kids will kill for air-pump shoes?

3. Emotional attachment to things as a substitute for relationships: As is true of people suffering from compulsive hoarding, stuff can dominate a person's life, at the expense of relationships and meaningful activities.

4. Compensation for low self-esteem, feelings of inadequacy. If one feels too short, or too fat, or unloved, there may be a turning toward stuff which is not therapeutic.

Remember, the research on happiness shows that happiness comes from sharing life with others, not from possessions per se. If possessions facilitate relationships (e.g., a large backyard for having friends over), they might be good for you.

Reversing Acquisitiveness

Now that you have thought about possessions and why you have them, what can be done to optimize your life? Is it possible to downsize your inventory of things in a constructive way?

Many years ago, I taught a course at a church on lifestyle optimization. I emphasized getting rid of things and focusing on relationships and causes. At the last class, an elderly widow stood up and announced that she had sold her mansion and most of her possessions, and now lived simply in a little town home with a cat and little else. She reported a peace and contentment she had not known while reigning over her old palatial house and its staff of servants. I think the other well-to-do members of the class were astonished that anyone had actually followed through on the recommendations presented. I am sure the widow was thereafter held in the highest suspicion by her former neighbors.

Now the act of reversing acquisitiveness in one's life has become a trend. While most try to display power and wealth through conspicuous consumption, a growing number of people have decided to practice what they call "conspicuous nonconsumption" or "simplicity chic." Their goal is to see how thriftily they can live. They take pride in how little they need to survive. Self-sufficiency used to be an American value, and these adherents of independence from rampant consumerism pride themselves on the positive effect their lifestyles have on the environment. They recycle, grow their own vegetables, and think of themselves as connoisseurs of life, focusing on quality rather than quantity.

Duane Elgin wrote *Voluntary Simplicity* in 1981. He recommends reducing consumption in order to conserve the earth's resources. The VS way advocates reducing the number of hours worked and increasing the time spent with family and community activities. Another popular book is *Living the Simple Life* by Elaine St. James. A careful study of such books could be helpful. Find and join an organization devoted to environmental preservation through reducing consumption. Unless a large number of us take action, the world will be bought and consumed before humans are finished using it, and you won't be able to order another one from QVC.

According to Marianne Williamson (1997, pp. 87–88), Americans are being tyrannized into assuming a state of passivity, not directly, but indirectly "through an endless dripping stream of pleasure that the system is able to provide us, much like a low-grade morphine pump pushed into our veins, making us think we can't live without it. Pleasure can be used to enslave a person as effectively as pain. And so, while we are not happy, perhaps we are having fun in some peculiar way or are so addicted to the pure adrenaline rush of contemporary culture that we no longer question the pain of it all." She urges spiritual renewal for America. Read her book.

Shaw on Civic Involvement

"What Englishman will give his mind to politics as long as he can afford to keep a motor car?"
                                                             Bernard Shaw

Homework: Action Plan—How Simply Can You Live?

List all your possessions that are not absolutely required for survival. Another way to do this is to identify all your possessions that a poor person would be unlikely to have.

For each of these possessions, determine its purpose. These purposes could be:

1. I own this for prestige and to make a *display* of money or power.

2. I own this because it is really an *expensive toy* that I like to play with.

3. I own this because it is *essential for my job,* to impress clients.

4. I possess this because it is a keepsake/inheritance from my dear grandmother/treasure/something I just couldn't get rid of even though I haven't seen or thought about it in 10 years. An item I am *emotionally attached* to.

5. I own this because it provides me with hours of *entertainment* in the form of eight-speaker sound and a 40-inch television picture presentation of spectator sports, which are important for me to watch for some reason that has nothing to do with making my life any better, although with some beer it sure seems to be a nice way to pass my life away.

6. I possess this because it helps me to be constructive, artistic, or nurturing to myself or others, or because it helps me share life with others. (These are the keepers; those items in categories one to five above should be considered for outplacement.)

Next, for each item, plan to get rid of as much as you can (discuss this with your spouse first). Sell what you can, give the rest away to charity. Remember, the idea is to keep only those things which will help you stay healthy and energetic, relatively comfortable, and help you relate positively to others.

Note: The goal is not poverty. Far from it. The optimal goal would be to have the highest financial resources (for economic security, college funds, retirement, charity) while at the same time living a very simple life in terms of *things*.

In addition to reviewing your possessions, you should also examine your checkbook and credit-card statements over the last six months to get an idea of what you have paid for that did not end up as a possession. This includes entertainment, vacation, and gourmet dining. Assuming you can afford a lot of this type of activity, ask yourself the question "Beyond my own enjoyment, did this enhance my happiness by helping me relate better to others, or by helping me learn something useful?" (See also the section on time management.)

Your checklist for possessions will look something like this:

Possession	Purpose (Display, Toy, Emotional, Entertainment, Self/other nurturance)	Keep or discard?	Sell or give away?	Replace? With what? Why?
43-foot sailboat	Display, Toy/Entertainment	discard	sell	Spend more time with charities. Find greater happiness.
BMW 7.31 ti	Display/Toy	discard	sell	1988 Pontiac 6000. Less likely to be robbed/stolen

As you *downsize* your materialism, you will be better able to *upsize* your relationships with family and friends. Someone once said, "What good does it do if you possess a whole bunch of stuff, but miss out on what's important in life?''

Start taking corrective action TODAY.

References

Bryan, G. B., Mieder, W. (1994). *The Proverbial Bernard Shaw*. Westport, CT: Greenwood Press.

Durning, A. (1992). Asking how much is enough. In LR Brown, et al. (eds), *State of the World 1991*. New York: W. W. Norton.

Elgin, D. (1993). *Voluntary Simplicity: Toward a Way of Life That Is Outwardly Simple, Inwardly Rich*. Quill.

Fromm, E. (1976). *To Have or to Be*. New York: Harper & Row.

Granfield, M. (1991). Having it all in America today. *Money,* October, p. 124.

Harris, T. G., Yankelovich, Y. (1989). What good are the rich? *Psychology Today*, April, p. 38.

Harwood Group (1995). *Yearning for Balance: Views of Americans on Consumption, Materialism, and the Environment*. Bethesda, MD.

Indermaur, D. (1995). Are we becoming more violent—a comparison of trends in violent and property offenses in Australia and Western Australia. *Journal of Quantitative Criminology*, 11, 247–70.

Laufman, L. (1998). Personal communication, July 23.

Morris, B. (1987). Big spenders: as a favored pastime, shopping ranks high with most Americans. *The Wall Street Journal*, July 30.

Myers, D. G. (1992). *The Pursuit of Happiness: Who Is Happy—and Why*. New York: William Morrow.

Shames, L. (1989). *The Hunger for More*. New York: Times Books.

St. James, E. (1998). *Living the Simple Life: A Guide to Scaling Down and Enjoying More* (reprint ed.). New York: Hyperion.

Veblen, T. (1994). *The Theory of the Leisure Class.* New York: Dover.

Watchtel, P. (1989). *The Poverty of Affluence: A Psychological Portrait of the American Way of Life.* New Society Press.

Williamson, M. (1997). *The Healing of America.* New York: Simon & Schuster.

13 | Finding Purpose in Your Job: Making Work Meaningful

GOALS: To think about your job, and perhaps to be motivated to take some action to make your work more meaningful. To think about volunteering as a way of finding meaning.

Thinking About Your Job

Since most of us go to work at least five days a week, fifty weeks a year, for decades, it is easy to get into a rut. We want out of the rut, but we are unsure of how to do it, or why we want to do it. Most people have a great need to reflect upon their career and redirect themselves. This redirection is not toward more earnings, but toward a sense of purpose in their work which provides meaning, and gives the satisfaction of having done something worthwhile with one's skills.

In our career ruts we experience the stress of work; we come home not secure in the knowledge that we have done something good, but mentally tired. We may hate our jobs while at the same time fear being unemployed.

I will now ask you to walk up out of the rut, onto a

hillside where you can look down and see the trench in which you have been slaving these many years. As you look down, I want you to fill in the following table about your work. (This recapitulates some of the information on job stress covered earlier in chapter 9.) For each aspect of work, fill in the cells with the "good" and "bad" facets. For example, a "good" thing about your supervisor might be that she praises you a lot for good work. A "bad" thing about her might be that she never rates you high enough for you to be eligible for a raise. If there is nothing "good" about a factor, leave that cell blank. *Note:* House spouses have a job, too.

Table for Evaluating at Your Current Job

JOB FACTOR	THE GOOD	THE BAD
Ability to control my work		
Job clarity (I know what work I am supposed to do)		
Role clarity (I know what my role in the organization is)		
Amount of work		
Difficulty of work		
Supervisor: mentor or mean?		

Job Factor	The Good	The Bad
Coworkers: cooperative or competitively hostile?		
Subordinates: eager to please, or rebellious?		
Noise, smells		
Chances for advancement		
Opportunities for training and education		
Job security		
Pay	a) too much b) about right c) none: I volunteer	d) not enough e) none: no job
My current employment status	(I have a job)	(I don't have a job but need one)
Opportunities to socialize on the job	☺	
The effect on humankind of what my company does	☺	
The meaning of my work to me: being able to do good work	☺	

JOB FACTOR	THE GOOD	THE BAD
The meaning of my work to me: my interest in this occupation	☺	
The meaning of my work to me: how my work affects others/ humankind	☺	

Now go back and think about what you have written. Discuss it and compare notes with your support-group members. One point in filling out this table is to show that people who have some really good things to put into the cells marked with the ''☺'' can put up with a lot of ''bad'' job factors.

Take combat for example. I was drafted to serve in Vietnam in 1969, but due to a back operation, was not able to go. But hundreds of thousands of Americans have fought in that and other wars under the most insufferable conditions. Only a small minority really complained and rebelled against their duty to their country. Why? Because they felt they were fighting for a cause they believed in: the defeat of an enemy that was threatening their cherished values of freedom and individual liberty (to say nothing of the threat to U.S. trade routes and to opportunities for economic exploitation of third-world nations).

When I was an engineer at NASA, thousands of government and corporate workers operated at their peak physical capacities and professional capabilities, putting in hours of overtime, to achieve man's first landing on another heavenly body. No one complained of the extra work. It was exciting. It was meaningful. We were working for a cause. Dale Carnegie (1970) has noted that it is not work itself that leads to fatigue, but boredom. When work is perceived as exciting and interesting, mental energy is limitless, and is constrained only by physiological demands for sleep.

If your social relationships at work are pleasant, this can make even the most loathsome jobs somewhat tolerable. On the other hand, even the most meaningful work can become repulsive if coworkers are unfriendly and antagonistic. If the social scene is negative, use the methods discussed in chapter 11 to try to make some friends.

Artists who create unique reflections of beauty and meaning, leaders who change the course of humankind for the better, inventors who devise better methods and machines, and authors who write self-improvement books are examples of people who feel their work is meaningful. They have a clear sense of purpose. Their work has a positive effect on humankind.

It was not too long ago in human history that most people had jobs that benefited humankind in obvious ways. They farmed, baked, made fabric, took care of children, taught, preached, or led the community. Only a very few people were employed in silly occupations such as making fancy clothes for royalty. Nowadays there are people who make money putting chrome decor on the side of Buicks, running tanning salons, writing romance novels, producing TV sitcoms, or playing spectator sports. None of these activities benefits mankind; they help others gratify desires for sensuous pleasures, or provide vicarious experiences for those who lack a real life of their own. However, the existence of such jobs provides gainful employment for many, and some cannot find other jobs. I am not trying to shame those who work hard in occupations which are frivolous and superfluous. Many are trapped in these jobs through no fault of their own.

Finding Meaning in a Meaningless Job

Not all workers can have jobs with obvious purpose and meaning beyond performing a function for an employer. For example, if you were an accountant with a large firm, you may check the profit-and-loss statements for several corporations every quarter for years and years. This is of obvious value to the corporations, but what does it mean to you? Perhaps you are one of those accountants who comes home after a hard day and exclaims, "Wow. What an exciting day. I really got those accounts receivable organized for the Humongous Corp!" If Humongous Corporation produces a high-quality product which is very meaningful and needed for humankind, and sells it at a fair price, then perhaps accountants can feel that they play an important part in providing these products to society. Or the corporation could be making an unfair profit selling a product they claim is good for health, even though they secretly know use of the product will gradually destroy one's liver.

Regardless of the meaningfulness of the ultimate product, you might feel you are just filling in a job slot that many other people could fill. There is no personal meaning to the work, and if you quit, nothing would change, as your associate, Bob, would take over the accounts. Recognizing that some people are stuck in such jobs, how is one to cope? Of course, it is good to look at one's blessings: you have a job, it pays money and provides health benefits, and you are surviving well compared with the homeless down under the freeway overpass. (Take them some food tonight.) There are probably some worse jobs you can imagine (for example, you could be flipping disks of animal flesh over a hot grill). You can feel blessed not to be doing those tasks.

Whatever you do for a living, if it seems unsatisfying due to lack of meaning, and if there is no easy route to another career, then you can at least do something to make life more bearable:

1) Don't continue to agonize about your situation. Agonizing almost never makes things better. Don't be caught up in the antiemployer sentiment commonly expressed by disgruntled workers.

2) If your job is so routine that you can fantasize while doing it, think of pleasant things, or listen to music or recorded books. If you are on a chain gang (figuratively or literally), sing songs about hoped-for freedom and the glory to come.

3) Try to improve your efficiency. This makes a challenge for yourself, and may have a positive effect on your boss. While some work slower or goof off because of the boring nature of the job, you will stand out like a bright light.

4) Never let the negative aspects of a job influence you to sabotage your company. Sabotage never helped anyone, and those who are caught will not find better jobs waiting for them after they are fired or imprisoned.

Looking for More Meaning

Some people may have the luxury in time and resources to consider changing to a more meaningful occupation. This is becoming a trend. For example, a top corporate attorney in New York City may quit to seek fulfillment running a small orchard in Vermont. People are reevaluating their jobs and asking themselves, ''Why am I spending so much time and energy in a job which has no meaning for me, which seems like drudgery?'' There is definitely a movement toward finding occupational meaning in the U.S. workforce. Some of the reasons are (Caudron, 1998):

1) Social forces have resulted in longer working hours, longer commute times, and thus less time for personal fulfillment outside the job.

2) Widespread layoffs have left large numbers of people with plenty of time to think about finding meaningful work. Layoffs reinforce the perception that corporate loyalty to employees is a thing of the past; it is more difficult to find meaning in helping corporations meet their goals.

3) Baby boomers, the largest group of U.S. workers, are now coming to an age at which they are naturally more contemplative. They seek to find themselves through a spiritual awakening, searching for something greater than themselves to believe in.

For a while, in the seventies and eighties, workers enjoyed new prosperity, and felt comfortable and satisfied in their new cars and homes. However, the materialistic orientation has not proved ultimately fulfilling. Workers find themselves in meaningless jobs working for companies that produce meaningless products. What is missing in these companies is a sense of community and a mission which goes beyond mere improvement of the value of stockholders' net worth. To motivate employees in these times, corporations are trying to develop a sense of team spirit and corporate identity, as well as participative management, so that workers can feel part of a larger whole, and experience a sense of pride in workmanship.

Being an employee of a corporation plays a more important role in personal identity than it has in the past. Jay Conger, a professor of business, has noted that involvement in extended families, civic activities, and religious endeavors has declined over the last few decades, making the workplace a more significant aspect of people's lives (Conger, 1994). Social interaction may be optimal at work, because it is one arena of life in which television viewing is not allowed.

Japanese Corporations Give Meaning to Work

After World War II, Japan had the task of rebuilding its industrial infrastructure. The Japanese were interested in how to develop industry quickly, and how to get a foothold in the world market throught competition (since they weren't allowed to conquer territories anymore). They hired productivity experts from the U.S. They developed many concepts, the best known of which is the team management approach. The larger team is the corporation, and the workers are trained to develop a devotion to their company. Employee loyalty is enhanced by policies of guaranteed employment for life. The smaller team is the work unit, where all employees participate in decision making. Workers feel they are part of the corporation, and have a stake in the success of their company, and indeed, of their country. Workers with this sense of purpose will work harder and longer. These approaches have led to a level of productivity about 12 percent higher than the U.S. Another factor has been the cooperation among the workers, the corporations, and the government to achieve the common goal of helping Japanese corporations attain dominance in world markets.

Contrast Japan with the United States. Here the workers and corporations often see each other as enemies, in a continuing struggle for higher wages versus net profit. Even with union power resulting in very high wages compared with the rest of the world, productivity is not enhanced, perhaps due to the adversarial relationship between labor and capitalists. The perception that one's work has meaning may be clouded by the perception that "hard work benefits my company, but not me."

However, even as participatory management principles are being applied in the U.S., giving workers a greater sense of purpose, economic forces and work stress are resulting in corporate hardship in Japan. Job stress is manifesting itself in family disruption, and companies are no longer able to keep employees for life.

Changing to a More Meaningful Career: How to Do It

There are five basic steps to changing careers if you are looking for more meaning:

1) Review your past (job and hobbies), and note what you were good at doing.

2) Review your past, and note what you most enjoyed doing.

3) Look at others, to determine what you might like to be doing that you have never done before. Interview them about their enjoyment of their work.

4) Among the things you would like to be doing, what has the most meaning for you?

5) Put all the above information together to select a career path that involves doing things that you can do well, that you enjoy, and that allow you to produce meaningful results. Getting paid a good salary wouldn't hurt, either.

There are many career guidance companies who will, for a fee, counsel you through this process. I recommend as a first step reading *What Color Is Your Parachute?* by Richard Bolles. This book is updated annually and contains chapters on the above steps, as well as a section on "how to find your mission in life." The book also covers in depth how to get a job in your chosen field.

Finding Meaning in Avocation

The age of the New Work may not be here yet, but most people have some spare time (turn off the TV!) to do something meaningful, even if it involves only an hour or two

---

Be Careful in Choosing a Career

In the classic comedy skit "Vocational Guidance Counselor," by Monty Python's Flying Circus, an accountant seeks help. He has been an accountant for twenty years and wants to do something a bit more exciting. He declares his desire to become a wild-animal trainer. The counselor informs him that to be an animal trainer, he must confront large, ferocious beasts with giant sharp claws and enormous teeth. Upon reflection, the accountant inquires about opportunities in the insurance business. Is your career fantasy in line with your true abilities and courage?

In another skit, "The Pet Shop," the shop owner, after a troublesome confrontation with a customer about a dead parrot, confesses that he never wanted to be a pet-shop owner in England. What he really wanted to be was a lumberjack in the wilds of British Columbia. How distant (in terms of skills and geography) is your current job from your "ideal" job? Is your ideal job something that you imagine to be more meaningful, or just more enjoyable? Interview lumberjacks before taking up the ax.

---

each week. Hobbies such as model railroading are fun, as are wood carving, butterfly collecting, and topiary. However, if you have been reading closely, you might have picked up on the idea that a sense of fulfillment and happiness in life may require that you do something that helps to improve the human condition.

Many retirees are in a good position to do something worthwhile with their spare time. Everyone wants to retire so that they will no longer have to work. I know many people who are spending the last twenty-five years or so of their lives sitting around swimming pools in Florida drinking tequila sunrises, playing bridge and dominoes. They seem happy. Perhaps for some it is the ideal life. But research shows that retirees who are doing volunteer work in their community are more likely to have a sense of purpose in life, and that a sense of purpose is inversely related to feelings of boredom (Weinstein et al., 1995).

The "New Work"

Philosopher Frithjof Bergmann has conceptualized a better future for the world of work (Crawford, 1997). He feels that the use of technology should not be just to make workers more efficient, but to reduce the oppressive, spirit-breaking power of boring and repetitive work. In his vision, there are three elements for vocation or avocation in a future time when technology allows everyone more discretionary time. First is "chores," the jobs that we must do for money and to make the economy run. The second element is the "hi-tech providing system" which allows a greater degree of self-sufficiency without the strenuous labor of farming for survival. The third element is the "calling" system. A future cultural and social framework will enable people to pursue a calling. A calling (Latin: *vocation*) is something that a person feels compelled to do out of a passion to be creative and useful in business, the arts, inventions, social and political change, or in learning or teaching. Callings might be funded by grants from foundations. In this way, at least a portion of one's career could be spent in a calling. Those who feel called to do work will do it with greater energy and creativity. The results of their efforts are likely to benefit humanity.

The National Commission on Civic Renewal, a panel of academics, business executives, and Washington insiders, has issued a report entitled ''A Nation of Spectators: How Civic Disengagement Weakens America and What We Can Do About It'' (1998). According to two of the report's chief authors, former Secretary of Education William Bennett and former Senator Sam Nunn, Americans' participation in civic, educational, or religious organizations has dwindled. Even though many Americans claim to be busy with work and family, the truth is that we now spend more time watching TV than ever since the glowing boxes invaded our homes. A sense of cynicism about politics and a sense of hopelessness about social problems has led to a state of passivity and whining. But a free democratic society cannot function properly without citizen involvement. And citizen involvement is an excellent place to find purpose and meaning in life.

In addition to advocating participation in community and religious organizations, the report recommends the recruitment of adults to act as mentors for the millions of youth who lack sensible direction. Other avenues for finding meaning might include membership and participation in environmental groups, visiting the elderly and sick, helping the homeless, or cleaning up the cities. The newspapers of most big cities have a special section each week listing a wide variety of opportunities for volunteering.

Another group in the forefront of enhancing citizen participation is the Center for Democracy and Citizenship, affiliated with the University of Minnesota. One project developed by the Center is Public Achievement, which involves teams of young people (ages 8 to 18) who are led to organize public-work projects that contribute to their community and schools. These kids are no doubt experiencing more meaning in their lives than if they stayed at home playing Mortal Kombat. Results of the project, in addition to the valuable help the children provide, is improvement in their self-concept, school performance, and participation in community life. The Center has also initiated the VCW (Value of Citizen Work) Project in an effort to identify strategies and tools that citizens can use to get involved in community building and community education, and to get others engaged.

This is America. You have the freedom to live a life of purpose. Don't squander it on passive entertainment. For more details on how to get involved, read a good book about it (Raynolds & Raynolds, 1988).

Homework

1. Write a brief story about how you got into your present career. To what extent did it happen by careful planning and seeking after your passions and interests? Or were you

unduly influenced by an incompetent high-school vocational guidance counselor? Talk about this with your support group.

2. Fill in a table that looks like this:

Table for Personal/Career Growth Possibilities

THINGS I WANT TO ACHIEVE	HOW THIS WILL BENEFIT ME PERSONALLY	HOW THIS WILL BENEFIT MY EMPLOYER
Learn Spanish	Interesting to do; will help me on vacation	Bilingual employees needed in South American department
Form a team of my coworkers, meet regularly about work	I will get more cooperation, and have more fun at work	Employer will get more productivity out of happier, self-managed team
etc.		

Discuss this table with your support group, then with your supervisor.

3. Read a book about volunteering. Make a list of all the possible ways for you to become involved in helping your community. Visit some of the more interesting ones. See what it's like. Talk with others who volunteer. Pick something to do and start off with two hours a week. See what it feels like compared with watching prime-time soap operas.

References

Bolles, R. N. (1998). *What Color Is Your Parachute? A Practical Manual for Job-Hunters and Career-Changers.* Berkeley, CA: Ten Speed Press.

Carnegie, D. (1970). *How to Enjoy Your Life and Your Job*. New York: Pocket Books.

Caudron, S. (1997). The search for meaning at work. *Training & Development,* (51, 9, 24–27).

Chapman, G., Monty Python (1989). *The Complete Monty Python's Flying Circus: All the Words!* Vol, 1. New York: Pantheon.

Conger, J. A. (1994). *Spirit at Work: Discovering the Spirituality in Leadership.* New York: Jossey-Bass.

Crawford, J. (1997). *New Work: An Option for the Future of Work.* Study guide. Lady Godiva Presse.

National Commission on Civic Renewal (1998). *A Nation of Spectators: How Civic Disengagement Weakens America and What We Can Do About It.* Washington, DC: National Commission on Civic Renewal.

Raynolds, J. F., Raynolds, E. (1988). *Beyond Success: How Volunteer Service Can Help You Begin Making a Life Instead of Just a Living.* Master Media.

Weinstein, L., Xie, X., Cleanhouse, C. C. (1995). Purpose in life, boredom, and volunteerism in a group of retirees. *Psychological Reports,* 76, 482.

14

Perseverance and Other Thoughts

GOAL: To realize that the best ideas and intentions need continuing effort to get results.

If you faithfully follow the recommendations of this book, you should have some chance of success. However, you should remember that humans are not totally rational beings, and the ability to make significant improvements in one's life will depend in part on the learning that took place in childhood. You should also remember that life change takes a continuing effort to avoid backsliding.

Why do some people persevere and others give up under the same conditions? There are many possible reasons:

1. Some people learned when they were children that extra effort didn't get them anything but grief; they may have had cruel parents who never rewarded their children for striving.

2. They may have grown up in a society that told them that they should just be workers at the local factory, and not to try to achieve anything significant.

3. They may have grown up in a society that told young children that living an insignificant life was a sign of low willpower and general inferiority. A childhood like this might cause an adult to lack motivation to try to make changes, or to give up too easily.

4. An unfortunate childhood might have led to such low self-esteem that even the slightest mistake causes severe shame and guilt, and a desire to quit all efforts at self-improvement. Since everyone experiences mistakes and setbacks, low self-esteem can prevent any real progress.

5. They may not know any of the motivational tools described in this book.

Perseverance can be achieved by:

1. Keeping records of behavior and outcomes faithfully so that you have a clear record of progress and problems.

2. Using others for support. It is very difficult to succeed all on your own, especially if you are the type who criticizes yourself too harshly. An encouraging support person is essential.

3. Maintaining a high level of energy.

4. Having a calm, positive attitude about problems that arise, and using problem-solving methods to work through them.

5. Maintaining an attitude that you will *never give up*. You will never give up because *it is more painful to give up and fail than to keep trying*.

Here is the self-evaluation table from chapter 1. Make copies. Fill one out now, and compare with your beginning status.

Table for Evaluating Your Current Life

LIFE AREA	REASONABLE GOAL
Intimate Relation	1 lifelong spouse, sharing/caring
Current Status	
What have I done for this?	
Family	Nurturing relationships with children/kin
Current Status	
What have I done for this?	
Friendships	1 or 2 good ones
Current Status	
What have I done for this?	
Sleep	8–9 hours/night
Current Status	
What have I done for this?	
Exercise	4–5 hours/week
Current Status	
What have I done for this?	

LIFE AREA	REASONABLE GOAL
Nutrition	Eat for health and enjoyment, avoid weight gain
Current Status	
What have I done for this?	
Relaxed body	Lack of tension and stress disorders
Current Status	
What have I done for this?	
Relaxed mind	Feeling of well-being, peace, clear thinking
Current Status	
What have I done for this?	
Organization	Following a careful plan to achieve specific goals, using time wisely
Current Status	
What have I done for this?	
Work	Job satisfaction from performance and usefulness of work
Current Status	
What have I done for this?	

LIFE AREA	REASONABLE GOAL
Purpose	Have good idea of what your life is about, which brings satisfaction
Current Status	
What have I done for this?	
Community	Active in one organization to help improve the human condition
Current Status	
What have I done for this?	
Religion	Practice a faith based on principles of love
Current Status	
What have I done for this?	
Well Being	Usually happy, optimistic; as result of above
Current Status	
What have I done for this?	
Energy	Able to feel energetic for 16 hours a day, with 3 or fewer cups of coffee
Current Status	
What have I done for this?	

Teddy's Comments on Effort and Involvement in Life

"The credit belongs to the man who is actually in the arena—whose face is marred by dust and sweat and blood—who knows the great enthusiasms, the great devotions—and spends himself in a worthy cause—who at best if he wins knows the thrills of high achievement—and if he fails at least fails while daring greatly—so that his place will never be with those cold and timid souls who know neither victory or defeat."

T. ROOSEVELT,
"Citizenship in a Republic."
Speech given at the Sorbonne, Paris, April 13, 1910.

> *Go Forth, Make Yourself Better, and Make the World a Nicer Place.*

If you would like to send a message to
the author, he can be reached at:

kgoodrick@hotmail.com

Ken Goodrick grew up as a "State Department" brat, living in many countries. After engineering school at Northwestern, he was a NASA engineer who helped on the Apollo lunar missions. He then became a psychologist, and directed employee counseling programs for large corporations. For twenty-one years, he was a researcher at the Texas Medical Center. He has received five NIH grants, written seventy-one scientific publications, and is currently on the faculty at Baylor College of Medicine.